# Undercover Nanny

Alison Henderson

# Undercover Nanny

ISBN-13: 978-171-936-9633
ISBN-10: 1719369631

Cover Art by Creative Author Services

Published by Alison Henderson
United States of America
May 2018

# DEDICATION

To my wonderful daughter, the Egyptologist.
Jessica, this one is for you.

# OTHER BOOKS BY ALISON HENDERSON

*Harvest of Dreams*

*A Man Like That*

*The Treasure of Como Bluff*

*Small Town Christmas Tales*

*Unwritten Rules*

*Boiling Point*

# CHAPTER ONE

Casey Callahan checked her watch for the third time in three minutes. She was late to meet the man who would change her life.

Okay, so maybe that was an exaggeration, but with luck he might help pay her rent for the next month or two.

She tugged her fuchsia knit hat lower, bent her head against the biting wind, and picked up her pace across the quad. Scores of down-clad, scarf-wrapped undergraduates pushed past her on the icy sidewalk on their way to class or the library. Chicago in late January was nobody's idea of fun.

She glanced at her watch again. Already five minutes late, and she still had three blocks to go. Professor Bainbridge's office in the Near Eastern Institute was on the opposite side of campus from her apartment. A major hair dryer malfunction that morning had set her back a good fifteen minutes. Time she didn't have to spare.

For the past six months, while she finished her dissertation, money had been short and anxiety high. She'd lost ten pounds, countless brain cells, and ultimately, her fiancé. When he broke off their engagement and moved to Portland, Peter had blamed it on her. He'd said she spent so much time inside her own head, she had nothing left for him. He was probably right. Although, to her way of thinking, he'd been just as bad.

The only thing that had saved her sanity — and her apartment — was her part-time job with the Phoenix, Ltd. Personal Protection Agency. The owner, Madelyn Li, liked the idea of having a psychologist on staff. She liked it so much she was willing to overlook Casey's lack of skills normally required of a bodyguard, such as hand-to-hand combat and advanced firearms training. Despite Madelyn's reassurances, so far Casey had mostly provided back-up for other agents or filled in when they needed a break on a long assignment.

The Bainbridge job would be different. That's why it was so critical to make a good first impression. Madelyn had chosen her specifically for her experience and credentials. Casey would be the lead — and only — agent on the case. The professor had requested an operative who could serve as both bodyguard and nanny to his preschool-age niece. He didn't want the little girl to suspect someone had been hired to protect her, and if Casey did her job properly, no one else would, either.

In addition to her shiny new PhD, Casey's primary qualification for the assignment was her research and training in child psychology. According to Madelyn, Professor Bainbridge had agreed to the contract as soon as he learned of her academic background.

Madelyn hadn't provided any specifics as to why the child needed protection. The little girl lived with her uncle, and Casey presumed the professor would fill in the blanks when she met him in person.

Which would be in about five minutes. The Near Eastern Institute occupied the corner up ahead. Built in the late nineteen twenties from smooth blocks of sand-colored stone, its Collegiate Gothic style and red tile roof matched the rest of the original campus buildings. The Institute housed the campus museum of ancient Middle Eastern art and antiquities, as well as faculty offices and classrooms for everything from ancient Egyptian hieroglyphics, to Mesopotamian Archaeology, to Modern Arabic.

Casey dashed up the steps and followed the crowd through the double oak doors. Scanning the spacious, high-ceilinged lobby, she spotted a young man whose black hair rose in short, stiff points, sitting behind an information desk.

She approached, slightly out of breath from her race across campus in the cold. "I'm Casey Callahan. I have an appointment with Professor Bainbridge."

The young man, probably a student, glanced up from his phone with a bored expression. "Second floor, on your right." He tipped his head toward a broad stone staircase with steps worn concave by the feet of generations of budding scholars.

As she turned and joined the stream of students heading up, her stomach tightened. Did she look too much like a student in her serviceable, low-heeled black boots, black knit slacks, and white puffy jacket? How would a client expect a bodyguard/nanny to dress? She could have worn a suit, but the only one she owned no longer fit as well as it once had. That was another item on her need-to-buy list as soon as she had the money.

When Madelyn had called about the job, Casey had looked Alec Bainbridge up in the department's online catalogue. An Egyptian archaeologist, he was young for a tenured professor — only in his mid-to-late-thirties — with hair that appeared to be blond in the black-and-white photo and round, horn-rimmed glasses. The old-fashioned glasses, along with his stern expression, reminded her of one of the original, early twentieth century explorers whose finds formed the basis of the collection at the NEI. All he needed was a dusty linen suit, a pith helmet, and a camel.

When she reached the second floor, she searched for his name on the heavily-carved, dark-stained oak doors. About half-way down the hall, she passed an open door and spotted him sitting at a desk, examining what appeared to be a large, wooden, model boat with a magnifying glass. He was dressed in a brown tweed jacket over a coffee-colored sweater vest, and the cool winter sun pouring through the tall, leaded glass windows seemed to tip the thick waves of his hair with liquid gold.

Most women she knew would kill to have hair that color, or at least spend hundreds of dollars in search of it. Alec Bainbridge probably got it from forgetting to wear a hat in the blazing Egyptian sun. What dirty trick of nature gave hair like that to a man?

He glanced up, set down the magnifying glass, removed his glasses, and frowned. "Ms. Callahan? You're late."

Her heart stuttered. His perfect hair was bad enough, but his eyes were also a color she'd never seen on a living, breathing person—the deep, dark blue of the ocean off Cape Cod in August. "I...I'm sorry."

He waved her in. "Don't stand around out there. Come in. I have a class in forty-five minutes."

She swallowed hard and tried to tamp down her nerves. The man might look like Adonis in the flesh, but looks were often deceiving, and she had probably blown her chance to make a good first impression. What if he sent her packing? Madelyn might be able to assign another agent, but Casey could kiss her job at Phoenix, Ltd. goodbye.

As she pulled off her hat and stepped into his office, she could feel static electricity teasing the fine strands of her hair into the air. *Winter hat hair. Perfect. Just perfect.* If she hadn't been running late, she could have stopped in the restroom downstairs and smoothed it back into place with a damp comb.

"Uncle Alec, her hair's like mine."

Casey swiveled to face a small blond girl dressed in pink-striped leggings and a sweatshirt with a cartoon picture of a cat, seated on the floor in the corner. The girl's round blue eyes and short, straight nose were refined, feminine versions of those of the man behind the desk.

Casey smiled. "Are you Grace?"

The child nodded.

"I'm Casey."

Grace lifted her gaze to the top of Casey's head. "My hair does that, too, when I pull off my hat. Uncle Alec's always stays where it's s'posed to, but mine flies every which-a-way."

Casey approached the girl, squatted beside her, and reached out to smooth the wayward curls of the child's pale, silky tresses. "Staying where you're supposed to is boring. I'd rather have fun hair like ours."

Grace tipped her head and regarded Casey with a matter-of-fact expression. "Sometimes my hair's too much fun. Uncle Alec says it's having a party on my head, and he has to put it in pigtails."

Casey pressed her lips together to keep from laughing then glanced at Grace's hand. "What do you have there?"

"It's a paper doll of an Egyptian princess from the museum store downstairs. She has different hairstyles and outfits. See?" She held up a book with pages of brightly printed ancient Egyptian costumes and accessories with tabs to hang them on the doll. Her rosy mouth slipped into a pout. "But I'm having trouble. I'm not very good with scissors."

"Maybe I could help you."

The girl's face brightened. "Yes, you —"

"Not right now, Grace," Professor Bainbridge interrupted. "I need to talk to Ms. Callahan for a few minutes." He turned to Casey. "I'll ask my teaching assistant to take her to play in the common room for a while." His hand was already on the receiver of the old-style desk phone. He punched in a number, said a few words, then hung up. "Maria will be right in."

Moments later a petite young woman with black hair that fell in loose waves past her waist popped into the doorway and held out one hand. "Hi, Grace. Shall we go play?" She spoke the words with a light, almost musical accent.

Grace stood, clutching her paper doll and the book of clothes. "I'm having trouble. Do you have good scissors?"

Maria's laugh was bell-like. "We'll borrow some from your Uncle Alec."

The professor pulled a pair from his center desk drawer and handed them to his niece, handles first. His expression and tone were as solemn as a judge. "Now remember, no running."

The little girl took the scissors with an eye-roll, punctuated by a dramatic sigh. "Uncle Alec, what do you think I am, a baby?"

"No, but I think you sometimes get excited, and your feet get carried away with you."

The TA rested a hand on Grace's head. "Don't worry. We'll be very careful."

"I know you will. Thank you, Maria. You can bring her back in half an hour."

The two disappeared through the doorway, deep in conversation.

"Now, Ms. Callahan, please sit down."

Casey started. She'd been caught up watching the interaction between Professor Bainbridge and his niece. As a psychologist, she admired his ability to maintain authority while meeting the child on her own level. And Grace's comments about her uncle were even more telling than his behavior. He clearly loved the girl, but more than that, he seemed to understand her. In Casey's experience observing parent/child interactions, that ability was rare among fathers of young girls, much less an uncle.

"Ms. Callahan?" Alec Bainbridge's lips pressed into a tight line, and he'd put his glasses back on.

Heat rushed to her face. "Yes. I'm so sorry." She slid into the chair facing him across the broad oak desk and folded her jacket in her lap before offering her hand. "Please call me Casey."

"Very well...Casey."

****

Alec examined the young woman across the desk as he shook her hand. It was hard to believe she was a trained bodyguard. Despite her firm grip, the first word that came to mind when he looked at her was *soft*. Unlike so many women these days, Casey Callahan had no hard angles. She wasn't fat by any means, but everything about her—from cheeks and lips still pink from the cold, to the line of her jaw and the curves of her body—was gently rounded. Smooth hair the color of dark honey pooled on her shoulders in a soft wave, and her warm brown eyes reminded him of top-shelf cognac.

How could a woman like this protect his little girl? He prayed it would never come to that.

He steepled his fingers on the desk in front of him. "What did Ms. Li tell you about the job?"

Relief filled Casey's eyes, and she straightened her spine. "Very little, really. She said you wanted an agent who could serve as both bodyguard and nanny for your niece. She didn't share any details about the nature of the threat."

*The threat.*

The muscles in Alec's throat tightened at the word. He took a sip of lukewarm coffee from the mug on his desk, then set it back on the coaster shaped like the mask of Tutankhamen, a gift from his sister when he'd completed his doctorate. "There was an incident at Grace's school the day before yesterday, a potentially dangerous incident." He regretted the snap in his voice, but the thought of any kind of harm coming to Grace pushed him to the tipping point.

Casey pulled a pen and a small notebook from her bag, crossed her legs, and fixed him with an expectant look. "What can you tell me about it?"

"A stranger told the front desk attendant he was a relative and tried to take Grace out of school." His stomach clenched. Speaking the words aloud brought the phone call from the school director back with sickening clarity.

"I assume the school's security protocols prevented that."

Alec nodded. "She's in morning preschool at the university-run Lab School, and they're extremely cautious. The man gave the name Robert Bainbridge and claimed to be my brother. Since that name wasn't on the approved sign-out list, the office refused to let him in and called me."

"Do you have a brother named Robert?"

"I don't have a brother at all. I told them to call the police and raced over there. The police took a report, but with no security camera images and only a vague description of a young man with dark hair, wearing a baseball cap and a hoodie, they didn't have much to go on. They told me to use extra caution where Grace is concerned." He took off his glasses and massaged his temples in an attempt to banish the incipient headache.

"That's disturbing, but you shouldn't worry too much. It sounds like the school handled the situation appropriately."

"They did, but there's more." He opened his top desk drawer, pulled out a folded sheet of paper, and handed it to her. "This was on my desk when I arrived the next morning."

While she read, the words formed in his brain as if they'd been burned there:

*If you want Grace to be safe, keep her away from school.*

He ran a hand through his hair. "Someone must have delivered it either early yesterday, or after I left the day before."

Casey's brows pinched together. "You don't lock your office?"

"Generally, yes, but that was the last thing on my mind when I rushed out of here to get to the school."

She scanned the note again. "The timing would suggest this is related to the earlier incident, do you have any idea why someone wouldn't want Grace to go to school?"

"None at all. It's absurd. It makes no sense." His voice rose, along with his anger. "If they're after money, they've picked the wrong target. I'm not wealthy." When she made no comment, he released his breath in a huff of frustration. "I have no choice but to follow the advice of the police and take the necessary precautions. It's all I can do."

"So, you called Phoenix."

"A friend suggested a bodyguard might be a good idea."

"You made the right choice. I'll do everything possible to protect your niece." She hesitated. "Does Grace know about any of this?"

"No, thank God." He slumped back in the chair and rubbed his eyes with one hand before replacing his glasses. "There's probably not much risk of someone trying to take her from school again, but I can't afford to ignore that note. I have to keep her home until I have some idea who's behind this and what they want."

"What have you told her?"

"For the time being, I told her a few older students at the school have come down with a serious flu, and her doctor says she has to stay home until there's no longer a risk she might catch it."

"I wonder how long that will satisfy her."

"Long enough, I hope. A couple of years ago, Grace was hospitalized with the flu. She doesn't remember much about it, but she remembers enough not to want to go through that again."

Casey glanced up from her notes. "Who else knows about these incidents?"

"Only the campus police and the staff at Grace's school are aware of the attempted kidnapping, or whatever it was. Because it didn't affect any of the other students, they didn't send an alert to the parents. I did share the situation with the mother of Grace's best friend—she's the one who suggested I call you—but I haven't told anyone here at the NEI."

"Have you shown the note to anyone?"

"No. I asked the department secretary and the student who mans the information desk in the lobby if anyone had been asking for me or looking for my office, but they both said no."

"So, the note was left by someone who knows the location of your office." Casey pressed her lips together. "I think you should report it to the campus police."

"I intended to do that yesterday, but I got caught up in trying to find a bodyguard agency whose employees didn't all look like hulking Secret Service agents." He exhaled heavily then met her gaze square-on. "To tell the truth, it slipped my mind again until this morning."

"That's understandable. In the meantime, what exactly do you want me to do?"

"Your boss indicated you would be able to serve as a live-in nanny, as well as providing around-the-clock protection for Grace."

She nodded. "Yes."

Alec regarded her closely. She seemed competent, but in some respects, he'd feel better if she were 6'6", with bandoliers crisscrossing her chest, an assault rifle in one hand, a machete in the other, and a Bowie knife clenched between her teeth. Unfortunately, that would frighten the bejabbers out of his four-year-old niece. "Do you have much experience with preschoolers?"

"I spent many hours interacting with children Grace's age as part of my dissertation research."

He narrowed his eyes. "Grace is not a lab rat."

As hot color flooded Casey's cheeks, a stab of guilt poked him in the chest. He was being unreasonable, but he was exhausted and on edge, and Grace's well-being had to be his primary concern.

Casey met his gaze head-on. "I simply meant I know what books, games, and toys children her age like."

He gave a knowing nod. "You'll find enough of those in her room to start your own preschool, but this is not a baby-sitting job. Don't think you can stare at your phone and expect her to play by herself. Grace needs engagement."

Casey rose so suddenly her chair teetered on its back legs before settling again with a thud. Her hands clenched, and a fine tremor ran through her body. "I am not a fourteen-year-old babysitter. I have a PhD in Child Psychology. All children need engagement, Professor Bainbridge."

Alec swore under his breath. What was wrong with him? His ability to keep his cool in difficult situations was legendary in archaeological circles. During last year's dig season, he hadn't even raised his voice when one of the workmen had offered him a pair of cows in exchange for one of the female students. Instead, he'd suggested his old motorbike would be much more useful than a silly young woman, and the man had agreed. Once the trade was made, Alec sold the cows and bought a new motorbike. Neither the student, her parents, nor the dean were any the wiser. Now, with this threat to Grace, his cool had deserted him.

He stood and gestured toward her cockeyed chair. "Please sit down, Ms. Callahan…Casey."

She eyed him with suspicion and remained standing.

He glanced away and made and effort to compose himself. "I apologize for being rude. I've tried not to let this situation get to me, but as you can see, I've failed. Grace is the most important person in my life. We're the only family each other has, and I can't stand the thought of anyone trying to hurt her."

Casey hesitated then resumed her seat. "I understand. She's a lovely child and obviously very bright. As for keeping her challenged, I can prepare a list of activities for your approval, if you like."

He sank back into his chair. "That won't be necessary. I'm sure you'll do a fine job."

Her tight expression eased. "Very well. When would you like me to start?"

Alec released the breath he hadn't realized he was holding. He'd been half-afraid she would refuse to take the job after he'd behaved like such an ass. As he met her calm, determined gaze, his decision crystallized. Casey Callahan might be young, but her competent, professional demeanor reassured him. She gave the impression of a woman comfortably in charge—the perfect complement to a lively, precocious child like Grace.

"The sooner, the better. Can you pack a bag and come to my house around noon? Here's the address." He scribbled the information on a scrap of paper and handed it to her.

She scanned the paper then tucked it in her purse. "That won't be a problem."

He rolled his chair back and stood, feeling much better than he had an hour earlier. "Excellent. I can probably get the department secretary to watch Grace while I'm in class. She's always looking for ways to help out. I'll bring Grace home for lunch and turn her over to you then."

Casey rose and shouldered her bag. "That will be fine."

When he offered his hand, she shook it firmly. He straightened when Maria and Grace appeared in the doorway behind her.

Grace held up her paper doll. "We finished cutting out Princess Tia's dresses. Is it okay to come back in?"

Alec glanced at Casey. "I think we're about finished here."

She gave him a short nod then bent down and smiled at Grace. "What a beautiful costume, Grace. Would you like to show it to me?"

The little girl marched in, followed by Maria, and held the doll close so Casey could see. "Her dress has gold sewing around the top. See? And look at her belt.

14

Maria says the blue stones are called lapis. Her hair's really fancy, too. It's a wig."

Casey touched the elaborate black hairpiece. "Maybe this is what you and I need for the days when our hair doesn't want to stay where it's supposed to."

Grace's eyes widened. "That would be great! Uncle Alec, can I get a big black wig like Princess Tia's?"

Alec patted the top of her head. "We'll have to see about that. Right now, I need to get to my class, and Ms. Callahan—"

A sharp rap on the door frame interrupted him. A man's face appeared in the doorway, followed by the short, dapper form of Dr. Fermin LeBlanc, Professor of Egyptology and chair of the department of Near Eastern Studies, who occupied the office next door. His thick, dark hair and goatee, accented by dramatic streaks of gray, made his leonine head appear to be overlarge for his compact body. He wore a charcoal wool jacket with one of his signature scarves in red, draped around his neck and flowing back over one shoulder.

Alec tapped his fingers on his desk as he struggled to suppress his exasperation. The man was notorious for his habit of popping into other faculty members' offices unannounced and poking his nose into their business. "Good morning, Fermin. What can I do for you?"

The officious busybody craned his neck and peered over Casey's shoulder until his sharp gaze fixed on the Middle Kingdom, Egyptian model funerary boat resting on Alec's desk. "I was going to ask if this was a good time to see the Fassbender boat. I've been anxious to examine it since it arrived."

*The boat.*

Alec had almost forgotten it in the chaos of the morning. The Near Eastern Institute had recently received the two-foot-long, green-painted, wooden boat— complete with removable oarsmen—as a bequest from the late collector Ernest Fassbender. Unfortunately, Fassbender's reputation was less than sterling. The Egyptian government asserted the boat had been looted during the Arab Spring unrest of 2011 and was demanding that it be repatriated. Alec had been charged with the task of authenticating the artifact before the museum agreed to return it to Egypt.

"I'm afraid I'm in the middle of something." He tipped his head toward the other occupants of his office.

"Another time, then. Soon." Fermin zeroed in on Casey with a smile of delight. "Is this a new student?"

Alec had to keep from rolling his eyes. Fermin fancied himself a ladies' man and didn't seem to grasp the concept of boundaries where female students were concerned. As far as Alec knew, the man had never crossed the line of propriety, but he couldn't blame the young women who tended to give him a wide berth. "This is Casey Callahan, Grace's new...er, nanny. Casey, Professor Fermin LeBlanc."

"So pleased to meet you, young lady." Fermin grabbed her hand and raised it to his lips.

Casey's brows flew up, but before she or Alec could react, Fermin had released her hand and stepped back.

Alec opened his mouth to speak when Grace announced in a loud voice, "I don't need a nanny!" She crossed her arms with a mutinous scowl.

He counted to three. Grace was past the tantrum stage, but the last thing he needed was a full-blown battle of wills with his strong-minded niece. "I have to work, and you certainly can't stay home alone until Dr. Allen says you can go back to school. We don't know how long that might be."

Before the child could respond, Nora Samuels, the department secretary, stuck her head through the doorway and peered at him over a pair of purple reading glasses. "Professor Bainbridge?"

*Great Ramses' Ghost.* His office had turned into a freaking three-ring circus.

"Nora, if you could give me a moment." He turned to Maria. "I'll need those student essays you're grading by tomorrow afternoon."

"Of course, Professor." She nodded and hurried from the room.

He turned to face his niece. "You and I will discuss the nanny issue later." Placing one arm behind Fermin's back, Alec herded him toward the door. "Check back with me tomorrow afternoon. I might have time to show you the boat then."

Fermin turned his head and gave Casey a hopeful smile as he stepped into the hallway. "I'll do that."

When he was gone, Alec turned to the stout, practical department secretary, trying to keep his frustration from his voice. "Now, Nora, what can I do for you?"

She leaned to one side, directing a quick glance at the boat on his desk. "I saw Professor LeBlanc headed this way and wondered if you needed help with anything."

Alec frowned. He had once persuaded a troop of armed Bedouin tribesmen to turn over a priceless Old

Kingdom stele in return for two well-used Jeeps. Why would he need help dealing with Fermin?

Nora was an odd duck. She seemed to take her duties very seriously, even though she was only filling in while the regular secretary was on maternity leave. But at the moment, Alec didn't have the time or inclination to worry about her work habits. "As a matter of fact, I do need someone to watch Grace for the next hour or so, while I'm in class."

"I'd be happy to help." She turned to Grace with a smile and offered her hand. "I have a box of graham crackers in my desk, and I know where we can get a coloring book of the Pyramids and some crayons."

Grace considered a moment, then nodded and took Nora's hand. "That sounds like school, and I like school."

After they left, Casey turned to Alec with a bemused expression. "Is it always so...um...lively around here? How do you get any work done?"

He shook his head. "I'm sorry about that. This place can be a real circus, but today does seem worse than usual. Maybe it's the full moon. I don't know what got into Grace. She usually has better manners."

Casey's smile was warm and confident. "Don't worry about it. Most children dislike change. She'll be fine once we get to know each other."

"I hope so. As for Fermin...he's a brilliant scholar, but he has a unique ability to make people uncomfortable. Especially women."

"I'll try to avoid him, but if that's impossible and he gets out of line, I can always tie him up with his own scarf." She raised one delicate brow. "Or shoot him."

Alec almost choked. Casey Callahan might look like the girl next door, but maybe she was tough enough for this job after all.

# CHAPTER TWO

Shortly before noon, Casey stood on the sidewalk in front of a three-story, blue-and-white Queen Anne Victorian, separated from the sidewalk by a classic white picket fence. She checked the house number against the address Professor Bainbridge had given her. This was the place. She ran her gaze from the wide front porch, to the diamond-paned, leaded glass windows, to the bands of decorative shingles cut in three different shapes and smiled. The paint might be faded and peeling in a few spots, but there was something homey and welcoming about the house's exuberant eclecticism.

She tightened her grip on the handle of her suitcase and rolled it up the front walk to the dark gray wooden steps. With each step she became increasingly conscious of a fluttering in her stomach. She wouldn't describe it as butterflies—more like an army of spiders, each wearing four pairs of tiny wooden clogs and dancing a jig. Although the resources of Phoenix, Ltd. were only a phone call away, she would be largely on her own for the duration of this assignment, responsible not only for the protection, but also the nurture and education of one very bright and determined four-year-old, who apparently resented her presence before she'd even set foot in the house.

She grabbed the handle of her bag with both hands and hefted it up the stairs, bumping each tread as she went. She'd probably packed too much, but with no idea how long the assignment might last, she'd brought enough for a couple of weeks, including the small pistol her father, a retired Boston cop, had given her when she'd started working for Phoenix. If she needed more clothes, her apartment was only a few blocks away, and Risa at the Phoenix Ltd. office could provide anything else.

Before her finger touched the doorbell, the lace curtain covering the oval, etched-glass pane in the front door twitched aside, and Grace's small face appeared. Casey smiled. Grace did not.

She adjusted her hold on the suitcase, expecting the door to open any second. When it didn't, she pushed the bell.

After a couple of minutes, Alec Bainbridge opened the door, wiping his hands on a dish towel. "Come in. I was just fixing Grace's lunch." He reached for her bag. "Let me take that. I'll show you to your room, then you can join us...unless you've already eaten." He turned and headed toward a wide oak staircase with elaborately carved balusters.

Grace stood behind her uncle and made a grotesque face by pulling the corners of her mouth and eyes together with her thumbs and forefingers. Casey responded by crossing her eyes, pushing the tip of her nose upward, and waggling her tongue, then followed

Alec up the stairs. "Thank you, but I think I'll wait. I'm not too hungry right now."

He continued to the second-floor landing, oblivious of the byplay going on behind him. "Suit yourself, but I'm not sure what you'll find in the refrigerator or pantry. I haven't had time to go to the store for a few days."

Casey turned and glanced down at Grace, who stood at the bottom of the stairs with her brows knit, her lower lip outthrust, and her arms crossed. "That's not a problem. Grace and I can go this afternoon. It will give her a chance to show me what she likes to eat."

Alec carried the suitcase into a sunny corner bedroom with tall windows on two sides and old-fashioned, floral-striped wallpaper in tones of rose and raspberry. Ordinarily she disliked wallpaper, but it looked at home with the antique, carved walnut furniture.

He surveyed the room. "I hope this will be all right. I'm afraid I haven't touched it since I bought the place. Grace and I don't have many guests."

"It's lovely."

He gave a brisk nod. "Fine. I'd better get back downstairs and finish lunch. I have a meeting this afternoon." He stepped into the hall, and Casey followed. "I'm next door to you." He pointed to the room occupying the other front corner of the house. "The bathroom is on the other side, and Grace's room is beyond that, at the back. Her playroom is on the third floor. Oh, and I have to warn you…don't leave any jewelry or valuables out in your room."

She frowned. The university might not be located in the best part of town, but the security system she'd noticed when she arrived should be sufficient to deter most garden-variety thieves. "We're on the second floor. You don't have a problem with cat burglars, do you?"

Alec's lips tightened. "Not cat. Monkey."

She halted. "What?"

"Balthazar."

"Who is Balthazar?"

He grimaced. "Follow me, and I'll introduce you."

He headed around the open center stairwell, past the bathroom and Grace's room, to a smaller room that might once have been a nursery or servant's quarters. In the center of the room stood a large kennel, the kind one might use to house a Great Dane—or a small polar bear. Standing on his hind legs and clasping the bars like a convict in a 'thirties prison movie was an angry-looking monkey who shrieked the moment he spied Alec.

"Meet Balthazar."

Casey took a couple of tentative steps forward but froze when the monkey glared at her and shrieked again.

Alec walked closer to the cage. "You don't have to be afraid. He needs a major attitude adjustment and will steal anything that's not nailed down, but he won't hurt you."

Balthazar bared his teeth in a wicked parody of a grin.

Casey kept her distance. "What kind of monkey is he?"

"He's a white-faced Capuchin from Costa Rica. They're exceptionally intelligent. I just wish this one could be persuaded to use his brainpower for good instead of evil. On a positive note, he's housebroken, more or less. We leave the door open when he's not locked in the kennel, and he comes back here to do his business. The downside of that is having to change the papers in the tray under the cage regularly."

"It's none of my business, but why keep him if he's so much trouble?"

Balthazar coiled his tail around one of the bars like a snake and sent her a simian death stare.

"He's only here for the term. He actually belongs to Tomas Huerta, a colleague of mine in the Anthropology Department. Tom adopted him after he was kicked out of a companion animal training course for being an anti-social little klepto. We agreed to monkey-sit this quarter while Tom is away digging in Central America."

"How does Grace feel about having a monkey in the house?" Casey knew how *she* felt. Balthazar's knowing black eyes and smug, yet hostile expression unnerved her.

"She's the main reason he's here. She's crazy about him." Alec gave a soft snort and shook his head. "Tom made sure to ask me when Grace was in the room. He knows how hard it is to say no to her."

"Why would anyone want to say no to me?" a small voice interrupted.

They turned to see Grace standing in the doorway. She marched up to the kennel and stuck her fingers between the bars to rub Balthazar's furry cheek. The monkey nuzzled her hand as he shot Alec a defiant look.

Alec glanced at Casey with raised brows, as if to say, *see what I mean*? Then he smiled at the back of his niece's small, blond head. "I know it's hard to believe, but sometimes I know more than you."

Grace turned her head and gave him a long-suffering look. "Oh, Uncle Alec, don't be silly." She returned her attention to Balthazar, who now wore a pitifully forlorn expression. "He hates being in this cage, and I don't blame him. Can't we let him out?"

Alec put a hand on her head and turned her toward the door. "You know the rules. Not while we're eating. When you're finished, you can help fix him a bowl of fruit."

Wondering what she'd gotten herself into, Casey followed them downstairs to a well-used white kitchen that looked like it had last been remodeled sometime in the middle of the previous century. A precocious child was challenge enough, but adding a monkey to the mix was a potential recipe for disaster. She had a sudden vision of Balthazar brandishing her shiny new Sig Sauer P238 and made a mental note to keep it locked in her suitcase whenever she and Grace were in the house.

While Alec finished making Grace's peanut butter and jelly sandwich, Casey sliced an apple from the blue ceramic bowl on the red tile counter. She arranged half the slices in a pinwheel design on Grace's plate and poured the child a glass of milk before taking a seat next to her at the kitchen table.

Grace pondered the apple slices. "This is pretty. It looks like a flower."

"I'm glad you like it. I try to make food fun." Casey smiled and took a bite of the remaining half of the apple without thinking. She was pleased to discover the dancing spiders in her stomach had settled down.

Grace leaned toward her and whispered loudly, "Uncle Alec doesn't make fun food. I don't think he knows how."

"Hey!" Alec raised his brows in mock injury.

Casey bent her head to Grace's. "While I'm here, we'll have lots of fun food, and you can help. Would you like that?" Grace's head bobbed, giving Casey a sudden inspiration. "Since we're all blondies in this house, we could bake a batch of blondies this afternoon."

Grace's pale brows pinched together in suspicion. "What are you talking about? I don't want to eat hair."

"They're treats. You've had brownies, haven't you?"

"Sure. My best friend Sophia's mom makes good brownies." She hesitated. "But she puts pee-cans in them, and I have to pull them out. I don't like pee-cans."

Casey bit back a smile. After all, pee-cans were serious business. "Blondies are kind of like light-colored brownies, and we won't put any pecans in ours."

"Okay."

"Good. Finish your sandwich, and after lunch we'll walk to the grocery store to buy what we need. We'll pick out something fun for dinner, too."

Alec plopped a quick kiss on his niece's head. "Casey, I don't want you to think I expect you to do all the cooking while you're here. Grace and I are used to fending for ourselves." He sent his niece a mock-serious look. "Even if I don't know how to make fun food."

Casey smiled. "It's not a problem. I love to cook. Besides, cooking is a great opportunity for Grace to practice her numbers and letters. She can sound out the words for some of the ingredients and learn about measurements."

"I already know how to read," Grace insisted.

"I'm glad to hear that, but I bet you don't know every single word."

"Well...maybe not every single one."

Alec glanced at his watch. "I've got to run. Grace, finish your lunch. I'll see you later this afternoon. Casey, I'd like to speak to you before I leave."

"Of course." She followed him to the front hall.

He grabbed his heavy wool coat from the closet, shrugged it on, and made quick work of the buttons. As he pulled on his gloves, he turned to face her. Taut lines framed his mouth, and his deep blue eyes had turned stormy.

She swallowed, wondering what she'd done wrong. "If you'd rather I didn't take Grace out..."

"No, no." He swore under his breath. "I can't hold her prisoner in the house until we figure out who tried to take her out of school, who wrote that note, and why."

"There isn't much to go on at this point."

"No. The note is the only potential clue. It must be connected, but I'm not sure it's even a threat. It almost reads more like a warning. At any rate, I'll turn it over to the campus police and let them worry about it. After that, all we can do is watch and wait, and I've never been good at waiting." His frustration was palpable.

"I know it isn't easy, but you can leave the watching to me. That's why I'm here."

"You'll be very careful when you take her out." It was more order than question.

"Absolutely. I'll be armed whenever we leave the house, and I promise I won't let her out of my sight."

"I trust you, but believe me, with Grace that's easier said than done."

Her lips twitched at the corners. "Would you worry less if I handcuffed her to me?"

Her attempt at humor seemed to relax him, and he responded with a wry half-smile. "Probably. Oh, and I should have asked upfront, but I hope it won't be a problem for you to work seven days a week. I'm sure I can work something out with the agency to send a substitute when you need a day off."

"That's fine, and I don't anticipate needing any time off."

"No demanding husband or boyfriend?"

"No." Her mind went to Peter. Even if he were still around, her former fiancé probably wouldn't have noticed or cared.

"Good." Reaching into his hip pocket, he pulled out his wallet and handed her several folded twenties. "This is for groceries. Get whatever you need. I should be home around five-thirty."

She gave him a bright, confident smile. "See you then." She closed and locked the door behind him then headed back to the kitchen.

Grace was finishing her last apple slice. "Can we let Balthazar out now? Uncle Alec said we could."

Casey wasn't sure she was ready to deal with an ill-behaved monkey up close and personal. "Maybe that should wait until we come back from the store."

"But you saw him. He's hungry *now*. He might *starve* if we wait." Grace collapsed on the table for dramatic effect.

Casey bit her lip to keep from laughing as she picked up the empty plate and glass and carried them to the sink. Grace was a master at the fine art of wheedling. "We wouldn't want that. If you get an orange and a banana, I'll help you cut them up."

The monkey began to shriek the minute he heard their footsteps on the stairs.

Grace shot Casey an indignant look. "See, I told you he's starving." She bounded up the last four steps, nearly spilling the bowl of fruit, and rushed into his room.

The second she burst through the door, Balthazar's shrieks became an almost conversational chatter. He reached through the bars and touched Grace's fingers. Alec had been right about the bond between the two.

Grace pointed to a key on top of a small table near the kennel. "That's the key to unlock his cage."

Casey would have preferred to poke the pieces of fruit between the bars, but since Alec had indicated Balthazar was allowed the run of the house when the family was home, she reluctantly unlocked the padlock. With deft fingers, the monkey removed the lock, swung the door open, and flew to Grace, who held him on her hip like a mother with a toddler, offering him chunks of orange from the bowl. Casey kept her distance and observed the interaction between the pair with fascination. Despite the lack of actual language, they seemed to have no problem communicating.

After Balthazar had finished eating, she picked up the bowl. "Put him back in the cage now, Grace, so we can go to the store."

There must have been something in her tone that tipped the monkey off, because he tightened his grip on Grace's hair and glared at Casey.

The child hugged him closer. "Can't we leave him out? It's mean to keep him in there."

Casey recognized limit-testing when she heard it and knew better than to knuckle under, especially while she and Grace were still taking each other's measure. "I'm sure he's used to it. Do you leave him out while you're at school and your Uncle Alec is at work?"

"No...but—"

"No *buts.*"

"Oh, all right." Grace disentangled Balthazar's fingers from her hair and put him back in the kennel.

*Whew. No tantrum. A win for the grown-up.*

Ten minutes later, Grace seemed to have forgotten her pique as they walked the three blocks to the grocery store. The sidewalk was slippery with packed snow, so Casey held the child's hand with one hand and a folding shopping cart with the other. Her pistol was stowed safely in her purse.

"What's your favorite thing for dinner," she asked as they waited for traffic to clear before crossing the only major street on their route.

"Chicken nuggets," Grace replied without hesitation. "Uncle Alec buys big boxes of them to keep in the freezer."

Casey winced. She wasn't surprised to hear Professor Bainbridge relied on the highly processed, frozen staple of working parents everywhere, but she could at least try do better. "I think we'll make real ones tonight."

Grace wrinkled her nose in disbelief. "Not from a box?"

"Nope. From real chicken. What's your favorite vegetable?"

"French fries."

"Besides that."

Grace pursed her lips and considered the question. "Carrots, I guess."

"Then we'll have real chicken nuggets and carrots for dinner. And our blondies, of course. Do you think Uncle Alec will like that?"

"He'll probably like anything he doesn't have to cook himself. I don't think he likes to cook very much. He usually sends me upstairs to play so I don't hear the bad words, but sometimes I hear them anyway."

Casey stifled a grin. "It sounds like it might be better for you and me to do the cooking while I'm here."

Grace eyed her with suspicion. "How long are you going to be my nanny?"

Casey hoped the professor was right and Grace was anxious enough about avoiding the hospital to accept his explanation as long as necessary. "I'm not sure. That's up to your doctor and your uncle." She met the child's skeptical blue gaze and smiled. "I'm not so bad...really. If you give me a chance, we can have lots of fun."

"We'll see."

Casey smiled at Grace's perfect imitation of an adult putting off a demanding child. She'd probably heard those words in that exact tone hundreds of times in her young life.

Once they were in the store, Grace perked up. She dragged Casey through the aisles, pointing out her favorite treats. Casey was able to nix several items on the grounds that the folding cart could only hold three bags of groceries, but she still ended up with a bag of gummy bears and a box of cereal with so much sugar her teeth hurt just looking at the picture on the front.

She'd just finished checking the contents of the cart against her list one last time when she glanced up and realized Grace had disappeared.

Her heart pounded in her ears as she scanned the dairy aisle for a small figure in a purple parka. She then moved on to the meat section, but there was no sign of the child. Could the would-be kidnapper from school have followed them into the store and grabbed her?

Abandoning the loaded cart, Casey raced up and down the aisles, swerving to avoid startled shoppers. She called out an apology after bumping an elderly woman's cart, then collided with a tall display of Cheez-its, sending red boxes skidding across the floor.

"Grace! Where are you? Grace!"

All she could think about was Alec Bainbridge. He obviously loved his niece with every fiber of his being and would be devastated if something happened to her. Hysteria rose in her throat, threatening to choke her.

Her breathing had shifted to short pants by the time she rounded a corner and spotted the small blond head at the bakery counter. A woman with long, wavy dark hair flowing over a bright red coat knelt beside the child. She had one hand on Grace's shoulder and was offering something in the other. As Casey ran toward them, she thrust her right hand into her purse, feeling for the cold metal of the Sig.

When she raced up, the woman straightened, but Casey kept her hand in her purse and focused her attention on the child. "Grace, where have you been? I've been looking all over for you." Sharp breaths separated her words.

Grace's eyes welled, and her lower lip quivered. "I wanted to get more bananas for Balthazar. Then I forgot where you were, and I got scared 'cause I couldn't find you."

The tightness in Casey's chest eased a fraction. "I'm sorry you were scared, but when you disappeared I was scared, too. We've got to stick together, remember?"

Grace nodded then her face brightened. "But it's okay because Maria found me, and she bought me a cookie."

Casey withdrew her hand from her bag and examined the young woman closely. It was Professor Bainbridge's teaching assistant.

Maria smiled at the little girl and ruffled her hair. "Grace and I are old friends. Aren't we, Grace?"

"Uh, huh."

Maria glanced back at Casey with concern in her dark eyes. "I've been her regular babysitter since she first came to live with the professor. Grace, you know you shouldn't wander off."

"I know." The resignation in the girl's tone suggested they'd had that conversation before.

Casey's took Grace's hand. "We need to get home."

"Can I still have my cookie?"

"You'll spoil your appetite. We're going to bake blondies this afternoon, remember?"

"Oh, yes. I forgot. Let's go." Grace tugged Casey's hand in the direction of the check-out lanes. "Bye, Maria."

Casey felt Maria's gaze on her back as they walked away. She turned to Grace. "Do you like Maria?"

"Uh, huh. She's nice. She lets me chew gum. Uncle Alec doesn't like gum."

Casey had to vote with Uncle Alec. She could easily imagine Grace swallowing her gum in the middle of an animated conversation or getting it stuck in her hair.

After retrieving the cart, they took their place in the checkout line behind a woman with a pair of cranky toddlers. Grace suddenly jerked Casey's hand. "The bananas!"

Casey sighed. "We walked right by them when we came in. Why didn't you ask then?"

Grace tipped her head with a classic, four-year-old, *duh* expression. "I didn't think of it then. I can only do things when I think of them."

How could one argue with logic like that?

Casey sighed again and asked the woman with the toddlers to watch their cart while they zipped to the produce section to grab the ripest bananas they could find. After checking out, Grace helped load the bags into the collapsible cart, and they headed home.

The weak afternoon sun had caused a thin layer of slush to form on top of the snow-packed sidewalk, making it extra slippery. Grace kept up an easy chatter about her friends at preschool, her favorite stuffed animals, and the toys she wanted for her upcoming fifth birthday, while Casey relived the initial terror of glancing up to find the child gone. She had failed her first test as a bodyguard—miserably.

What would the professor say when he found out? Although his niece was unharmed, he was bound to be angry. At the very least, he would lose all confidence in her ability to do her job. After all, he had given her fair warning that Grace could be a handful. Casey's stomach churned as she pictured the inevitable conversation. By the time she and Grace reached the house, her stomach was in knots.

As she opened the front gate, an unbidden thought popped into her head and curled around her brain like a wisp of smoke. Did she really have to mention the incident? After all, Grace was fine, and no harm was done. By the time she'd unzipped her coat, she realized she was being cowardly and childish. Of course, she would tell Alec what had happened. He had every right to know. Truth was not a disposable commodity. If he fired her, so be it. The coffee shop on the corner of campus was always hiring.

Once she had put the groceries away and locked her Sig back in her suitcase, she allowed Grace to let Balthazar out of his cage and take him upstairs to the third-floor playroom. Within minutes she discovered Alec was right—the monkey was extremely clever. He was also incorrigibly naughty. And he liked crayons. He *really* liked crayons.

After a frustrating hour spent trying to keep him from eating the crayons or drawing on the walls, Casey glanced at her watch. "Grace, it's time for Balthazar to go back in his cage."

"Oh, but—" Grace hugged his furry little body to her chest, while he glared at Casey and screeched.

"If we don't get those blondies in the oven soon, they won't be ready in time for a snack before dinner, and Balthazar might get hurt if he runs loose in the kitchen while we're baking."

Grace jumped up, keeping her grip on the monkey. "That would be bad. Uncle Alec told me it's my job to help keep Balthazar safe."

Balthazar wrapped his legs around her waist and grabbed two tiny fistfuls of her hair.

Grace worked to disentangle his fingers as she headed for the door. "Bad boy, Balthazar! You know you're not supposed to do that." She continued her lecture until the unrepentant monkey was safely back in his cage.

Casey searched the kitchen drawers for an apron and eventually settled on an oversized tea towel to tie around Grace's neck before they set to work. Soon the tantalizing aromas of melted butter and brown sugar filled the kitchen. By the time the blondies were cool enough to eat, it was nearly four o'clock—definitely too late for such a substantial snack—but she cut two small squares anyway and poured them each a glass of milk.

"I love these." Grace's words were muffled by a mouthful of blondie.

"I thought you would, and you did a great job helping."

As Casey ate the last crumb off her plate, she heard the front door opening and closing, and her pulse shot up. Either they were being burgled by a robber with a key, or the professor was home early. She rose and set the dirty dishes in the sink.

Moments later Alec strode into the kitchen. He set his briefcase on the floor. "Hello, ladies. How was your afternoon?"

Grace hopped down from her chair and ran to greet him with a hug. "Busy. Balthazar and I colored, then Casey taught me how to bake blondies. You can have one—they're really good. Oh, and one more thing—I got lost."

Alec straightened and pinned Casey with a steely glare. "Lost?"

# CHAPTER THREE

Alec's frown deepened. Four hours. Casey Callahan had only been in charge of Grace for four hours, and his niece had already managed to get *lost*. He tried to keep his tone calm to avoid upsetting his niece. "What exactly happened?"

Grace's expression was almost bored. "I was looking for bananas for Balthazar."

"Alone?"

"Casey was busy reading. I was only gone a minute, but then I got lost." Her face brightened. "But it was okay. Maria found me. She bought me a cookie, but Casey wouldn't let me eat it because we had to come home and make blondies. They're really good. Do you want one?"

"Maybe after dinner. Why don't you go play with Balthazar for a while? I'm sure he would be glad to see you." He turned to Casey. "Casey and I need to talk."

She acknowledged the statement with a silent nod.

Grace grabbed a banana from the fruit bowl and turned imploring eyes on Casey. "Can I take him a treat? He's really good at peeling them himself. You should see him."

Casey's lips barely curved. "Go ahead. I'll watch Balthazar peel a banana another time. I need to talk to your uncle."

"Okay." Grace raced out of the kitchen and thundered up the stairs.

Alec turned to Casey. He took no pleasure from the apprehension on her face, but she had managed to lose Grace in *only four hours!*

He motioned toward the kitchen table. "Let's sit."

She sat facing him with her hands clasped in her lap and tension radiating from her stiff posture.

"Tell me what happened this afternoon."

She glanced away and cleared her throat then lifted her chin. "There isn't much to tell. We had almost finished our shopping, and I stopped to check my list one last time. When I glanced up, Grace had disappeared. I searched the store and found her in the bakery section with your TA. Maria was buying her a cookie."

The cavalcade of emotions across her expressive face belied the simplicity of her explanation.

"She vanished...just like that?"

"In a split second, without a sound."

"That sounds like Grace." He softened his tone. "I warned you."

"You did. And I failed." She dropped her gaze to her lap. "I'll understand if you decide to call Ms. Li and request another agent. In fact, I'll make the call myself."

She looked so dejected, he almost felt guilty. Then he remembered what was at stake. "I don't think we need to do anything that drastic yet, but I am concerned. You told me you had experience with children her age."

She rested one elbow on the table and speared her fingers into the smooth, molten honey of her hair. "I do, but in the preschool lab in the Psychology Department, not in a busy store. I clearly don't know as much as I thought."

"Grace is fast."

Casey met his gaze with renewed panic in her warm brandy eyes. "She almost scared the life out of me—literally. I swear my heart stopped when I looked up and she was gone."

"You learned an important lesson the hard way. Now you have some idea what it means to be a parent."

Her pretty lips compressed into a tight line, and she shook her head. "After today, I'm not sure I'll ever be ready."

"No one's ever ready. There's no way to prepare yourself for the fear of losing your child."

"I suppose not."

"Was Grace crying?"

"No. I think she was relieved to see me, but she didn't seem terribly upset."

"Grace might not always show it, but she feels things deeply. She had barely learned to walk when her mother died. I'm sure she doesn't remember Sara, but sometimes I'll find her holding her mother's picture, just staring at it." And it half-broke his heart every time.

Casey reached for his hand then pulled back as if she regretted the impulse. "Even if she doesn't remember, I'm sure Grace is curious about her mother.

Does she ever talk about her or ask questions about her?"

"Not much. Grace knows her mother died when she was a baby, and I've told her that her mother loved her very much, but I don't want to give her more information that she can handle."

"Adults are often surprised by how much children can handle."

He leaned back in his chair as the memories rolled through his brain. "My sister was a naïve and irresponsible twenty-three-year-old looking for a good time when she fell in love with the drummer in a local band back home in Indiana who moonlighted as a drug dealer." He glanced across at Casey. "What is it about women and bad boys?"

She raised one shoulder. "The allure of the forbidden?"

He snorted in disgust. "Well, it didn't work out too well for Sara. When she got pregnant, he took off. Since both our parents were gone, she came to live with me. Shortly after Grace's first birthday, her father re-appeared. Three days later, he drove his motorcycle into the back of a semi at seventy miles an hour." Alec paused and swallowed hard. Even after three years, the words caught in his throat. "Sara was riding behind him. They both died instantly."

"I'm so sorry." Casey's voice was gentle, and her eyes glistened.

He straightened his cuff and glanced at his watch without seeing it. "At any rate, you can see why I haven't shared the full story with Grace."

Casey nodded. "I'm sure she'll want to hear it someday, but you'll know when the time is right."

He shoved his chair back from the table with a sigh and pushed to his feet. "I guess I'd better have another talk with her about the dangers of wandering off."

She rose, too. "I'm so sorry about this afternoon, Professor. I swear it will never happen again."

"You should probably call me Alec, at least when we're at home." He allowed his lips to tip up on one side. "Now that you've seen how easily Grace can slip away, I'm sure you'll be more careful in the future."

When she returned his smile, a dimple appeared in her left cheek. "Those handcuffs are sounding better all the time."

"I wouldn't rule them out," he replied as he headed toward the stairs.

He found Grace and Balthazar playing dress-up in the third-floor playroom. Grace was dressed in her favorite blue princess costume, and the monkey wore a pointed headdress with a wispy pink scarf hanging from the tip. When Alec entered the room, Balthazar glared at him and shrieked.

"Grace, I need to talk to you."

She turned back to arranging the play dishes on her child-sized table. "Okay, but we're having a fancy dinner and a ball."

"I'm sorry, but you'll have to take a break from the party. This is important."

When she faced him, her lower lip quivered. "Am I in trouble?"

*Stay calm. You don't want to scare her.* Parenting could be a real balancing act sometimes. "Why do you think you might be in trouble?"

She reached over to the monkey and straightened his hat. "At the store, I didn't tell Casey where I was going."

"Why not? You know you're not supposed to go off on your own."

"I was only going to be gone a minute."

"That doesn't matter. We've talked about this before. Sometimes it only takes a minute for something bad to happen."

"But nothing bad did happen," Grace insisted. "Maria found me and bought me a cookie."

"What if someone else had found you, someone you didn't know?"

She gave him a pitying look for being so dense. "Uncle Alec, I'm not a baby. I know not to take cookies from strangers."

He could go on with what-ifs in an attempt to make his point, but his head was starting to hurt. Little-girl logic could do that to a man. "Promise me you won't wander off alone again."

"Okay, I promise."

"You'd better mean that, because if I don't think you're grown-up enough to be trusted, I'll have to take Balthazar to live at the vet's until Professor Huerta comes home."

Grace's eyes rounded, and her mouth fell open. "You wouldn't!"

"Only a very trustworthy person can be responsible for taking care of an animal."

"You can trust me. I promise I won't go anyplace by myself ever again!"

He smiled and reached for her to give her a hug. "We'll talk about it again in a few years. Maybe by the time you're this tall," he held his hand at shoulder height, "you can go out by yourself."

A look of relief crossed Grace's face. "Good. That won't be long then. You tell me all the time how fast I'm growing."

Alec kissed the top of her head. "That you are." *Much too fast.* "Let's go down and see what Casey is fixing for dinner tonight."

"But Balthazar and I haven't finished our ball."

Alec glanced at the monkey, who was chewing the end of the scarf on his headdress. "I think Balthazar's getting hungry. He's eating his hat."

Grace snatched the headdress from his head. "Bad monkey! You can't play dress-up any more if you eat the costumes."

Balthazar bared his teeth in a cheesy grin.

Alec helped Grace change out of her princess dress and put her toys away. After stopping on the second floor to deposit Balthazar in his crate, they went down to the kitchen. Casey stood with her back to the door, cleaning carrots at the sink. The sun's dying rays filtered through the window in front of her, warming the silhouette of her hair like a soft, golden halo. The tune she was humming under her breath sounded like Bon Jovi's "Living on a Prayer." Alec had been just a kid when his mother used to dance around their trailer, belting out that song at the top of her voice.

"So, what did you and Grace choose for dinner?"

Casey started, and the vegetable peeler clattered in the sink. She spun around, pointing a carrot at him like a cornered convict with a shiv. "Don't do that! You nearly gave me a heart attack."

He grinned. "Sorry."

"We're making chicken nuggets, Uncle Alec," Grace piped up. "*Real* ones, not frozen from a box."

He raised one brow at Casey. "Oh?"

Her cheeks turned pink. "Um, yes. I thought it would be fun for Grace...not that there's anything wrong with frozen nuggets."

"Of course not."

He perched on a stool next to the counter, scrolling through his office email on his phone while stealing glances at Casey and Grace. Casey had tied a big towel around the child's neck and found a plastic milk crate for her to stand on so they could work together. Grace watched Casey cut the chicken into bite-sized pieces, then helped measure the salt and bread crumbs for the coating. She beamed when Casey let her shake the nuggets in the plastic bag all by herself.

When the chicken was ready for the pan, Casey lifted Grace off the crate. "Hot oil can be very dangerous, and we don't want you to get burned. Why don't you set the table while I fry these? Then you can help pour the milk."

Watching the pair, Alec's chest tightened. Was Grace's life incomplete because she had no mother? Was this what family life was supposed to be like? He certainly had no model to follow from his own childhood. His mother had spent most of the time she was home lost in a bottle of cheap scotch, leaving him to tend to his and Sara's basic needs. He'd done his best, but it hadn't been enough.

A few minutes later, they took their seats at the kitchen table, and Casey served dinner. The first bite surprised the melancholy right out of him. "Wow, these are delicious!"

The dimple re-appeared in her cheek. "Better than pre-packaged and frozen?"

"Hey, I do my best."

She smiled at Grace, who was wolfing hers down. "You do a great job." She tapped the child's wrist with her forefinger. "Grace, slow down. You'll choke."

Alec popped a carrot into his mouth. Ordinarily, he hated cooked carrots, but these were delicious.

"I added a little honey and mint."

"It works for me."

After they finished dinner, Casey rose and gathered the dirty plates. "Grace, would you like to serve the blondies?"

The little girl scooted out of her chair and returned, balancing the plate as if the golden squares were made of spun glass instead of flour, sugar, and eggs. She set the plate in front of Alec very carefully.

He made a show of choosing the best-looking one. "These are beautiful, Grace. Did you help make them?"

"Uh, huh. And they're yummy."

She was right. Alec ate a couple of bites then met Casey's gaze with an appreciative nod. "These were an excellent project. What's on the agenda for tomorrow?"

Grace's eyes brightened. "I want to go to the zoo!" She turned to Casey. "When I have a vacation from school, Uncle Alec always takes me to the zoo."

Casey frowned. "It might be a little cold for that."

"Winter is the perfect time to see the penguins."

Casey didn't look convinced. "Well—"

"Maybe Sophia can come!"

When Casey sent him a questioning glance, Alec replied, "Sophia is Grace's best friend. She lives a couple of blocks over." He turned to Grace. "I'll make you a deal. If you help clean up the dishes, I'll call Mrs.

Chiang and see if Sophia is available tomorrow afternoon. Okay?"

"Yay!" She wriggled to the floor and began a silly, sideways waddle. "We're going to see the penguins! We're going to see the penguins!"

Alec slipped off to the living room and placed a quick call to Carolyn Chiang. Carolyn was a professor of Art History, and her husband George was an anesthesiologist at the University Hospital. She'd been a bastion of support since Alec's first overwhelming weeks as an instant single parent. Over the past four years, the Chiangs had become like family. Carolyn was the only person he'd called after receiving the anonymous letter, when he'd been consumed by panic and unable to think straight. It was she who'd suggested he consider a bodyguard for Grace.

A couple of minutes later, he returned to the kitchen. "You're all set for the zoo tomorrow. You can pick Sophia up at one o'clock." He hesitated then frowned. "I didn't think to ask if you have a car. I guess I could try to rearrange my afternoon schedule to drive you."

Casey gave him an impish smile. "Don't worry. I don't own a car, but I have something better—a chauffeur."

He lifted one brow. Was she an heiress in disguise, slumming it as a bodyguard?

"I'll have a Phoenix, Ltd. car and driver pick us up. It's one of the services our firm provides."

The tension eased from his shoulders. He liked the safe, secure sound of a professional driver and company car. "Sounds good. Have fun with the penguins."

****

Shortly before one o'clock the next afternoon, the doorbell chimed. Grace beat Casey to the door because she'd been bouncing around the living room in her hat, parka, and mittens for half an hour, beyond excited about the trip to the zoo.

Casey opened the door to a tall, freckled redhead, dressed all in black and wearing a chauffeur's cap. "Hi, Risa."

Risa was the receptionist, researcher, IT department, and principal driver for the Phoenix, Ltd. personal protection agency. No bit of information was too obscure, no client request too outlandish, no technology too complex for Risa. She was the acknowledged Queen of Everything. Once, she had greeted Casey at the front desk wearing a cardboard crown decorated with glitter and rhinestones.

Risa addressed Grace with a smile. "I see you're ready to go."

Casey pulled her coat on and picked up her bag. "She's been ready since she woke up."

The little girl stared at Risa, then at the black Town Car parked at the curb, then back at Risa. "Are you driving us in a movie star car?"

Risa laughed. "Not exactly, but kind of. Come on, I'll show you." She reached for Grace's hand and walked beside her while Grace skipped down the front walk singing her penguin song.

Casey locked the door and set the alarm before joining them at the car. After settling Grace in one of the two child safety seats she'd requested for the back seat, she joined Risa in front and gave her the Chiangs' address. Two minutes later, she and Grace stood on the front porch of a classic Chicago brownstone. When the Chiangs' housekeeper opened the door, Sophia burst past her, clad in hot pink from head to toe, the perfect contrast to her long, straight black hair. The girls greeted each other as if they'd been separated for months instead of a couple of days, then ran to climb into the back seat of the car. They kept up their excited chatter all the way up Lake Shore Drive until Risa pulled into the entrance of the Lincoln Park Zoo.

"What time shall I pick you up?" she asked, as Casey wrangled the girls out of their car seats.

"How about four o'clock?"

"Perfect. I'll meet you here." She flashed a lopsided grin. "Oh, and good luck. I have a feeling you'll need it."

The girls wanted to go straight to Penguin Cove, so Casey checked the map near the entrance before taking each one firmly by the hand and heading out. She was not going to allow a repeat of yesterday's incident in the grocery store.

As soon as they spied the penguin exhibit, the girls tore loose and raced toward the huge plate-glass windows with Casey in hot pursuit.

"Grace, Sophia, slow down!"

When she caught up, they were giggling, noses pressed against the glass.

"Look at that one," Grace exclaimed, pointing to one animal, who kept sliding into the water, then popping back up onto the snow-covered rock ledge like cork from a champagne bottle.

A few small groups of mothers with preschoolers also clustered in front of the windows, but the big, concrete-floored room had a hollow, empty feeling. Weekday afternoons in the dead of winter were clearly off-peak hours for visiting the zoo.

"Hello, ladies," a deep voice said from behind her.

Casey's body jerked as she sucked in a short breath. When she spun around, she found herself staring up at what had to be the most beautiful man she'd ever seen. He was perfectly proportioned — tall, with just the right amount of muscle. Thick black hair fell away from his face in casual waves. His nose was strong, his lips full and sensuous, and when he smiled, his white teeth formed a dazzling contrast to his warm, olive-toned skin. If someone had told Casey he was Michelangelo's *David* come to life, she wouldn't have been surprised.

"H-hello."

Mr. Perfect offered his hand. "I'm Theo."

She grasped his palm, marveling at its warmth in the chilly room. "Casey."

A small hand tugged on Theo's sleeve. "We're not ladies."

He gave Casey's hand a brief squeeze before releasing it, then turned the full wattage of his smile on a frowning Grace. "No? Are you penguins, then?"

Grace's frown dissolved. Apparently, no female could resist this man's charm. "No, silly. We're girls."

Theo glanced from Grace to Sophia and back. "Well, you look like beautiful ladies to me. Tell me, do you like the penguins?"

Both girls nodded.

"These are special penguins from South Africa, and we have twelve of them here at the zoo."

Casey noted his navy-blue pants and shirt with the simple plastic name badge that read *Theo*. He must be a docent or one of the zookeepers. He certainly seemed well-informed.

"Notice how you're inside, but the penguins are outside," Theo continued. "This is a special open-air exhibit. The rocks were designed to mimic the birds' natural habitat in South Africa." He flashed Casey a smile that would have steamed up her glasses, had she been wearing any, before returning his attention to the girls. "Do you know what a habitat is?"

Sophia assumed a bored, yet superior, expression. "Everybody knows that. A habitat is where they live."

Theo rewarded her with a glittering smile. "That's right. You're very smart girls."

Grace and Sophia looked at each other and giggled.

Theo talked about the penguins for several more minutes then turned to Casey "I'm just finishing my shift and was headed to the cafeteria for a cup of coffee. I wonder if you'd like to join me." He flashed a charming grin at the girls. "I hear they make wonderful hot cocoa and chocolate chip cookies."

*Say yes,* her ego whispered in her ear.

An unwelcome little voice quickly responded. *You're working. You have two preschoolers in tow. You can't accept, no matter how spectacular he is.*

Her ego tried to make excuses. *It's not a date. The girls are hungry. It's a snack. Besides, maybe he finds me attractive.*

The annoying, rational little voice scoffed at the idea. *You're cute enough, but get real...*

*But I haven't had a date – or even a non-date – in months,* her ego whined, *not since Peter left, and Theo's drop-dead gorgeous.*

*And he was waiting here, just for you? Dream on.*

*Oh, shut up.*

Before she could reply to his invitation, each girl grabbed an arm and began tugging. "Can we? Can we? Please, please."

Casey couldn't resist the excited look of anticipation on their upturned faces. To be honest, she didn't try too hard. Little voice of reason be damned. It had been ages since she'd spent time with such an attractive man. Okay, it had been forever. "I guess we have time." She glanced up at Theo with a tentative smile. "Lead the way."

The warmth of his answering smile curled her toes inside her boots.

He swept one arm ahead in a theatrical gesture. "This way, ladies."

Grace and Sophia danced a few steps ahead, while Theo walked beside Casey. "Is the pretty little blonde your daughter?"

Hmm. Not a very impressive pick-up line. Maybe her catty inner voice was right, and he wasn't interested in her after all. "No. I'm the...uh...nanny."

"Ah." He nodded. "She must keep you on your toes."

"She does." Casey chuckled. "But overall she's delightful and very well-behaved."

"Of course." When he shook his head, the perfect waves of his hair swayed in wavy perfection. "I only meant she's quite lively."

"She is that."

She caught up with the girls in a couple of brisk steps and took each by the hand. They continued to converse happily as they followed Theo toward the cafeteria. As they approached the entrance, she sensed movement out of the corner of one eye. An indistinct figure appeared in a shadowed hallway and lingered for a couple of seconds, watching. Then it turned and disappeared around a corner.

# CHAPTER FOUR

Alec was grumpy—he admitted it. For starters, he still had that damned note in his desk. As soon as he'd returned to the office the day before, after settling Casey with Grace, he'd called the campus police to report it. The dispatcher had told him that since it wasn't an emergency, an officer wasn't available to take the report right away. No one had shown up that afternoon or the next day, and he had no idea if, or when, someone would. How was he supposed to put an end to the threat to Grace if the police couldn't be bothered?

That afternoon he'd ended up with four undergrads in his office, all wanting help with their Middle Egyptian grammar. Normally, that would have been Maria's job, but she didn't seem to be around. Every time he glanced up, Nora Samuels seemed to be hovering outside his office. And to top things off, he had been right in the middle of an explanation of proper word order when Fermin LeBlanc strolled in wanting to see the Fassbender boat. It was all Alec could do not to grab him by his gray and yellow paisley scarf and fling him into the hallway.

His mood hadn't improved when he'd arrived home to find Casey and Grace still out. They'd been gone four hours. How long did it take to look at a bunch of penguins? He had gone upstairs to clean Balthazar's cage when he heard the heavy *thunk* of a car door slamming. A couple of minutes later the front door opened, and Grace's happy chatter preceded her into the foyer. The minute Alec unlocked the cage, Balthazar shot out and scampered down the stairs to greet her. Alec followed at a more measured pace.

He found Casey hanging their coats in the front hall closet. Her soft cream-colored sweater and faded jeans hugged her curves perfectly without being too tight. When she turned to greet him, her smile evaporated.

"I thought you'd be home an hour ago. What took you so long?" As soon as the words left his mouth, he wanted to call them back. His prized self-control seemed to have deserted him the past few days. If he didn't find it again soon, she was going to think he was nothing but an arrogant, demanding jerk.

*What does it matter what she thinks of you? You're paying her to do a job.*

*It matters.*

Her lips thinned, and a tiny muscle in her jaw flexed. "It's rush hour, and there was an accident on Lake Shore Drive."

He consciously relaxed his face, hoping for a more amiable expression. "Of course, I should have realized. Since I'm spoiled by being able to walk to work, I forget about rush hour."

Before Casey could reply, Grace bounded into the room wearing Balthazar like a backpack. "Hi, Uncle Alec."

His smile was reflexive, a natural response to her cheerful energy. "Did you have a good time at the zoo? How were the penguins?"

"They were funny. There was one who jumped in the water and popped back up, over and over. Sophia and I called him Poppy. And Casey met a new boyfriend named Theo. He looks like a movie star and bought us hot cocoa and chocolate chip cookies."

His gut tightened.

Grace hitched Balthazar higher on her back. "Is dinner soon? I'm starving."

They both turned to Casey, who froze with a blank look on her face. "I...uh...haven't had time to think about dinner yet."

Alec made a snap decision. Opening the pantry, he pulled out a box of crackers and offered one to Grace. "This should tide you over until the pizza arrives."

"Pizza! Yay!" She snatched the cracker.

"You and Balthazar go up to the playroom. I'll call you when it gets here."

Cracker in hand, she whooped and raced out of the kitchen with the monkey clinging to her back, sporting a toothy grin.

"Thanks for the quick thinking...about the pizza."

Alec turned. "It's my standard fallback. As I told you, cooking is not part of your job description." He leaned one hip against the counter, crossed his arms, and waited.

Casey studied her fingers for a moment as they twisted the silver patterned ring on her right hand then raised her eyes to meet his. "I suppose you'd like to hear more about our trip this afternoon."

"According to Grace, you met a new boyfriend who looks like a movie star."

"Theo's hardly my boyfriend."

"Then who is he?"

A pair of tiny lines appeared between her brows, and her lips pursed. "I think he was a zoo employee or docent. He was wearing a uniform with a name tag and seemed to know a lot about the penguins."

"Grace said he bought you cocoa and cookies. That seems like a strange thing for an employee to do, no matter how attractive he thought you were."

She bristled. "He had just finished his shift and invited the three of us for a snack. It was perfectly innocent."

Alec doubled down. "He was a stranger."

A muscle in Casey's jaw tightened then released. "He wasn't going to do anything. We were in a public place, and I had my gun in my purse. The girls were so excited by his offer, they might have raised holy hell if I'd said no. I can assure you, Grace was perfectly safe."

"What if he'd grabbed her and run?"

"I held her hand while we followed him to the cafe, and I and sat next to her, across the table from Theo. I knew the situation was unusual and was on guard the whole time. It would have been impossible for him to make a move before I could act."

Alec released a heavy breath, dropped his arms, and straightened. "It sounds like you had the situation under control."

"I did."

He ran a hand through his hair and glanced away. "I'm sorry, but it's hard to stop worrying."

She took a step toward him and rested a hand on his arm. "I understand. Did the campus police come by about the letter?"

He shook his head. "No. Apparently they're too busy. Hopefully, someone will find time to take the report tomorrow."

She dropped her hand, but a worried look came into her eyes. "I hope so, too." Then she smiled. "Now about that pizza…"

He relaxed a bit and returned her smile as he reached into his pocket for his phone. "I'll get right on it."

Later that night, as he lay in bed hovering on the edge of sleep, loose, random thoughts careened through his brain like balls in a pinball machine. He reached for them but was too tired to hold any one long enough to focus on it. Images of Grace, the letter, Casey, and the Fassbender boat swirled in his head until he was dizzy. His last conscious thought before falling into a restless sleep was that he was tired of reacting. He needed to take action, but exactly what action remained beyond his grasp.

The next morning, instead of taking the time to eat his usual bowl of oatmeal with his niece, Alec filled a travel mug with coffee and grabbed a sesame seed bagel from the bakery bag on the counter, pausing only long enough to plant a quick kiss on Grace's sleep-rumpled head before dashing out the door. He made it to the NEI in record time and was at his desk before eight o'clock, determined to bring some measure of control to the turmoil that had taken over his life in the last three days.

First on his list was a call to the director of Grace's school to let her know Grace would be staying home for a while. He'd gone back and forth all night about how much information to share and ultimately decided to stick with the truth. Fortunately, Mrs. Romero was a straightforward, no-nonsense woman, not given to overreaction or unnecessary drama. Alec stressed there was no threat to the other children, and he intended to do everything in his power to keep it that way. She thanked him and said everyone missed Grace and hoped the situation would be resolved as soon as possible. By the time he hung up the phone, the knot in Alec's gut had eased a fraction. His world was beginning to regain some semblance of order.

He glanced at his watch. It was barely eight-thirty. He made a quick call to the campus police, who assured him an officer would be over within the hour to take his report. With luck, he still had time to go down to the basement, retrieve the boat from the vault in the archives, and get some work done before the cop showed up.

Between his computer and the books in his personal library, Alec was able to conduct much of his research in his office while the artifact remained safely locked away. Today, though, he wanted to spend some time with the actual piece, and he wanted to do it in comfort. The archives were maintained at fifty degrees — the optimal temperature for preserving museum relics — which was miserably cold for people. Even the light cotton gloves he wore to handle antiquities weren't much help. Besides, the natural light in his office was better for examining fine details than the harsh overhead lights in the interior basement room.

Other faculty and staff members were starting to arrive as he headed down the broad stone stairway.

"Morning, Indy!"

He grimaced and suppressed the temptation to return Howard Boardman's customary greeting with a one-fingered salute. Howard taught Mesopotamian Archaeology and never tired of comparing Alec to Indiana Jones in mock tribute to his home state. At the Near Eastern Institute Christmas party a couple of years ago, Howard had gone so far as to present him with a floppy brown fedora, to the delighted howls of the rest of the department. Alec had laughed and replied that all he needed now was a bullwhip, but the joke had long since grown stale as far as he was concerned.

Nevertheless, he dipped his chin in acknowledgement. "Howard."

Twenty minutes later, he was back in his office gingerly removing the delicate wooden boat from its protective crate when a series of loud raps sounded on his closed door. He sucked in a sharp breath but held tight to the boat.

Before he had a chance to respond, the door opened, and Fermin LeBlanc stuck his head in. When his gaze landed on Alec's desk, his eyes widened, and his goatee twitched. "Ah, I see you're working on the boat. May I come in?"

*Sure. Why not? I don't have anything important to do this morning.*

Alec forced his features into what he hoped was a pleasant, collegial expression. "Of course."

He glimpsed a figure clad in dark green lingering in the hallway as Fermin came through the door, but it disappeared before he could be certain. It had better not be another student wanting help with grammar, because he had no time to spare for that today.

Fermin pulled a pair of pince-nez glasses from the inside breast pocket of his jacket and balanced them on his nose.

*Who the hell wears pince-nez glasses? What a pretentious ass.*

As the annoying little man leaned over Alec's desk toward the Fassbender boat, the fringe on his brown silk scarf brushed a pile of papers, sending the top one sailing to the floor. Fermin tilted his head and stroked his goatee as he leaned in, until the tip of his nose nearly touched the carved wooden figure standing at the prow ahead of the sixteen miniature oarsmen. "Definitely Middle Kingdom—probably Eleventh or Twelfth Dynasty, I'd say."

Alec eyed the artifact, carved to resemble funerary boats of the time made from papyrus stalks lashed together. "Stylistically, I'm leaning toward Twelfth Dynasty, sometime around 1980 B.C.E. Dating is difficult when you have no idea when or where the piece was excavated, and that assumes we're not dealing with a top-quality fake constructed from ancient materials taken from artifacts of lesser value. As a first step, I've sent a sliver from the bottom to the Illinois State Geological Survey lab in Champaign for radiocarbon dating."

Fermin straightened and raised his brows. "I'm surprised the director authorized the expense. If the boat proves authentic, it will have to be returned to Egypt, and if not, the museum can't display it anyway."

"Not necessarily. If it turns out to be a fake, the director is thinking of using it as the centerpiece of a new educational display on forged antiquities."

Fermin's posture stiffened almost imperceptibly. "That could be interesting. How much progress have you made so far?"

A colorful Arabic curse popped into Alec's mind. The man had a real knack for turning even a simple question into a high-handed demand.

He bit back his instinctive response, reminding himself there was no point in antagonizing his colleague unnecessarily. As department chair, Fermin held the reins of the budget. "It's a complicated process. Dating is only part of the puzzle. There's also the issue of proving the provenance. Even if the piece is as old as it looks, is this the boat the Supreme Council of Antiquities claims it is? If we can prove it isn't, the Museum will be able to legitimately keep the boat."

"That would certainly make the trustees and director happy."

Alec nodded. "I'm sure it would. The Egyptian authorities believe it was looted from a provincial museum during the unrest of 2011, but their documentation is minimal—almost as skimpy as Fassbender's."

Fermin's lips parted in a knowing smile. "I was well acquainted with Ernest. Did you know that? He had a great passion for antiquities, but he could be a sly old dog."

*To say the least.* "He also wasn't much of a record-keeper. His will stated he bought the boat in 1975 from a dealer in Hamburg, who bought it from a dealer in Cairo in 1962. Since antiquities purchased legally before 1970 aren't subject to the current laws, we have to do everything we can to determine the legitimacy of Fassbender's claims."

Fermin fingered his goatee again, stroking it to a point. "That won't be easy after all this time."

*Tell me about it.* "We have the name of the alleged German dealer, but he died twenty years ago. I've been working with the German authorities to try to track down his records, but so far we haven't found much."

Movement in the doorway caught Alec's attention, and he peered over Fermin's shoulder at a matronly figure clad in a forest green sweater over a gray wool skirt. "Can I help you with something, Nora?"

Nora Samuels hesitated in the hallway. "I have that grant proposal typed up and ready for your signature, Professor Bainbridge, but I don't want to interrupt."

Alec frowned. The proposal wasn't due for three weeks. The regular department secretary would simply have left it in his box in the main office. Maybe because Nora was new, she wanted to make a good impression by being extra efficient.

He glanced at Fermin. "I think we're about finished here."

"I suppose, although I would like to examine some of the details more closely when you have time. Do you keep the boat here?"

Even a linguist with minimal archaeological experience like Fermin should know better than that. Was the man accusing him of slipshod handling of a valuable artifact? Alec's spine stiffened. "Only when necessary."

Fermin raised his chin with a sniff. "I'll have try to stop by at a necessary time, then."

"Feel free, but I'll probably be quite busy. The director is expecting my report in the next few weeks,

UNDERCOVER NANNY

so…" Alec lifted his shoulders in a you-know-how-it-is shrug.

Fermin's eyes narrowed. "That soon?" He dropped his gaze to the boat and fiddled with the ends of his scarf for a moment before stepping back from the desk. "Well, it appears you have your task cut out for you. I hope the rest of your work doesn't suffer."

Alec gritted his teeth. "I'll manage."

The officious little man turned and bustled from the room, brushing past Nora, who still hovered outside the door. Alec sighed and waved her in.

She glanced over her shoulder, down the hall. "Professor LeBlanc likes to keep a close eye on the workings of the department, doesn't he? I seem to run into him every time I leave my office."

Alec made a point of avoiding department gossip and wasn't about to be drawn into a potentially career-damaging conversation about Fermin's terminal nosiness. "He likes to keep busy, and he isn't teaching this quarter."

Nora's glance sharpened over her purple reading glasses as she presented the document she held. "Here's that grant proposal."

He took it. "Thank you. I'll drop it off after I've had a chance to check it over and sign it."

Her mouth tightened. "Of course." But she made no move to leave.

"Was there something else?"

Her lips parted then clamped shut again. She shook her head. "No. Let me know if you need any revisions."

Alec smiled. "Will do. Thanks again." As she strode from his office in her sensible Miss Marple shoes, he shook his head. Nora was a character, but so was nearly everyone else at the Institute. She wasn't much odder than most.

The small desk clock he'd received as a prize for winning an essay contest in high school showed eight-fifty. The campus police officer could show up at any time, but with the director's deadline looming, Alec couldn't afford to waste a minute. He retrieved a magnifying glass from his desk drawer and began to examine the artifact.

The green paint on the sides of the boat and the white on the figures' loincloths were remarkably well-preserved. Not a single piece appeared to have ever been broken. The expressions on the oarsmen's faces showed their devotion to the task of rowing the soul of the departed to the cult center of Osiris at Abydos. The boat looked more like a barely-used child's toy than an ancient relic from the reign of Amenemhat I. But Alec knew better than to give too much weight to an artifact's condition. There were too many other variables to be considered.

Several minutes later another knock interrupted his concentration. At this rate he would be lucky to finish his evaluation before June. When he glanced up, a tall, dark-haired young man in the uniform of the campus police stepped through the doorway.

"Professor Bainbridge?"

"Yes. Please come in."

The officer approached his desk with the fluid grace of a natural athlete. His gaze bounced down to the boat on the desk then back to Alec before he unzipped his padded jacket and removed a small pad and pen. "You called about a threatening letter."

"Yes." Alec opened his middle drawer and removed the envelope. "I found this on my desk yesterday morning."

The officer slipped on a pair of blue nitrile gloves before accepting it. He sucked a breath in through his teeth as he scanned the short message. "Have you taken any precautions based on this?"

Alec nodded. "I've removed my niece from school for the time being. She's at home with a nanny."

The young man jotted a few words in his notebook. "And have you received any other messages, or noticed anything out of the ordinary, or anyone behaving oddly?"

"There was an incident the previous day when an unauthorized man tried to pick her up from school. The school called the police, and one of your officers took a report. Since I found the note shortly after the incident, I believe there may be a connection."

The young man scribbled a few more words. "I'll refer this to the detective assigned to that case, and she'll be in touch if she has any questions or information."

"Thank you."

"Is there any other specific action you'd like us to take at this point, sir?"

Alec wasn't sure what he'd expected. The cops weren't likely to set up round-the-clock surveillance on his office in case the note-writer left another message, and he had no further clues to offer. "I guess not. I'll wait to hear from your detective."

The officer slipped the envelope and letter into a plastic zip-lock bag and tucked it into his inside jacket pocket, along with the notebook. "Is there anything else?"

"Not that I can think of." Alec rose and offered his hand across his desk. "Thank you, Officer—" He glanced at the plastic name tag pinned to the man's coat. "—Foster."

The young man gave his hand a firm shake. "You're welcome, sir." He reached into his pocket and pulled out a business card. "And if there are further developments or you have any questions, please give me a call. I'll be happy to coordinate the department's efforts in the case for you." As he turned to leave, his gaze settled on the Fassbender boat, and he bent down to take a closer look. "That's an unusual boat. Does it belong to your niece?"

Alec walked around the side of the desk "It's a piece I'm working on—an artifact from the museum."

The officer straightened with an engaging grin. "I guess I shouldn't touch it."

Alec didn't return his smile. "That would be a good guess. It doesn't look it, but that boat is almost four thousand years old."

The young cop drew back. "I never would have guessed. I'm surprised you keep it in your office. Aren't you worried someone might steal it?"

Alec bit back his growing impatience. The officer might carry a gun, but he didn't look much older than some of the grad students. *I guess all kids love toy boats.* "We have excellent security here."

"I'll leave you to it then." The young cop patted his jacket over the pocket. "Be sure to call if anything else happens."

"I will. And thank you for coming."

Officer Foster headed toward the door. "Just doing my job."

After he left, Alec rose from his chair and closed and locked the door. He had no appointments or classes the rest of the day and desperately needed a few uninterrupted hours to examine and record the techniques the ancient artist had employed to join the pieces of the miniature boat together.

At five o'clock he leaned back in his chair, removed his glasses, and rubbed his eyes. He'd been able to confirm the construction of the boat was appropriate to the time period in question. He'd also received an email from the German authorities with a couple of intriguing bits of information about Ernest Fassbender's alleged antiquities dealer. All in all, not a bad day's work. He pushed to his feet, stretched, then kneaded the small of his back with both hands. He couldn't remember the last time he'd sat working for so many hours straight.

He packed the boat away in its protective crate, and by the time he had returned it to the archives, most of the other offices were empty and the building was nearly deserted. He pulled his coat on, wrapped a scarf around his neck, said goodnight to the guard on duty at the front desk, and headed out.

When he reached the bottom of the steps and turned east, a frigid, gusty wind off the lake smacked him in the face, hurling tiny stinging pellets of snow against his exposed flesh. He pulled the scarf up over his cheeks and nose but left his eyes uncovered. The last thing he needed was a broken ankle from a misstep off the curb. Pedestrians going the opposite direction blew past him as he bent his head into the wind and pushed ahead.

Normally he enjoyed the walk home after work. It gave him an opportunity to unwind and switch gears before diving into an evening of domestic duties. Since there was very little parking around the NEI, a number of the professors used ride-sharing services, even for short commutes, but Alec had always considered that absurd for a six-block walk. Not tonight. Tonight, he would gladly have footed the bill for a door-to-door limo ride.

At the end of the next block, he turned left and headed north, thankful the wind no longer buffeted him head-on. His right cheek and ear were numb, but at least he could see. Halfway down the block, the skin on the back of his neck prickled—and it wasn't due to the cold. A car passed him, but the sensation of being followed persisted. He stubbornly refused to turn back into the wind to check. If someone was following him, he hoped they were as miserable as he was.

He glanced up ahead to his house in the middle of the next block. Warm light glowed through the living room windows, and the porch light illuminated the front steps. Casey must have turned it on for him. He pictured her working in the kitchen with Grace to put dinner together and smiled, despite the fact that the movement threatened to crack the skin of his face like a thin layer of ice. In a few short days, he'd grown accustomed to her presence in their lives. When this business of the letter was resolved—and that couldn't come a minute too soon—maybe he could talk her into seeing him on a social basis. Casey appealed to him more than any woman had in years. She and Grace seemed to get along well and, since she had graduated, she was no longer off-limits as far as the university was concerned.

Headlights coming from behind lit the street ahead and pulled him back into the moment. He slowed his step, but the car didn't pass. Its wheels crunched slowly on the packed snow several feet behind him, just keeping pace. Maybe someone was looking for an address. He paused in front of the gate to his house and turned just as the car sped up and drove past, showering his pants with slushy ice. Swearing, he squinted, trying to see the driver in the brief glow from the streetlight in front of the house next door, but all he could make out was a dark silhouette.

*Who does a thing like that? Jackass.*

He pushed through the gate, slammed it shut behind him, and stomped up the front walk, muttering under his breath.

# CHAPTER FIVE

When Casey heard Alec's key in the lock, she called upstairs to Grace, "Your uncle's home. Time to put Balthazar in his cage and come down and wash your hands."

As the door shut behind her, she turned and saw Alec stomping his feet on the small rug in the foyer while he brushed snow out of his hair. Clumps of dirty slush slid from his pants to the rug.

He dropped his backpack and looked up. Raising his arms to his sides, he glanced at each sleeve. "Can you get me a towel? I'm melting all over everything."

He was. The tiny crystals that caked the folds of his coat in a thin white layer were turning to sparkling droplets as she watched.

He shook his head like a wet dog "A towel? Please?"

"Of course."

She hurried to the kitchen and grabbed a clean towel from the drawer. Just as she returned, Grace bounded down the steps and threw herself at her uncle.

"Uncle Alec!"

He put a hand out to stop her. "Better keep your distance, kiddo. I'm soaked."

"That's okay. I'm still a little wet from giving Balthazar a bath this afternoon." A simian shriek emanated from the small room upstairs at the sound of his name.

Alec glanced at Casey with raised brows as she handed him the towel. "You gave Balthazar a bath?"

She nodded. "We did. He wasn't entirely cooperative." *And if I never bathe a monkey again, it will be too soon.*

Grace pinched her nose and scrunched her face. "We had to. He was stinky."

"He gets that way sometimes," Alec agreed. He glanced toward the kitchen with a hopeful sniff.

Casey shook her head. "I hate to disappoint you, but—"

"We're going to Sophia's!" Grace bounced in place.

"Carolyn Chiang called this afternoon and invited us over for make-your-own pasta night. We're already late."

She felt a nip of guilt at the expression on Alec's face—cold, tired, and hungry, with a hint of burgeoning rebellion. "I guess I could call Carolyn and cancel."

"Noooooo!" Grace did her best grief-stricken-waif-on-the-verge-of-collapse impression.

Alec glanced upward with a sigh then back at his niece. "We'll go."

She hugged his leg. "Yaaay!"

He peeled Grace off. "I need to change my pants before we go."

When he returned, Casey handed him his black down parka. "I hung your wet coat in the bathroom to dry."

"We're bringing spaghetti," Grace chimed in. "I'll go get it." She sped off toward the kitchen and returned with a box of dried spaghetti.

Alec grumbled as he slipped on the dry parka. "The weather is foul."

Casey knelt to zip Grace's coat and pulled her hood over her head. "I think we'll make it. It's only a few blocks."

"I almost broke my neck on the walk home. We're taking the car. I'll get my keys."

Casey flipped on the back-porch light, and Grace led the way down the narrow, concrete path that bisected the small backyard, to the detached garage off the alley behind the property. After securing his niece in her safety seat, Alec and Casey climbed into a solid-as-a-tank white Volvo SUV and drove the three blocks to the Chiangs' brownstone where they were lucky enough to find a parking spot nearby. Sophia met them at the door, grabbed Grace's hand, and dragged her toward the kitchen, conversing at warp speed.

The interior of the Chiangs' house was the complete opposite of its historic exterior—all simple, pure, minimalist modern in tones of black, white, and gray with bright splashes of primary colors here and there for interest. But the minute Casey stepped into the foyer and began unwinding her scarf, a warm, cozy feeling engulfed her. The tantalizing aromas of tomato sauce, basil, and oregano transported her back to Mario's Tuscan Kitchen, the Italian restaurant down the block from her parents' house in Boston. Her taste buds perked up, and her mouth began to water.

Directly behind her, Alec gave an appreciative sniff. "I'm dying. I'll never make it to dinner."

A petite woman with fashionably shaggy, cropped black hair approached bearing a tray of raw vegetables, chips, and dip. She shoved the food at Alec. "Here. Eat. There will be no dying in my living room. And take this down to George in the family room. I'm sure he's dying, too." Alec took the tray, popped a carrot stick in his mouth, and headed for a door tucked beneath the stairs. The woman smiled and offered her hand to Casey. "Hi, I'm Carolyn. We've spoken but never met."

Casey shook her hand. "It's so nice to meet you. I'm Casey."

"You can hang your coat here—" She motioned to a coat tree by the door. "—then I think we'd better get into the kitchen before the girls try to boil the pasta water by themselves."

Casey followed Carolyn down the hallway to the ultra-modern, sleek white kitchen at the back of the house, where they found Sophia teetering over the sink on a step stool, trying to fill a huge stockpot with water. She was wet to the elbows, and water darkened the front of her pink shirt.

With speed and dexterity born of experience, Carolyn intervened and pushed the faucet lever, shutting off the water.

"We were just trying to help," Sophia complained.

Carolyn lifted her off the stool with a flourish and set her on the floor. "And I appreciate it, but you'll freeze in that wet shirt. Run up and change, then you and Grace can set the table. Now scoot." She gave her daughter an encouraging nudge in the direction of the doorway. The girls ran off, and seconds later their footsteps pounded up the stairs.

Carolyn wiped the black granite counter in front of the sink and turned the water back on to fill the pot. "Let's see how much progress we can make before they get back." She tipped her chin toward the stove where three sauce pots steamed on the gleaming six-burner range. "Can you give those a quick stir? We've got basic Marinara, Alfredo sauce with peas because it's Sophia's favorite, and Puttanesca for the more adventurous."

Casey chose a wooden spoon from the holder on the counter. "That's an awful lot of food." She lifted the lid of the closest pot, gave the bubbling Marinara a couple of stirs, then turned down the flame.

Carolyn approached with the stockpot. "Trust me—it will barely be enough. Sophia's two older brothers eat like starving vultures." She set the pot on a free burner and turned it on. "This is for the spaghetti. We've also got bowties for the kids and some spinach rotini. Everyone can mix and match their favorites."

Casey laughed. "I always wondered what anyone would do with six burners. Now I know."

Carolyn returned with two more pots of water, and soon all six were steaming away. Her lips twisted in an apologetic, yet hopeful expression. "I know it's kind of like playing whack-a-mole, but do you mind keeping an eye on these while I make the salad?"

Casey grinned and picked up another spoon. "Sure. I'm fully armed."

She alternated lifting lids to check the sauces with stirring the pasta to keep it from sticking. It was fun cooking with someone again. It reminded her of the last time she'd been home. That had been—what—

almost two years ago? Last Christmas she'd been too busy preparing to defend her dissertation, and the year before, she and Peter had gone to visit his parents for a few days.

Peter. She'd hardly thought of him in days. For the past couple of months, she'd kept herself too busy to analyze the break-up or grieve. Peter had accused her of dissecting their relationship to death on his way out the door, and maybe he was right. Sometimes it sucked to be a psychologist. Insight wasn't always everything it was cracked up to be.

*But that was then, and this is now.* She was in a warm, cheerful kitchen with an open, friendly woman, helping cook dinner for people who were rapidly becoming more than just a job.

She turned and glanced at Carolyn's back as she chopped lettuce next to the sink. "Alec told me you're an art historian. What's your field—Chinese Art?"

Carolyn turned, chef's knife in hand and an impish glint in her eyes. "You might think that, but you'd be wrong. I teach classes in Italian Baroque painting and sculpture—wrote my dissertation on Bernini."

"I wondered about the pasta dinner."

Carolyn laughed. "Everyone seems to expect General Tso's Chicken or Peking duck when they come over. My mother tried to teach me Cantonese cooking when I was growing up in San Francisco, but I really learned to cook when I spent a year in Rome. George and the kids love pasta, but desserts are my favorite. I make some mean cannoli, if I do say so myself. You'll be able to judge for yourself after dinner."

"That sounds wonderful. I haven't had cannoli since I left Boston."

Carolyn had returned to chopping the mound of romaine. "You're from Boston? I never would have guessed. You don't have much of a Beantown accent."

Casey gave a rueful laugh. "My mom worked hard to make sure I didn't. You should hear my dad—he's a retired Boston cop. Sometimes even I have a hard time understanding him."

"And you became a bodyguard—an interesting career choice for a young woman. Following in your father's footsteps?"

Casey lifted the lid of the Puttanesca pot and gave the olive-laden sauce a stir. "Actually, I'm following in my mom's. She's a high school social worker, and I just finished my doctorate in psychology."

"Congratulations! I know what a huge accomplishment that is." Carolyn tilted her head with a tiny frown. "But that makes the bodyguard job even more surprising. I know the academic job market's tight, but after all the work you put in to get your degree, I would have expected to find you teaching or in a clinical position."

"This is just temporary. I've applied for a number of psychology jobs, and I'm waiting to hear back."

"I wonder why Alec neglected to mention your credentials when he told me he'd hired you to help out during this situation with Grace."

"Between the incident at school and the letter, I think he's pretty shaken."

"I don't blame him. I'm worried, and she's not my child. Although sometimes I feel like Alec and Grace are members of the family." Carolyn dumped the mound of greens into a giant wooden salad bowl. "You haven't had enough time to get to know Alec well, but he's a special man."

"I know he's very good with Grace."

"He adores her. Has he told you anything about how she came to live with him?"

"He told me a little about his sister's death."

"It was tragic." Carolyn shook her head. "We met Sara when she moved here. She was a sweet girl, but flaky."

Casey thought about Grace's keen-eyed ability to cut straight to the heart of a situation and tell it like she saw it. "Grace doesn't seem to take after her mother."

"No. She's much more like Alec." Carolyn laughed. "We've called her Occam's Razor since she started to talk."

Casey had heard of Occam's Razor—the philosophy that the simplest answer was usually the best. It was an apt nickname for the sharp little girl.

Carolyn added a couple of sliced radishes to the salad bowl. "I bet he didn't tell you he and Sara grew up in a trailer park in Indiana. Their father died young, and their mother drank herself to death a few years later, when Alec was a senior in high school."

Casey's thoughts flew to her own close-knit family. She could only imagine how she would have felt if she'd lost both parents so young—bereft, lonely, and frightened. "He never mentioned it. That must have been devastating."

Carolyn began halving a pint of cherry tomatoes. "He took care of Sara by himself, forgoing a scholarship to a prestigious college back East to go to the nearby state university until she graduated from high school. Sara wasn't interested in college, so she got a job, and Alec moved to Chicago for graduate school, then got a job teaching here when he finished."

"At least he wasn't too far away." Casey checked the bubbling Alfredo sauce and turned down the heat.

"True, but with school and the months he spent digging in Egypt every year, he didn't see Sara very often—not until she got pregnant. I know he still feels guilty about that, as if he would have been able to change her life if he'd been more involved."

"I doubt he could have changed anything. I've never known a woman that age who toed the line because her big brother told her to." Casey teased a strand of spaghetti from the boiling pot and tasted it. Done. She turned off all six burners. "We're ready here. Do you have a colander?"

Bending over, Carolyn pulled a big green plastic colander from a lower cupboard and set it in the sink. "Here you go." While Casey made her way across the room with the first steaming pasta pot, Carolyn gave the salad a quick toss with a pair of big, wooden forks. "I'll put this on the table. The serving dishes for the pasta are over there." She pointed with her elbow to a trio of simple white bowls lined up on the butcher block-topped kitchen island.

Before Casey had finished filling the bowls, Sophia and Grace raced into the kitchen.

Carolyn didn't glance up from the salad dressing she was whisking in a glass bowl. "Set the table, please, then you can call Daddy and Uncle Alec and your brothers to dinner."

The girls carried red placemats and a pile of paper napkins to the farmhouse-style table. Forks came next, then big white plates—carefully delivered one at a time. By the time the table was ready, Casey had filled the serving bowls and poured glasses of milk for the children and water for the adults. Carolyn was just setting the salad bowl in the center of the table when Sophia and Grace returned with Alec, George Chiang, and a pair of gangly pre-teen boys.

Carolyn wiped her hands on a towel. "Casey, these two monsters are my sons Henry and Caleb, and this is my husband, George. George, Casey is Grace's new nanny." She placed a very slight emphasis on the last word.

George Chiang nodded and smiled as he shook Casey's hand. "Welcome to the lychee nut house." Tall and solid, he was the opposite of his petite wife, with smooth, broad features and a high forehead beneath a helmet of thick black hair. He also had a Puckish smile and an infectious laugh that immediately won Casey over.

Dinner was casual and lively. While Alec, George, and Carolyn discussed a controversial new university proposal regarding faculty leaves, the boys entertained themselves by poking each other and practicing their burps. The girls ignored them and huddled together, deep in conversation about Grace's upcoming fifth birthday.

"What kind of party are you going to have?" Sophia asked before popping a forkful of Alfredo-drenched bowties into her mouth.

"I'm not sure." Grace twirled a strand of spaghetti around on her fork. "I think maybe a zoo party so Balthazar can come."

"That would be awesome—a party with a real monkey." Sophia nodded vigorously. "Can we dress up? I want to be a penguin!"

A vision of Balthazar with cake and ice cream sent chills up Casey's spine. "Grace, I don't think—"

"No monkeys at your birthday party," Alec inserted with finality.

"Awww." Grace frowned and stabbed an innocent cherry tomato with her fork.

She might be past the age for tantrums, but she wasn't too old to spend the remainder of the evening in an epic pout. Casey searched for a way to re-direct the conversation. "I love the idea of a zoo party with costumes." She glanced at Alec. "Doesn't that sound like fun?"

His eyes sparkled when he smiled. "Indeed, it does."

She flashed him a quick smile of gratitude then returned her attention to Grace. "So, when is your birthday?"

The little girl perked up. "February tenth. I'm going to be five."

That was almost two weeks away — plenty of time to put together a cute party for a few preschool friends.

Grace's eyes suddenly rounded with excitement. "I know! Maybe your new boyfriend Theo could come. He knows all about zoos."

Before Casey could deflect the inevitable questions, Carolyn rested both elbows on the table and leaned toward her. "Theo? Do tell."

"We met him at the zoo," Grace chimed in.

Sophia giggled. "He looked like a movie star."

George Chiang raised both brows and rounded his eyes in exaggerated surprise. "You mean like Olaf or the Beast?"

"Daddy." Sophia heaved a dramatic sigh. "I know what real movie stars look like. I've seen the pictures in Mrs. Greenberg's magazines."

"Our housekeeper is a big fan of *People Magazine*," Carolyn explained.

"Ah." Casey turned to Grace. "I have no idea how to contact Theo, but even if I did, I wouldn't. We don't really know him, and your party should be for your friends. Wouldn't you like to see your friends from school?"

Grace nodded. "If they're not sick. Dr. Allen says I shouldn't be around sick people."

Casey and Alec exchanged a quick glance over her head. *So far, so good.* He gave his niece an encouraging pat. "Don't worry about that. I'm sure their parents wouldn't let them go to a party if they were sick."

Grace seemed mollified. "Okay. But if we're going to be zoo animals, do we have to eat yucky things like bamboo and fish?"

Casey laughed. "No, but you and I can bake a zoo cake. What kinds of animals should we put on it?"

"Zebras!"

"Giraffes!"

"Lions!"

"Penguins!"

Grace and Sophia stumbled over each other with suggestions, both for the cake and costumes. Talk of the party consumed the rest of the evening. By the time they were ready to leave, Casey's head was brimming with ideas, and Carolyn had volunteered to help with the whole thing.

The excitement had taken its toll on Grace, and she fell asleep on the short ride home. After parking in the garage, Alec extracted her from her car seat and carried her, draped over one shoulder, up the walk to the back steps while Casey searched for her key. She found it quickly in the light from the old-fashioned fixture over the back porch. It did a great job illuminating the yard about ten feet out from the house but turned the rest into an eerie tableau of wavering shadows.

As they approached the porch, Casey noticed a line of footprints in the snow around the perimeter of the house with occasional diversions toward the larger windows. She elbowed Alec and tipped her head to direct his attention as she opened the back door.

He hesitated with a frown before stepping into the kitchen then whispered, "Probably the boys next door."

She hadn't realized they lived next to a couple of budding Peeping Toms. She'd have to remember to close the shades in the evening. Shaking her head, she followed him in and locked the deadbolt.

Alec had already crossed the kitchen, heading toward the stairs as she reached up to disarm the security system. She did a double-take, and her fingers froze over the pad. The lights were off, both red and green. They'd been in a hurry when they left for the Chiangs' house, but she distinctly remembered setting the alarm, and it had appeared to be working fine then.

"Alec." Her loud whisper carried across the room.

He stopped and turned, brows raised.

"The alarm's off."

He shifted Grace's limp body to improve his grip. "We probably forgot to set it."

She shook her head. "No. I'm sure I set it." She tried pushing several of the buttons, but nothing happened. "The system isn't turned off—it's dead. There are no lights, and it isn't responding."

Grace stirred, and he patted her back, murmuring something against her hair. "It's an old system—it came with the house. Maybe it finally gave up. I don't see any sign of an intruder. The door was locked, and nothing appears to be disturbed."

Unease slithered up Casey's spine, raising the hairs on the back of her neck. "Maybe, but given the footprints outside, we can't afford to take any chances. You stay here with Grace, while I check the house to make sure there's no one here."

He frowned. "You shouldn't do that alone."

"It's my job. Remember? Just be ready to get Grace out of the house if I shout."

Fortunately, they'd left several lights on, so she didn't have to creep around in the dark. She slipped upstairs to retrieve her Sig before making her way, room by room, from the basement to the playroom, checking every closet and under all the beds. When she stuck her head in Balthazar's room, he shrieked a loud greeting. After she was satisfied no one was hiding in the house, she returned to the kitchen, where Alec stood with Grace still asleep on his shoulder.

"It's all clear."

He nodded and headed toward the front hall. As she watched him ascend the stairs, another idea took shape in Casey's mind. Hoping she was wrong, she fetched a flashlight from the junk drawer at the end of the counter and headed outside. First, she checked the tracks. They were much too large to belong to the neighbor children unless they were the spawn of Bigfoot. Swinging the beam of the flashlight across the snowy yard, she was able to make out the intruder's path, then she examined the prints close to the house. Unfortunately, she and Alec had obscured any evidence that might have been left on the walk or back porch. However, once she'd finished her investigation, the conclusion was inescapable. Her stomach knotted at the thought of Alec's reaction.

Before going back inside, she flashed the light around the fenced perimeter of the yard in a final attempt to dispel the sensation that someone was watching from the shadows but saw nothing. She took her time walking up the back steps, planning what to say. When she stepped into the kitchen, she found Alec sitting at the kitchen table with a piece of pink construction paper in his hand and a troubled look on his face.

She pulled off her gloves, stuffed them in her pockets, unwound her scarf, and unzipped her jacket before joining him. "What's that?"

He handed it to her. "When I stopped in my room to drop off my wallet and keys, I found this on the dresser."

It was a crayon drawing of a girl, lying on a bed, with big, fat teardrops falling from her eyes onto the floor like a fountain. Printed across the bottom in childish block letters were the words, *Don't let this happen*.

"Did Grace draw it?" Casey hoped not. Grace seemed well-adjusted and essentially happy. It broke her heart to think the child might be harboring that kind of sadness.

"I don't think so." Alec traced the figure with one finger. "This doesn't look like her drawings — she never draws stick figures — and she would have added more detail. When she draws her room, she usually adds things like her rug and the window with curtains and includes Balthazar or a couple of her favorite dolls. And this doesn't look anything like her printing."

Casey examined the drawing more closely. "It does look like something an adult might do, trying to make it look like a child's drawing. Grace didn't see it, did she?"

He scrubbed a hand over his face. "No, thank God. She was already in bed."

She pulled out a chair and sat across from him. "You're sure you've never seen this before."

"Positive. And I know it wasn't on my dresser before we left. I couldn't have missed it."

Casey caught her lower lip between her teeth. The implications of the drawing and what she'd discovered outside sent a chill down her spine, even in the toasty kitchen. "I hate to say it, but I think someone was in the house tonight."

Alec frowned. "They would have needed a key. The door was locked."

"Yes, but the security system wasn't working, and while you were putting Grace to bed, I went outside to poke around a little."

"And...?"

"The phone line to the security system has been deliberately cut."

# CHAPTER SIX

The muscle in Alec's jaw tightened several times as he tried to decide how to respond to Casey's news. When he finally spoke, she released her breath in a rush.

His gaze bored into hers. "Are you certain?"

She nodded. "I traced the line from the pole to the point where it enters the house. It has definitely been cut, straight through, probably with a knife of some kind."

He clenched his right hand into a white-knuckled fist, released it slowly, and swore.

She swallowed hard then continued, trying to sound calm and professional. "As you know, it's an older system, the kind that transmits over phone lines. A new, wireless system would be more secure."

His words had the edge of a diamond-toothed saw blade, and his nostrils flared, but he didn't explode. "I'll call the company in the morning and arrange to have one installed."

She gave a crisp nod. "Good. If you'd like a referral to a top-notch company, I can call my boss first thing."

When he met her gaze, his sea-blue eyes had taken on an Antarctic chill. "I still want to know how they got in. All the doors and windows were locked."

"Whoever it was must have had a key. Who has a key to the house besides the two of us?"

"Carolyn Chiang is the only other person."

Casey knit her brows. "We were with her all evening, so it couldn't have been her. Besides, I can't believe she would have had anything to do with this."

"Neither can I. She's been a rock for us since Sara died."

"Think back. Have you ever given a key to anyone else—say a plumber or electrician—to do some work while you were away?"

"No. Never. My schedule is flexible enough that I can arrange to be home."

She thought for a moment. "Does anyone at the NEI have access to your keys?"

He opened his mouth then closed it, shaking his head.

"What?" she prodded.

"Sometimes I leave them in the pocket of my coat and hang it in my office, but someone would have to know where the keys were and risk being caught going through my pockets. Then they'd have to take the same risk returning them after making a copy. It's not impossible, but it's hard to believe anyone at the Institute would do that."

He was right—it did sound unlikely—but since the whole situation appeared senseless on its face, they had to consider every possibility. "I think we should try setting a trap."

He sat a little straighter, and his attention sharpened. "What do you propose?"

"Have the locks changed, then leave your keys in your coat pocket again. We can set up a nanny cam in your office to see if anyone tries to take them. The cameras are relatively inexpensive, and we might get some answers."

Alec's gaze thawed, and his lips relaxed. "That's an excellent idea."

Casey hated to dampen his enthusiasm, but she wanted to make sure he kept his expectations realistic. "There's no guarantee we'll learn anything. Whoever broke in tonight might not have a reason to try again."

"True, but since we don't know their purpose this time—beyond trying to frighten or intimidate me—I think we should give the camera a try. We can install a couple here, too—maybe over the exterior doors—along with the new security system."

"If you like, I can make all the arrangements with my boss in the morning. I'll call a locksmith first thing, and Phoenix, Ltd. has the connections to get security installations done on an emergency basis. I'll also call the phone company to repair the line." Her words sounded competent and professional, even to her own ears. She must have absorbed more of Madelyn's training than she realized.

As the tension in his body eased, he almost seemed to deflate, like a man who had been through an ordeal and could finally let his guard down for a time. "That would be great. I'll admit I don't know much about these things. I've never needed to."

A glow kindled deep inside Casey. Knowing she'd lightened his load lightened her own. "My job is about more than protecting Grace. You're my client. I want to spare you as much worry as I can."

"Your client...yes." His eyes held an odd hint of surprise.

She hesitated, uncertain how to respond.

Alec shifted his gaze to the drawing on the table and tapped it with his forefinger. "It feels good to do something proactive instead of sitting around waiting for whoever's behind this to make the next move." He reached for her hand and gave it a squeeze. "Thank you."

His hand was big and warm, hardened from years of digging in the desert to expose the secrets of a people long dead. Its strength kindled a sudden glow somewhere in her middle, but before she had time to enjoy the sensation, he released her. She started to push her chair back from the table to rise but stopped when he crushed the pink paper in his fist.

She frowned. "Why did you do that?"

"I don't want to look at it."

"Neither do I." The image turned her stomach. "But you need to give it to the police. It has to be connected to the note."

He smoothed the crumpled paper. "You're right. I let my anger get the better of me. The officer who took the report this morning gave me his card. I'll call him tomorrow to see if he can stop by and pick this up, too. I'm not sure how much the police can do, but at least they'll have it."

"You never know. My dad was a cop in Boston for twenty-five years, and you'd be surprised what the smallest piece of evidence can do for a case. In the meantime, maybe the nanny cam will turn up something useful."

"Let's hope so."

She rose and slipped off her jacket. "I'm going to make some coffee. Would you like a cup?"

Alec pushed to his feet. "Sure. I'll see what I can find on TV. I don't see much chance of falling asleep tonight."

Casey hoped he would be able to sleep. He was paying good money for the peace of mind her presence was supposed to provide. With the alarm system out, the least she could do was stay up and stand guard. She'd pulled plenty of all-nighters over the past decade for much less worthy causes than a little girl's safety. A good book and three or four cups of strong coffee should keep her going until morning.

As she put the kettle on the gas range and turned the knob to ignite the flame, she couldn't get the sight of the footprints and severed phone line out of her mind. Disabling the security system went well beyond a prank. It represented a significant escalation from anonymous letter-writing, and she had to wonder why. Was it simply intended to reinforce the original message, or was it a more direct threat of action to come? Had Alec inadvertently done something to challenge or provoke the nameless antagonist? Or could her own presence be a factor?

She could almost hear Peter's voice in her head. *You're over-thinking again, Casey.* But she wasn't—she knew it.

She carried the steaming mugs into the living room, where Alec was watching an army of slavering zombies trying to overrun a small Alaskan town.

He accepted the cup she offered and motioned to a spot beside him on the comfortable camel-colored sofa. "Have a seat. I thought this might take our minds off things for a little while. It's about as far from the South Side of Chicago as you can get."

She settled back against the cushions at the opposite end, but the sofa wasn't long. With a little stretch, she could reach out and touch the hand he'd draped casually across its back. It felt odd, sitting so close to him, just the two of them. In the short time she'd been working for him, they had never been alone together for any length of time. They'd quickly fallen into a routine where she cleaned up the kitchen after dinner while he handled Grace's bedtime routine. After Grace was settled, he usually went to his study to work on course plans or read, and Casey retired to her room.

But not tonight. Tonight, it seemed important to stick together, to form a united front against whoever wished them ill.

They discussed the most effective weapons to use against zombies and had a rousing debate about the merits of popcorn vs. Milk Duds as the perfect movie-watching snack. At nine o'clock, Alec found a classic 'forties film noir on a cable movie channel, and conversation dwindled as they watched the hard-boiled dick outfox the slippery dame and her no-good, ex-con boyfriend.

When the final credits rolled, Casey glanced over and saw he'd slid down until his head lolled against the back cushions. His eyes were closed, and even breaths slid in and out between barely-parted lips. She eased up from the sofa, tiptoed over, and carefully removed his horn-rimmed glasses, setting them on the end table. Then she lifted the soft chenille afghan from the back of the big leather armchair and draped it over him. He stirred and mumbled in his sleep but didn't waken.

She turned off the lamp near his head then headed to her room to get the book she'd been using for bedtime reading. On her way back downstairs, she stole a peek into Grace's room to make sure she was asleep.

A monkey-shaped nightlight near the bed cast a warm yellow glow across the child's peaceful features. Awake, Grace was bright, precocious, and occasionally challenging, but asleep, she looked every inch the perfect angel. As the little girl's chest rose and fell with each soft breath, an unnamed emotion crept in, wrapped its tendrils around Casey's heart, and squeezed. How had she come to care so much for the little imp in a such a short time?

One thing she knew for certain—nothing was going to happen to this child. She wouldn't allow it. Resolute, she headed toward the stairs with her book. She'd left her P238 in the kitchen, so she made a quick detour to pick it up.

The old house was dark except for one lamp in the living room and a small light in the kitchen. Taking care not to disturb Alec, she settled back on the sofa and opened her book but found it hard to concentrate. The wind had picked up, occasionally causing a board to creak or a branch from one of the leafless shrubs outside to scrape across a window pane. Once an hour, she got up and walked the perimeter of the house from room to room, checking the windows and peering outside. A couple of times, the slow-moving headlights of a police car on patrol glided down the street. Otherwise, all was quiet.

After she'd repeated the cycle several times and returned to the sofa with a fresh cup of coffee, Alec stirred and started awake. "Huh...what?" He pushed himself upright and reached for his glasses. "What time is it? I must have fallen asleep."

Casey smiled and closed her book. "A little after three, and yes, you did."

He narrowed his eyes in a slight frown. When his gaze dropped to the Sig lying on the coffee table, his frown deepened. "Do you really need that while I'm here? What if Grace saw it?"

"Grace is fast asleep, and yes, I need to have it available. The security system is down, and it looks like a stranger was in the house tonight. I need to be able to protect Grace—and both of us, for that matter— if that person should come back."

Alec ran a hand through his hair, enhancing the waves. "I don't like it. This is my house, and protecting my family is my job."

"I understand, but this is what you're paying me to do, and I don't clock out the minute you walk in the door. What did you think you were getting when you hired a bodyguard for Grace—a grandmotherly caretaker who would scold the bad guys away?"

"Maybe," he admitted with a sheepish look.

Casey took a sip of her coffee with one raised brow. "I don't know any, but I could ask my boss to try to find one for you."

His lips curved in a slow smile, and he shook his head. "Not a chance. She sent the right person the first time." He reached for her hand. "You're exactly what we need." Something indefinable flared in his eyes, and his sleep-rasped voice flowed over her like melted butterscotch.

Butterflies shimmied in Casey's stomach, and she withdrew her hand. "Um...you should go to bed. There's still time to catch a few hours' sleep. I'll keep an eye on things down here."

He didn't move. "I should stay with you."

Not a good idea, especially with the hungry way he was looking at her and the erratic effect it was having on her pulse rate. "You need your rest. I'm sure you have a busy day ahead. I'll be fine." She tried to lighten the mood with a mischievous smile. "I am much younger, after all. You know how energy and stamina decline after thirty."

He grumbled something under his breath that sounded suspiciously like, *I'll show you stamina*, then cocked his head. "If thirty's the tipping point, you can't be too far from decrepitude yourself."

She tossed her hair with a semi-superior flip. "Five months. All the difference in the world."

He scrutinized her face as if searching for flaws. "I'm barely seven years older than you. We'll see how perky you are then."

*We will?*

She swallowed but couldn't bring herself to break eye contact. His comment seemed to imply he thought they would have some kind of relationship in seven years.

*Don't be ridiculous. It was just a throw-away comment, a figure of speech.*

Abruptly, Alec's expression shuttered. He tossed aside the afghan she'd draped over him and rose. "I think I'll take your advice and head to bed. You know where to find me if you need me."

Before she could come up with a suitable response, he left the room. She leaned back against the sofa and craned her neck as his legs climbed the steps and disappeared upstairs. When he was gone and all was quiet, she settled back and picked up her book, but the words blurred together. She blinked several times and set it aside. Anxiety squeezed her stomach, turning Carolyn's light and delicious cannoli into a lump of lead. She felt as though she and Alec had crossed some kind of dangerous, invisible line.

By six-thirty, she was exhausted, cranky, and miserable. She winced as she finger-combed the knots from her hair. What a wasted night. She had continued her hourly patrols, but no one had tried to break into the house. In fact, as far as she could tell, not a single soul in the entire neighborhood had ventured out all night.

The sound of the shower running upstairs jarred her from her funk enough to trudge into the kitchen and start the coffeemaker. Then she picked up her Sig and headed to her room to return it to her suitcase and grab a quick shower before Grace awoke. When she returned to the kitchen, she found Alec at the table, munching a piece of toast while he checked the morning headlines on his phone.

He glanced up with a pleasant, neutral expression, as if their conversation the night before had never taken place, but the lines between his brows and dark circles beneath his eyes suggested he hadn't slept much more than she had. "Good morning. I'm afraid I took the last slice of bread."

Casey poured coffee into a large red ceramic mug with a laughing brown-and-yellow cartoon monkey. "Grace and I will run to the store after I make the arrangements we discussed for the security upgrades here and at your office."

"Mmm, hmm." He returned to his reading.

"I'll call you with the installation schedule."

He nodded but didn't look up.

She bit her lip to avoid snapping at him as exhaustion and frustration bubbled to the surface. How could he remain so calm and detached? Someone was threatening his niece. Someone had broken into his house. Security might be her job, but if he didn't care, why should she? She set her half-full mug back on the counter with enough force to send most of the remaining coffee sloshing over the side. Swearing under her breath, she snatched a paper towel to mop up the mess.

Alec's voice interrupted her mid-swipe. "I trust you."

She turned to face him with a questioning frown.

His gaze had warmed, though his expression remained neutral. "I'm not worried about the alarm system and cameras. You said you would take care of them, and I know you will."

"Thank you." She made an effort to appear as unconcerned as he claimed to be, but inside she was cheering. After the night she'd had, his vote of confidence was a welcome boost.

"I also know you'll do everything in your power to make sure no harm comes to Grace."

"That's why I'm here."

"Yes, but I've watched you with her. I know she's more than a job to you."

Was he unusually observant, or was she that transparent? She had only just recognized her feelings herself. Either way, there was nothing to be gained by denying them. "I've grown very fond of her."

He rose and began gathering his dirty dishes. "I'm glad. She's fond of you, too."

Casey rested one hip against the counter. "I'm not so sure of that. She's usually on her best behavior around you. You don't see her when she's in challenge mode."

Alec deposited his dishes in the sink with a short laugh. "Don't forget, I've raised Grace alone for almost four years. I know all her tricks."

She had to give him that. "I suppose you do."

He finished rinsing his dishes and turned. He was only a couple of feet away, so it was an easy reach to take the mug from her hand and set it on the counter with careful deliberation before facing her. "She's glad you're here—I can tell." He stepped closer. "And she's not the only one."

As he bent his head toward hers, Casey froze, her pulse spiking erratically. What was he doing? Unless she was hallucinating, he was about to kiss her.

"I'm hungry, and so is Balthazar."

Alec jerked back, and they both turned to face the small figure still wearing her rumpled shirt and pants from the day before, holding the front paw of an aggrieved-looking monkey.

Casey recovered first. "Oh...of course, you are. How about banana pancakes for you and plain bananas for Balthazar?"

"You know Uncle Alec doesn't allow Balthazar at the table when we're eating."

Casey grabbed the bunch of bananas from the bowl on the counter, ripped one off, and handed it to the child. "You can take him back to his cage and feed him, then get dressed. By the time you're ready and back down here, your breakfast will be on the table."

Grace grinned. "Great!" With the banana in one hand and Balthazar's paw in the other, she bounded up the stairs accompanied by excited monkey chatter.

Casey smiled as she watched the pair disappear then turned to Alec. What should she say after their interrupted...whatever it was?

He met her gaze with an impassive expression that belied the turbulence in his eyes. After a long, awkward moment, he shifted his weight, and she got the sudden impression he was about to try again to kiss her. Nerves on edge, she side-stepped him and opened the door of the pantry cupboard to get the box of pancake mix. "If I know Grace, she'll be back in no time. I'd better get busy."

He stepped back out of her way as she opened the refrigerator to retrieve the milk. "I've never made her banana pancakes." His voice held a hint of regret.

She set the milk carton on the counter and turned. "You've done an incredible job with Grace. Don't let anyone — including yourself — tell you otherwise."

He glanced away, shifting his attention to the window over the sink. Beyond the glass, the snowy yard was brightening as dawn approached. "I've tried to do my best. Four years ago, I knew nothing about toddlers in general and little girls in particular, but now I can't imagine life without her."

Casey regarded his profile, with its high forehead, strong nose, and sculpted cheekbones. Like one of his ancient statues, his features could have been carved from granite. Then a muscle in his jaw twitched, giving him away.

When he turned back, his eyes reminded her of a winter storm at sea. "That's why this stupid business makes me so angry. I would do anything…anything…to keep her safe."

"We're doing everything we can think of."

"I know…I only hope it's enough."

The overhead lights in the kitchen cast shadows on the planes and angles of his face, bringing them into sharp focus. Casey's heart contracted at the stark signs of pain and worry. She laid a gentle hand on his arm and ventured a small smile. "Try not to worry. I'm sure I can arrange to have the cameras installed today. With luck, we'll finally get some answers."

His answering smile was bleak, but at least he tried. "I'm more than ready. I'll see you this evening."

She followed him to the front door, watching as he donned his coat and picked up his backpack. "I'll call to let you know when the appointments are scheduled."

He hesitated at the threshold. As his gaze met hers, his lips parted then closed. Whatever he was thinking, he'd decided to keep to himself. He gave one last nod, turned, and headed down the porch steps.

Casey closed the door behind him. She'd assured him they were doing everything possible to protect Grace, but were they? She was so inexperienced, how would she know? Maybe if she discussed the situation in detail with her boss when she called about the cameras she'd feel more confident. Right now, she'd better get back to the kitchen. Those banana pancakes weren't going to make themselves.

The rest of the day passed in an exhausted blur. After breakfast, she sent Grace to the playroom with Balthazar and a selection of pots and pans to play restaurant. She needed privacy for her call to Phoenix, Ltd.'s downtown headquarters. Her boss, Madelyn Li, offered a few suggestions and volunteered to pull in a favor to get the new security system and cameras installed that afternoon. Casey called Alec to update him on her progress then waited for the locksmith, who showed up a little before ten o'clock. The telephone repairman appeared shortly thereafter, and the security system installation crew arrived after lunch, finishing around three-thirty.

By the time the installers left, stress and the sleepless night had caught up with her. She was weaving on her feet and could barely hold her head straight. She corralled Grace at the kitchen table with hot cocoa and a plate of cookies and fixed a cup of strong tea for herself.

Grace dunked a cookie in her cocoa. "I'm bored. Can Sophia come over?"

Casey's head was beginning to pound. She struggled to focus on the insistent little face across the table. "Not today, Grace. It's too late. Maybe tomorrow."

"But—"

"No buts. How would you like to stretch out on your bed and watch a movie?"

The little girl shot her a suspicious look. "That sounds like a nap, and I'm too big to take naps."

*I'm not.*

"It's not a nap. It's quiet time. I'll put on that pirate movie you love."

Grace perked up. "The one with the monkey that Uncle Alec won't let me watch because he says I've already watched it a million times?"

Casey gave her a tired smile. "That's the one."

"Oh, boy! Yes, yes, yes!" Grace downed the rest of her cocoa in one gulp and raced up the stairs whooping.

After settling the child with her movie, Casey made her way back down and collapsed on the living room sofa.

*My eyes are so scratchy. I'll just rest them for a minute or two.*

The next thing she knew, her eyes flew open, and she sat up. The room was dark and still. What time was it? She turned on a lamp and checked her watch. Five-fifteen. Alec would be home soon.

*Grace.*

She ran to the bottom of the stairs and called. "Grace, is your movie over?"

No response.

How long was the movie? Casey couldn't remember, but she didn't hear any sound coming from Grace's room. She ran up the stairs and threw open the door.

The television was off, and the room was empty. Maybe Grace had gone back to her playroom. Casey called up the third-floor staircase but got no reply.

Her heart thumped wildly.

"Grace!"

The silent house mocked her.

# CHAPTER SEVEN

Casey's heart raced, and her pulse pounded erratically in her ears. Struggling to catch her breath, she grabbed the newel post for support as her body tried to decide whether to faint or vomit.

*How could this have happened?*

How could someone have broken into the house and kidnapped Grace without her hearing? She ran to the kitchen but found the door safely secured. Returning to the front hall, she rested her hand on the carved glass knob.

It turned. The front door was unlocked.

She hadn't had a chance to read all the material about the new alarm system and coordinate with the monitoring center yet, but surely, she'd remembered to lock the door after they left.

She flung it open and burst onto the porch, but there was nothing. No Grace. No note. No telltale footprints. The alarm installation crew had thoroughly disturbed last night's snow, making it impossible to make out fresh tracks.

She sank down on the top step, dropped her head, and thrust her hands into her hair. Incipient tears froze in the corners of her eyes. Damp, biting cold seeped through the thin denim of her jeans, numbing her flesh, but she didn't care. Her mind refused to focus beyond the overwhelming questions. Where was Grace, and what was she going to tell Alec?

A soft jangle from inside the house interrupted her misery. She twisted to peer through the open door. When it sounded again, her brain identified the tone as the phone in the kitchen. What if the kidnappers were calling with a ransom demand?

She sprang to her feet and bolted through the open door. When she reached the kitchen, she lunged for the handset and pressed the *TALK* button.

"Hello." She expelled the word in a rushed wheeze.

"Hi, it's Carolyn Chiang."

*Carolyn Chiang. Not the kidnappers.* Casey's brain fought through the fog of fear to come up with a coherent response. "Hi" was the best she could manage.

"I just got home, and the girls are pestering me to let Grace stay for dinner. Is that okay with you?" Children's voices vied for attention in the background. "Shh, you two," Carolyn ordered.

Casey sucked in a deep breath then released it slowly to clear her head. Sheer relief coursed through her veins.

*Grace is at Sophia's house. She isn't missing.*

There would be time later to discover the how and why. For now, it was enough to know she was safe. At that moment all Casey wanted was to see Grace, to hold her, and she didn't want to wait another minute.

"Let's put that off until another night. Tell Grace I'll be right over to pick her up."

"Okay. I'll have her ready."

As she returned the phone to its stand, she heard the front door open and footsteps in the foyer. She met Alec in the hall. He had dropped his backpack on the floor and was unbuttoning his coat. His cheeks were reddened from the cold and the exertion of his brisk walk home.

He greeted her with a frown. "The door was unlocked."

Her heart skittered. How could she face him after what she'd allowed to happen? Brushing past without meeting his gaze, she grabbed her jacket from the hall closet. "I just stepped outside to check the temperature. I'm on my way to the Chiangs' to pick up Grace." Before he could do more than nod, she was out the door and half-way down the walk.

Grace was zipped into her purple parka and waiting at the door with Sophia and Carolyn when Casey arrived. She crossed her arms and glared. "I'm hot...and I want to eat with Sophia."

Carolyn met Casey's exasperated expression with a rueful glance then patted Grace's head. "We'll do it another night soon."

"But I want to—"

Sensing an incipient show of will, Casey took the little girl's hand in a firm grasp and pulled her toward the steps. "We'll talk about this on the way home. Now, thank Mrs. Chiang for having you over."

"She wasn't even here," Grace grumbled under her breath.

"Grace..."

She tugged against Casey's grip then capitulated. "All right. Thank you, Mrs. Chiang."

Carolyn smiled. "You're welcome any time. We'll see you soon."

Casey maintained her hold on Grace's hand even after they reached the sidewalk. After this afternoon's scare, she was determined not to let the child out of arm's reach again. She also needed to find out exactly what had happened.

She kept her voice casual. "Grace, what were you doing at Sophia's house."

Grace kept her gaze focused on the snow-slicked concrete. "Playing." Her voice was small, with no hint of her previous rebellious bravado.

*She knows she's in trouble. Good.* "I guessed that, but how did you get there?"

"I walked."

"By yourself?"

"Uh, huh." Grace scraped the toe of her boot against a clump of frozen ice.

"Why?"

"I was lonely."

Casey's heart tightened at the sad little voice.

"And bored."

*Ah, now we get to the heart of the matter.* "You have a mountain of toys in your playroom, and I was home."

Grace responded with an accusatory frown. "You were asleep. Besides, I'm tired of staying home all the time. I'm tired of not seeing Sophia and Olivia and Hallie every day. I want to go back to school."

"I know you do, but we need to talk some more about what you did this afternoon. It was very dangerous."

Grace stared at a squirrel bounding through the deep snow in a neighboring yard.

Casey tugged her hand to get her attention. "Does your Uncle Alec allow you to walk to Sophia's house alone?"

Grace glanced up with determination in her china-blue eyes. "No, but he thinks I'm still a baby. I'm not. I'm almost five. I know the way. I didn't get lost."

"That might be, but what do you think he'll say when we tell him?"

The child's eyes widened, and her mouth dropped open. "We can't tell him! Please, don't tell him!"

"Will you promise not to leave the house without me again?"

Grace answered with a vigorous nod. "I promise! I promise!"

Casey pulled off her glove and offered her hand with the little finger extended. "I have to be sure you understand how serious this is. Will you pinky swear?"

Grace hesitated, then followed suit. "Pinky swear."

With their fingers locked in an unbreakable covenant, Casey pinned the little girl with a hard look. "You know you can't break your promise now."

Grace gave a solemn nod.

"Good. Now, let's go home and see what we can scare up for dinner."

"Scare up?" Grace giggled. "I know — we can make eyeball salad with grapes. We did that at school for Halloween. It's really scary!"

"Sounds perfect." Casey knelt to put Grace's mitten back on then gave her a quick hug before taking her hand again for the rest of the walk home.

\*\*\*\*

Alec sat at the white-painted kitchen table staring at the framed photo of Sara holding baby Grace without seeing it. If he'd been a drinking man, he would have drowned his worries in a bottle of scotch, but he'd learned young what the results of that could be. As it was, he sipped a glass of iced Perrier as he tried to formulate a course of action. He had to do something to end this string of threats. Anger and frustration had pushed him to the brink.

The sound of the front door opening, accompanied by chattering feminine voices, interrupted his thoughts. A couple of minutes later, Grace bounded into the kitchen with Casey following in her wake.

She plastered herself against him, grabbed his waist, and squeezed. "Hi, Uncle Alec!"

Alec returned the hug. "Hi, yourself. Did you have fun with Sophia?"

"I always have fun with Sophia." She pulled free and regarded him with a questioning gaze. "But sometimes I get bored. I want to go back to school. When will Dr. Allen say it's okay? I promise I won't get sick."

Something in her eyes tugged at his heart. He reached out to ruffle her feathery blond curls. "I know you'd never get sick on purpose, but we have to be careful. You don't want to end up in the hospital again. I'll call the doctor's office tomorrow and see what he says."

This situation had to end, and soon. They both needed life to return to normal. When a small voice in the back of his brain reminded him that their normal life didn't include Casey, he was surprised by the pang the thought brought.

Grace gave a single, decisive nod. "Good. Now let's eat. I'm starved. Mrs. Greenberg said it was too late for a snack, and Casey wouldn't let me stay for dinner."

After a quick dinner of the best mac and cheese Alec had ever eaten, accompanied by a bowl of peeled green grapes Grace kept referring to as eyeballs, he allowed himself to be talked into letting Balthazar join them while he read a record number of bedtime stories. By the time he finished the sixth story, Grace had nodded off, but Balthazar was still going strong. He monkey-cackled all the way back to his room, harassed Alec while he changed the papers in the cage, then tried to steal the key when Alec locked the crate for the night.

Alec headed back downstairs in search of Casey and found her in the living room, cuddled up on the sofa with a book in her hands, her head lolling to one side, and her eyes closed.

"Are you awake?"

She stirred and blinked. "Huh?... Yes...of course." She swung her legs around and placed her feet on the floor.

He plopped down in the leather armchair across from her and stretched his neck from side to side. "Last night was a helluva night."

"It was."

"And today wasn't much better."

Her mouth tightened briefly then relaxed. "Were you able to turn the drawing over to the campus police?"

He nodded. "The same young cop stopped by to pick it up. He didn't seem impressed but said he'd pass it along to the detective."

"I guess that's the best we can hope for. Did you have a chance to check the video from the new security camera in your office before you left?"

"Yes, but nothing useful turned up there, either. Maria left a stack of student papers on my desk while I was at lunch, and Nora Samuels stopped in and looked around but didn't touch anything. I left my coat hanging in plain sight, but nobody went near it."

"You can't expect instant results. You have to give it time."

"One week." His voice snapped in the quiet room. "No more."

Alec's frustration grew steadily as each passing day produced no results. It was all he could do not to rip the camera out and smash it to pieces. But he'd promised to give it a week, so he swallowed his temper and counted the days.

On the evening of the seventh day, after Grace was in bed, he brought it up again. "It's been a week, and we've got nothing. The camera idea isn't working. We have to think of something else."

Casey had joined him in the living room and sat curled on the sofa with her feet tucked beneath her while he sprawled in his leather armchair. "I agree." She paused and shifted position to see him better. "The culprit won't know about the new locks until he or she tries to use the old key again. Maybe you could mention to a few people that you had an attempted break-in and had the locks changed. That might stir up something."

"That's not a bad idea, but I'm sick of waiting for some faceless whackjob to decide he's ready to act." He opened and closed his fists. "I just want this nightmare to end."

Casey unwound her legs and stood. "I'm going to make myself a cup of chamomile tea. It's supposed to be calming. Would you like some?"

"Sure. Why not? I could use a little calm right now."

"Good." She smiled and headed for the kitchen.

By the time she returned, something she'd said earlier had triggered a new idea. He wasn't sure it was a good one, but he was ready to try anything.

He picked up one of the mugs. "I have an idea that might help bring this situation to a head sooner rather than later."

She settled back on the sofa. "Yes?"

"I can't imagine these threats are coming from anyone connected with Grace's school, but if I call the director and let her know Grace will be returning to class, then spread the word around the NEI, whoever's behind this will know we've decided to ignore their threats. That might make them angry or panicked enough to act."

Casey kept her gaze trained on him as she set her mug on the coffee table. "By act, you mean try to harm or kidnap Grace."

"Well…" He wanted to make something happen, but not *that* something.

She crossed her legs and leaned forward, resting one elbow on her raised knee. "What happens if you send her back to school? I would go with her, of course, and I'm prepared to do whatever is necessary to protect her, but we don't know what this person—or people—really wants." She uncrossed her legs and straightened before leaning back against the sofa. "I'm not prepared to risk an armed confrontation in a school full of children or on a public street, and I don't think you are, either."

"Of course not," Alec snapped. "I'm not crazy. I have no intention of sending her back until I'm sure it's safe for everyone."

Some of the tension left Casey's body as she relaxed against the cushions. "So, your thought was to try to provoke a response."

"Exactly." He pushed to his feet and took a few steps in front of the fireplace before turning. "Look. I've got to do something. Grace is frustrated staying home, and I had to stop myself from punching Fermin LeBlanc this afternoon."

Alec's already thin patience grew thinner while the mantle clocked loudly ticked off the seconds.

Finally, Casey responded. "Okay."

"Okay?"

"Yes. I don't see any increased risk in putting the word out, as long as it's just a ruse."

"I'll do it. Tomorrow." Feeling as if a weight had been lifted, he rose to his feet. "I'm going to head upstairs. I have some reading to do for my next class. Not surprisingly, I've had some trouble concentrating lately."

She tipped her chin toward his half-finished tea. "Why don't you take that up with you, and I'll set the alarm system."

"Will do." He picked up the mug. Halfway to the stairs, he stopped and turned. She still stood in the living room, watching him. "And Casey, thanks for everything."

Her eyes reflected the warm amber glow of the lamplight. "Just doing my job."

He hesitated a moment longer, wishing he could read the thoughts behind her serene expression. Were he and Grace just a job to her? Deep in his heart, he hoped not.

The next morning, Alec awoke with a start. It was almost eight o'clock. He had slept more than ten hours. He couldn't remember the last time that had happened. At least yesterday's brain fog had dissipated. He felt sharp, even edgy, ready to take on all comers.

When he walked into the kitchen, he found Grace and Casey at the table eating blueberry waffles.

Casey jumped up. "Sit down. I'll fix yours right away."

He motioned to her to sit. "Finish your breakfast. I may not be much of a cook, but I do know how to make waffles." He turned to Grace. "Right?"

She rolled her eyes at Casey. "He burns them. Every. Single. Time."

"Hey," Alec responded with wounded dignity. "They're well-toasted."

Grace's snort elicited a laugh from Casey.

He poured a cup of coffee and sipped it while his waffle cooked. Not wanting to prove Grace's point, he kept checking the color and managed to pry it from the iron before any actual smoke appeared. He brought his plate to the table and took his usual seat at the end. After slathering butter on the steaming waffle, he reached for the syrup. "What do you two have planned for today?"

Grace waved her fork. "We're going to the library. Casey promised they have books about dragons."

"I bet they do. That sounds like fun."

"We'll be very careful," Casey added.

Grace took a swallow of milk then set her cup down with a frown. "Why do we have to be careful? How could we get hurt at the library?"

Alec and Casey exchanged a quick glance before he smiled at his niece. "You might slip on the icy steps going in, or a book might fall on your head."

Grace pressed her lips together and huffed a breath out her nose. "Uncle Alec, you're so silly. You know I have grippy boots—you bought them for me. And books only fly off the shelf and land on your head in the movies."

"Of course. What was I thinking?"

"I don't know." She pushed back from the table and climbed down from her chair. "I'm going to brush my teeth."

He watched her with wistful amusement. She was growing up so fast. The thought brought a tightness to his chest.

As long as he drew breath, no one was going to hurt her. Ever.

"I'll keep her safe."

He turned at Casey's quiet statement. "We both will."

Ten minutes later he walked out the door with his new house key in his pocket and determination in his step. When he arrived at the NEI, he stopped by Nora's office before heading upstairs to his own.

She glanced up from her computer and peered at him over the top of her glasses. "Good morning, Professor Bainbridge. What can I do for you?"

*Make it casual.* "I remember you saying you lived near the university. I was wondering if you'd heard anything about break-ins in the neighborhood."

Her eyes narrowed, and her gaze sharpened. "No, nothing specific. Have you had a problem?"

"Someone tried to break into my house last week. I had to change the locks."

"Was anything taken?"

"Not that I could tell." *Actually, they left something.* "The whole thing was pretty strange."

"Maybe someone or something scared them off."

"Maybe." He paused. "There is something you might be able to help me with, though."

Nora brightened. "Of course."

"Grace's fifth birthday is coming up, and I'm drawing a blank when it comes to presents. The older she gets, the more trouble I seem to have. I wondered if she'd mentioned anything special to you."

Nora tapped her pen against her desk. "Well...I remember her saying she'd like a wig like the Princess Tia paper doll you bought her."

For some reason, the image of Balthazar wearing a long black wig popped into Alec's mind, and he grimaced. "Grace does like to play dress-up, but I think I'll pass on the wig. We're having a party for her on Friday, and I want it to be special. She's been out of school for a while and is missing her friends. Fortunately, she'll be able to go back next week."

The lines between Nora's straight, no-nonsense brows deepened. "I didn't know she'd been sick."

"She hasn't." The woman was almost as nosy as Fermin and seemed to thrive on department gossip. He was counting on her to spread the news. "I guess I'd better get to work. Thanks for your help."

As he left her office, she called after him, "You can never go wrong with books!"

114

Alec was hanging his coat on the hook on the back of his office door when Maria stuck her head through the opening. "Professor Bainbridge?"

"Back here."

She leaned around the side of the door, casting a quick glance at his coat. Purple smudges shadowed her eyes, and her smile had a brittle edge. "I wondered if you needed help with anything this morning."

His first instinct was to suggest she go home and get some sleep but decided that would be overstepping. "It would be a big help if you could pull and organize the slides for my lecture on Wednesday. I'll get you a list."

She followed him to his desk. He was rifling through a notebook, looking for the correct lesson plan when Fermin strolled in, looking like an ad for some over-the-top European menswear designer, as usual.

The corners of his prim mouth turned down when he glanced at the surface of Alec's desk. "Ah, Bainbridge. I'd hoped you'd be working on the Fassbender boat. I'd really like to take a closer look at it."

Would the man never let up? He was as persistent as a hungry mosquito. "I plan to, as soon as I have a chance to retrieve it from the archives."

Fermin lifted his chin with an injured sniff. "I don't know why you don't just keep it in your office. It would be so much more convenient."

Alec's blood pressure shot up until it pounded in his ears. "The boat is potentially one of the most important artifacts the Institute has ever received."

Fermin's chin rose higher. "The building has a top-notch security system. Surely you aren't suggesting someone inside would steal the boat from your office."

Alec found the list of slides he was looking for, removed the page from his notebook, and handed it to Maria before returning his attention to his annoying colleague. "I don't intend to give anyone the opportunity. Not only would the loss be a huge blow to the NEI, but I hate to think how our insurers would react."

"Hmm. I suppose that is a consideration." Fermin stroked his goatee.

Maria sidled toward the door, paper in hand. "I'll have this ready for you by the end of the day, Professor."

Alec rose from his chair. "Thanks, Maria." Before she stepped into the hall, he added, "Oh, by the way, Grace's birthday is coming up. She's beyond excited, and I know she'd love it if you came to her party. Since she's starting back to school on Monday, we're planning the party for late Friday afternoon."

The list fluttered from her fingers to the floor. She quickly bent to retrieve it, and when she straightened, her face was nearly as white as the paper.

Afraid she might pass out, Alec hurried around the side of his desk, but Fermin reached her first and grasped her elbow. "Are you all right, my dear?"

A hint of pink returned to her cheeks. "Uh...of course. I was running late this morning, and I skipped breakfast—"

Fermin tightened his grip. "We'll have to take care of that immediately, young lady. Come with me, and I'll buy you coffee and a roll at the café."

Maria cast a helpless glance over her shoulder as the older man steered her out the door and down the hall.

Alec watched until they disappeared down the stairs. Fermin bent his head toward hers and seemed to be talking, though Alec couldn't make out the words. He had a brief impulse to rescue his teaching assistant, but Fermin was basically harmless. Annoying, definitely, but too effete to be dangerous.

After making a quick call to Mrs. Romero, the director of Grace's school, to tell her the child would be returning to school Monday, he spent the rest of the day reviewing his lecture notes for his next class, drawing and notating the fine construction details of the oarsmen on the wooden boat, and thinking about the ancient Egyptian tortures he'd like to try on the bastard who was threatening his niece.

He left his office unlocked with his coat hanging behind the door during the lunch hour, but the surveillance camera showed no activity when he checked it at the end of the day. Granted, the information he'd planted might take a couple of days to make its way to the right ears, but his patience had long since run out. After collecting his coat and turning off the lights, he pulled his office door shut with enough force to send a bang reverberating through the empty corridor.

Seconds later, Fermin LeBlanc stuck his head out his own door. "Anything wrong, Bainbridge?"

Alec gritted his teeth. "No. The door just got away from me."

Fermin's mustache twitched above tight lips. "Oh, well then...I suppose I'll see you in the morning."

"Yes. Good night."

Alec's black mood abated when he arrived home and Grace greeted him at the door with one of her new library books. "Look at this, Uncle Alec." She thrust the book into his hands before he could get his coat off. "We got two dragon books and this one about a monkey like Balthazar who lives in Costa Rica. I can read most of the words by myself."

Alec dropped his bag and took the book. "You'll have to read it to me after dinner."

She tugged on his sleeve. "I want to read it to you now!"

"Okay, okay, but let me hang my coat up first."

As he opened the closet door, the kitchen telephone trilled in the background. A moment later, he heard Casey's muffed voice. He glanced toward the living room as she walked in carrying the handset.

"It's for you."

He took the phone. "Hello."

"You're making a big mistake." The voice sounded distant and weirdly distorted.

Alec frowned. "Who is this?"

The caller ignored his question. "It wouldn't be smart to send Grace back to school."

"What do you want?" he demanded, his gut churning with fury.

"Soon. Very soon," the voice crooned. "But don't ignore this warning or you'll be sorry."

# CHAPTER EIGHT

Casey regarded Alec with alarm. Tight lines bracketed his mouth, and the knuckles of the hand holding the phone were white. "Who was that?" she asked. "The voice sounded strange."

Instead of answering, he glanced at his niece. "Grace, has Balthazar had his dinner yet?" His voice cracked.

The child's eyes widened. "Oh, no! I was reading my books, and I forgot."

"Why don't you go up and feed him now. I'll come to your room in a few minutes, and we can read the monkey book together."

"Can Balthazar read with us?"

Alec hesitated. "Sure."

"Awesome!" She raced to the kitchen, came back with a small bowl of orange quarters from the fridge, and pounded up the stairs, calling the monkey's name.

As soon as Grace was out of earshot, Casey touched his hand "Let's go into the kitchen, and you can tell me about the call. I assume you'd rather not talk in front of Grace."

"You assume right."

When they reached the kitchen, she turned on the light in the oven and bent over for a quick peek. "The pot roast will be ready in an hour or so, but I can make you something to drink if you like. Maybe a cup of coffee or a soda?"

"I'll stick with water. The last thing I need right now is to get any more wired."

She grabbed a pair of glasses from the cupboard, tossed in a few ice cubes and slices of lemon, and filled them with water. "So, who was on the phone?"

"I wish I knew."

"Do you think it was our letter-writing, house-breaking friend?"

Alec took a swallow and grimaced. "I assume so. The person told me I was making a mistake, sending Grace back to school."

"Could you tell if the caller was male or female?"

"No. Whoever called was speaking through some kind of voice-altering device."

"Can you remember the exact words? Maybe they inadvertently gave us a clue."

He took another long swallow then set the glass on the counter. "Like I said, the caller told me I was making a mistake sending Grace back to school. When I asked what they wanted, the voice replied, 'soon, very soon,' and said I'd be sorry if I ignored this warning."

Casey considered the implications. "That's good."

He stared at her. "There's nothing good about it. The SOB threatened Grace."

"Yes, but don't you see? Our plan is working. We stirred things up, forced whoever is behind this to make a move."

"I'm not sure how that helps. We don't know any more than we did before."

"Oh, but we do," she insisted. "We've narrowed the field of possible suspects from every resident of the city of Chicago to someone connected with either Grace's school or the Near Eastern Institute."

He gave a soft, derisive snort. "I guess you could look at it that way."

She resisted the urge to shake him. Maybe stress was blinding him to the big, blue dancing elephant in the room. "The important part of the call was not the warning." She kept her tone calm and patient. "The important part was the 'soon, very soon.' Whoever is behind this is finally getting ready to show his hand."

After a second Alec straightened, and a new light sparked in his eyes. "You're right. And it's about damn time. I can't believe any of this actually has to do with Grace. She's just a way to get at me—the best way, straight to the heart. Someone wants something from me, and as soon as we know what it is, we can figure out how to deal with it."

"See? If you look at the situation the right way, we actually have something to celebrate." She clinked her glass to his in a mini-toast.

As they raised their glasses to drink, their gazes tangled and locked. Mesmerized by the fire in Alec's azure eyes, Casey's lips parted, but no sound came out. Seconds ticked by before either moved.

In what seemed like slow motion, he took the glass from her fingers and set it on the counter alongside his before resting his hands lightly on her shoulders. "I'm glad you're here. I don't know how I would have gotten through this ordeal alone."

Under the intensity of his gaze, something under her ribcage fluttered, and her lips suddenly felt dry. Before she could stop it, her tongue swept out to moisten them. She tried to glance away but couldn't. "I...uh...I'm glad I'm here, too."

*Pathetic. You sound like an inane twit. Yes, he's a client, but he's also a man – a very attractive man who needs and appreciates you.*

"Casey." Alec's deep voice interrupted her internal scold.

She blinked. "Mmm?"

His knowing smile curled her toes. "Stop thinking."

She registered a slight pressure on her shoulders as he closed the distance between them. Spellbound, she watched his well-sculpted mouth descend towards hers until his features blurred. A split second before their lips met, her lids drifted closed.

Strong arms wrapped around her back, pressing her against his hard chest with exquisite care. As sensation took over, her brain lost focus.

*Warm. He's so warm. I'm so warm. No, I'm on fire.*

"Casey?"

She jerked back against the hard band of Alec's encircling arms, but he merely tightened his hold. Together they turned toward the small voice.

Grace stood in the kitchen doorway, wearing a quizzical expression. "Is Uncle Alec your new boyfriend now?"

Heat rose in her cheeks as her dazed brain searched for words. "Um...no...we were—"

"She isn't sure yet," Alec replied. "What would you think if she was?"

Grace shifted her gaze from him to Casey and back then shrugged. "It's okay, I guess. But you promised to read my new monkey book, and Balthazar is getting tired of waiting."

Alec's slow nod acknowledged the seriousness of his transgression. "You're right. I'm sorry." He gave Casey a subtle squeeze before releasing her and took off toward Grace at a lope. "I'll race you upstairs!"

She squealed and tore up the steps.

Alec paused for a split second at the foot of the stairs and turned to Casey. "Later." Then he pounded up after his niece.

Casey stared after him, struggling to wrap her head around what had just happened. She had kissed a client. Was that grounds for dismissal? She didn't recall anything about it in her employment contract, but since her boss had ended up marrying one of her own clients, she would probably understand.

And what had Alec meant by "later?" They would talk *later*? They would pick up where they left off *later*? The thought of either option brought the army of clog-dancing spiders back to her stomach. Half of her couldn't wait to find out, while the more rational side vowed to avoid the issue at all costs.

By the following afternoon, her reckless half was more than a little irritated. Shortly after turning her world inside out, Alec had come down to dinner with Grace, acting like the whole incident never happened. No furtive glances over the pot roast. No secret smiles. Nothing. After putting Grace to bed, he retreated to his study to work on some research, leaving Casey to fume and wonder whether the kiss had been a figment of her imagination.

The next couple of days were just as frustrating. Every day Alec shook his head when she asked about results from the surveillance camera in his office, and they received no further communications from the anonymous caller.

Thursday afternoon, while Grace and Balthazar watched her favorite animated explorer show, Casey stole a minute to check her email and found a message from the Wiseman Institute. Her heart began to pound double time. She had applied for a therapist job at the prestigious residential treatment center in November and had done a preliminary Internet video interview in early January. With so much happening in the intervening month, she'd put it out of her mind. Now, they were asking her to come to Boston for a final, in-person interview in a couple of weeks. They'd even purchased her plane ticket!

It had looked like her dream job when she'd first applied—a well-regarded institution in her home town. Her mother had been thrilled. But since Alec and Grace had come into her life—or more accurately, she had come into theirs—the thought of moving half-way across the country felt more like a sentence than a gift. She had no idea where her relationship with Alec might be headed, but if she managed to find a full-time job in Chicago, at least she would be able to continue to see him after her current assignment ended.

But how could she pass up the Wiseman Institute? She had spent the last seven years of her life training for a job like that. Most of her classmates would kill for the chance to work there. She reminded herself she couldn't be the only finalist, and she might not get the job anyway. She owed it to herself and her future to give it a shot. She quickly responded to the email before she had time to talk herself out of it.

As soon as she hit *Send*, she wondered if she'd made a mistake and simply given herself one more thing to worry about. Fortunately, she had the preparations for Grace's birthday party to distract her. With plenty of input from Grace and the invaluable assistance of Carolyn Chiang, she had put together a guest list, phoned the children's parents, and planned and shopped for refreshments. She and Grace had also designed and painted scenery to match the zoo theme.

Grace had decided she wanted a monkey costume, so Casey threw herself on the mercy of the Chiang's housekeeper. Mrs. Greenberg turned out to be a seamstress extraordinaire and whipped up a whimsical approximation of a mischievous Capuchin in a couple of days. Sophia had chosen to go as a penguin and, as the day of the party neared, both girls' anticipation approached all-out frenzy.

Carolyn Chiang had no classes on Friday, so she and Sophia arrived shortly after lunch to help transform the living room into a barrier-free zoo, complete with jungle, Antarctic, and savannah habitats. The girls bounced and giggled and generally got in the way while Casey and Carolyn moved furniture and set up the painted cardboard backdrops. Casey and Grace had made the cookie dough the night before and stored the prepared cookie sheets in the refrigerator with the rest of the party food. At two-thirty, they slid them into the oven to bake, filling the house with the irresistible aroma of melting chocolate chips. Alec showed up at three o'clock to be on-hand when the gaggle of lions, zebras, kangaroos, and even an ingenious meerkat appeared at three-thirty.

The first activity was a treasure hunt for animal-themed prizes through the zoo habitats. Each discovery produced a chorus of squeals so loud Casey was sure they could be heard in the next block. After every guest had a prize, they trooped into the kitchen to make finger paint selfies of themselves in their costumes. Alec had donated several old shirts for paint smocks to protect the partygoers' costumes, but nearly as much paint ended up on the floor as on the paper. Carolyn was in charge of hand-washing, and by the time the masterpieces were spread out on the table to dry, the kitchen sink sported every color in the rainbow.

Next, it was time for zoo chow. Casey herded the giggling crew into the dining room, where she'd filled trays with sandwiches cut into animal shapes with cookie cutters, along with grapes and carrot sticks. They nibbled at the food but seemed to have more fun playing with the sandwiches than eating them, saving their real enthusiasm for the zoo cake and chocolate chip cookies.

Casey had just set the last slice of cake in front of the meerkat when the doorbell rang. She glanced at her watch. It was only five-thirty, and the party wasn't scheduled to end until six. Maybe something had come up, and someone had to leave early.

As the hungry beasts devoured their cake, she slipped out of the room and headed for the door, leaving Carolyn and Alec to supervise. She didn't see anyone through the curtain, and when she opened the door, no one was waiting. Perplexed, she took a step outside and glanced up and down the sidewalk but again saw no one. She was about to go back inside when Alec appeared in the doorway.

"Who was it?"

"I don't know. I didn't see anybody."

He stepped out, looked around, then bent to pick up something sitting against the house, beside the door. When he straightened, his expression was thunderous.

"What is it?"

He raised his hands. One held an envelope with *Grace* printed on the outside. In the other was a stuffed toy monkey. Or more accurately, the body of a stuffed toy monkey. Someone had ripped the head off.

Bile rose in the back of Casey's throat, threatening to gag her. What kind of person would do that to a child? And on her birthday!

"You can't let Grace see that," she murmured.

"I don't intend to. I'd like to burn it. Or better yet, stuff it down the throat of whoever put it here." Fury vibrated through every word.

"What's in the envelope?"

He lifted the flap and pulled out a card with a colorful picture of an owl saying, *Who's having a birthday?* "It looks like a birthday card."

When he opened the card, a folded piece of paper dropped to the porch deck. Casey picked it up and read the note printed in heavy block letters.

*Leave the Fassbender boat on your desk Monday night, with your office door unlocked. Fail to do this, and your niece will pay the price. Tell no one, or the consequences will be on your head.*

*Yes.* Casey's pulse skittered. *Success.* Finally, they knew what their adversary wanted. Now, they just had to figure out a way to deflect his or her attention away from Grace.

She handed him the note. "You have to give these to the police."

Alec swore as he scanned the note. "I'll call them later. I'm not going to ruin Grace's party by having the police show up."

"That's probably all right. There isn't much they could do right now, anyway. We didn't see anyone, and the security cameras weren't turned on because of the party."

"Speaking of the party, we'd better get back inside." He opened the door and held it for her. "If they've finished their cake, Grace can open her presents. I'll stow these somewhere out of sight."

Casey drew a deep, shuddery breath. "I feel like I just drank a gallon of espresso. It isn't going to be easy to carry on with the party as if nothing happened."

"We have to—for Grace."

By the time the last guest had left, Grace was burned out on excitement and half-sick from eating her weight in sugar. She went through the motions of helping to clean up, but as soon as Alec and Casey moved the sofa back into position, she collapsed on it, the tail of her costume hanging limply over the side. Her monkey headdress lay discarded across the back.

Alec nudged her aside a couple of inches and sat down. "All partied out, kiddo?"

"Uh, huh."

He brushed one hand across her pale, fine curls, causing them to spring up. "But did you have a good time?"

"Uh, huh."

"I think your friends had fun, too." He swiveled to face Casey, who was re-positioning the arm chair and floor lamp. "Those finger-paint selfies in their costumes were inspired."

She straightened with a half-laugh. "Maybe, but the kitchen floor will never be the same."

"Uncle Alec?"

"Mmm, hmm."

"I had fun with my friends today. Did Dr. Allen say when I can go back to school?"

His jaw flexed. "Soon. Very soon." He pushed to his feet and reached for her hand. "How would you like to go up and see Balthazar before bath time and bed?"

"Oh, yes! I know he's sad because he didn't get to come to the party."

"Here." Casey handed her a bunch of grapes from the refreshment table. "You can take him these. They're much better for him than birthday cake."

The little girl giggled when Alec hoisted her up with an arm beneath her bottom.

"You're almost too big for me to carry anymore, now that you're five."

"Nooooo! I love it when you carry me!"

"Then you'd better stop growing." He nuzzled her neck with a growling sound that elicited more giggles as he swept her up the stairs.

While Alec handled bedtime duty, Casey put the living room and kitchen back to rights. It was amazing how much chaos six preschoolers could create when they were having fun. As she scrubbed the remains of red, yellow, and green finger paint from the kitchen counter and mopped the floor, she pondered their next step. It might not be her place to recommend a course of action to Alec—he'd hired her to protect Grace, period—but the toll the stress of the situation was taking on both him and Grace weighed heavily on her. She wanted to help them return to their normal lives, even if those lives might not include her.

The thought brought a sudden pang of loss so sharp her throat tightened. When Madelyn had assigned her this job a few short weeks ago, she'd been nervous and excited to be working on her own for the first time. She'd never imagined what the reality of becoming a part of this little family would come to mean.

"She's asleep." Alec ambled into the room with a kangaroo-shaped peanut butter and jelly sandwich in one hand.

Casey straightened from squeezing out the mop. Worry had darkened and hollowed the flesh around his eyes, but their expression held new purpose. In fact, the air around him fairly crackled with energy. Skirting a damp spot on the floor, he leaned against the kitchen table and bit the head off the whole wheat marsupial like a hungry T-Rex.

She got two glasses down from the cupboard and glanced over her shoulder. "How about a glass of milk to go with that?"

He smacked his tongue against the roof of his mouth a couple of times. "Good idea."

She brought the milk-filled glasses to the table and handed him one before taking a long draught from the other.

He drained his glass and set it on the table. "We're close. I can feel it. We're going to catch this freak."

"You aren't planning to follow the instructions and leave the boat out, are you?"

"Of course, not. But he'll have to go into my office after hours to figure that out, and we'll get him on the camera."

"Do you think you should notify the director of the museum about the note?"

"I considered it, but I don't want to alarm him when the boat will never be at risk."

"True, but the director might want to inform building security to keep a close watch Monday night, especially on the hallway outside your office."

"I'm sure he would, but what if the thief gets nervous and doesn't act this time? That doesn't make the problem go away. It just leaves Grace open to ongoing threats. I'm ready for this to be over. Now."

*Even if it means we never see each other again.* As the thought flashed through her mind, she mentally berated herself for thinking about anything other than Grace's safety. "I understand." She tried, but failed, to keep the hint of poignancy from her voice.

Alec pushed up from his perch on the table. "Casey."

When he reached for her, she froze. She watched his fingers close lightly around her wrist as if it were happening in slow motion to someone else. When he gave a gentle tug, she went. Straight into his arms.

He cradled her against his chest and pressed a light kiss against her hair. "I know I told you before, but I have to tell you again—I'm so glad you're here."

She was, too, even if it was only for a short time.

He drew back and stared into her eyes for an eon before bringing his mouth down on hers with a low groan. His arms tightened around her back, pressing her against his chest, and sensation took over. As her breasts met the resilience of firm flesh stretched over solid muscle, one large hand stroked the length of her spine while the other rose to cup the back of her head. He adjusted the angle and dove in for more. As her lips responded, her blood pulsed rhythmically through the sensitive parts of her body.

And then, it was over.

**** 

Alec dropped his hands and stepped back. Casey stood blinking at him like a stunned owl.

"I'm sorry," he said. *Or, at least I should be.*

"Why?" A tiny tremor rippled through the single word.

"I shouldn't have done that." While he wasn't technically her employer, he could get her fired with a single phone call. He had never taken advantage of his position with a woman, and he wasn't about to start now. Stress was no excuse.

He half-turned, braced both hands against the counter, and dropped his head. "Sometimes, I forget you're here on a job. I crossed the line—I'm sorry."

"I'm not. Alec, for better or for worse, we're in this together."

He straightened and met her frank gaze. The kiss might have knocked her off-balance for a minute or two, but she was back on her customary even keel— calm, practical, and perceptive. The perfect partner at a time like this. Relief eased some of the weight pressing down on him. "I'm glad you feel that way. One way or another, we're going to find this bastard and take him down."

She nodded and held out her hand. "Together."

He grasped it and held tight. "Together."

Early the next morning, Alec called Officer Foster and was relieved when the young cop offered to meet him at the NEI to pick up the new note and the decapitated monkey. He was glad to get both out of the house and off his mind, at least temporarily.

When Foster read the note and examined the toy with stuffing protruding from the stub of its neck, the officer grimaced. "Whoa, I don't know what to say. That's creepy, Professor. This situation is getting serious."

Alec couldn't agree more.

The rest of the weekend centered around Grace, and Alec was glad for the diversion. Whenever he had a free moment, his thoughts returned to Monday evening like a tongue to a sore tooth, ratcheting up his anxiety another notch each time. Happily, his niece seemed oblivious to his mood. She was excited to play with her new toys and insisted on having Sophia over to help break them in.

Alec had taken Nora's advice and found a pop-up book about ancient Egypt with a real imitation ruby on the cover, and Casey had somehow managed to come up with an explorer's costume, complete with a khaki field hat and binoculars. By Sunday evening, all three of them were played-out.

Monday moved at a glacial pace. Alec taught a graduate seminar in the morning then sat through an interminable faculty meeting in the afternoon. He didn't have time to work on the Fassbender boat, but it and the anonymous adversary were never far from his mind. At the end of the day, he checked the camera one final time, closed his office door without locking it, and walked away. He'd done everything he could until the thief showed his hand.

That night, he tossed and turned, playing out various scenarios in his mind until finally drifting into a fitful sleep sometime after four-thirty. When his eyelids scraped open three hours later, the muscles in his shoulders ached, and his mouth tasted like cotton dipped in camel droppings.

By the time he had dragged himself out of bed and spent ten minutes under water so hot it nearly peeled the skin off his back, he felt almost human. Grace and Casey were half-way through breakfast when he arrived in the kitchen.

When Casey started to rise, he gestured her to stay seated. "Sit down and finish your oatmeal while it's hot. I can take care of myself."

He poured a cup of coffee and popped a couple slices of bread into the toaster.

When he took his seat beside her, Grace switched from eating to wheedling. "Can Sophia come over to play this afternoon, Uncle Alec?"

Alec glanced across at Casey and raised a brow in question.

She smiled then turned to Grace. "We'll call and ask after you brush your teeth and feed Balthazar."

"Yay!" Grace stuffed down the rest of her oatmeal in two bites and raced out of the room.

Casey took a sip of her coffee, then put the cup down and regarded him with concern. "How are you feeling?"

He blew out a breath. "About as good as I look. You?"

"Nervous. Excited." She lifted one shoulder in a deceptively casual shrug.

"Me, too." After downing the remainder of his coffee in a single gulp, he rose from the table, pulled on his coat, and shouldered his backpack.

Casey had followed him to the door. "Call me as soon as you look at the tape."

He nodded, resisting a sudden urge to kiss her. "I will."

Weaving around the icy patches on the sidewalk, he half-ran the several blocks to work and arrived at his office damp with sweat beneath his wool coat and breathing heavily. The closed door taunted him. What would he find inside? After a long pause he turned the knob.

His office appeared untouched, but what had he expected? That the perpetrator would trash the place in frustration? He dropped his pack next to his desk and plucked the nanny-cam from its hiding place. His heart pounded as he downloaded the data to the computer on his desk and opened the file.

# CHAPTER NINE

The compact surveillance camera had been situated to capture his desk as well as the door to his office. Alec held his breath as he stared at the closed door on his computer screen. When the image appeared static for a couple of minutes, he fast-forwarded until he detected movement. The round, burnished brass knob turned, and the door slowly pushed inward until a hand appeared holding the edge. He waited for a face or body to follow.

*Come on. Come on!*

Then—just as slowly as it had opened—the hand withdrew, and the door closed.

*Nothing. All that anticipation...all for nothing.*

He resisted the urge to throw the computer monitor across the room. His hopes had been riding on the camera to provide the first real clue to the culprit's identity. And what did it show? A hand. And not even a whole hand—just four fingers. He couldn't even tell if they were male or female.

How had the intruder known the boat wasn't on the desk without being able to see it? Had the person used some kind of mirror or other device? Or had the camera angle been off by a few degrees and missed the critical view?

He pulled out his chair and flopped into it. He had to call Casey—she was as anxious for the results of their trap as he was. How would she respond to his news, or lack thereof? She was bound to be disappointed, but she had such a levelheaded temperament, she probably wouldn't even raise her voice. It took every ounce of self-control he possessed not to put his fist through the wall. If it were only about the boat, he would be concerned but not emotionally invested. Because the threat involved Grace, his fight-or-flight response had been stuck in fight-mode for weeks.

He gritted his teeth and picked up his phone. *Might as well get it over with.*

As he had expected, Casey took the news calmly. According to her—and she was right—there was nothing to do now except wait for a reaction from the note-writer.

Alec made it through the rest of the morning by closing his door and burying himself in a series of emails and phone calls to Germany and Egypt regarding the origins of the Fassbender boat. It was a fascinating artifact, but he couldn't wait to be rid of it. Regardless of the outcome of his research, as soon as he finished, he could turn full responsibility for the boat over to the museum director. The thieves would no longer have anything to gain by threatening Grace, and this whole nightmare would end.

A little after one o'clock, he slipped out to the cafeteria to grab a sandwich to eat at his desk. When he returned, the first thing he noticed was a white envelope in the middle of his desk. He raced over, snatched it up, withdrew a single sheet of white paper, and read: YOU'LL BE SORRY. The block letters were hand-printed in the same style as the note in Grace's birthday card. The initial jolt of fear from seeing it again was quickly followed by a surge of triumph.

*I've got you this time!*

There was no way anyone could have put the paper on his desk and remained outside the view of the security camera.

*The camera.*

He spat out an Arabic curse having to do with the personal anatomy of a donkey. In his disgust at failing to catch the criminal earlier, he had left the camera turned off and lying on his credenza instead of returning it to its hiding place in the bookcase. Another lost opportunity. And one more piece of useless evidence for Officer Foster's growing file. In disgust, he tossed the note in his top drawer. He would deal with it tomorrow.

By five o'clock, his foul mood had become thunderous. He'd nearly thrown Nora out of his office twice and barked at Fermin when the man dared to poke his head in to ask if Alec would like to join him and Howard Boardman for a drink at the Faculty Club before heading home.

*I've got to get a grip. Grace will worry and wonder what's wrong.* He buttoned his coat and wrapped his scarf around his neck. *And there's Casey...*

When he stepped out of the building, the air held the tantalizing hint of spring that sometimes comes from an unseasonably warm day in mid-February. A sheen of sweat coated the sidewalks and streets instead of the usual icy film, and even the exhaust fumes seemed less toxic.

Alec closed his eyes and sucked in a deep breath. As he exhaled, he reminded himself things could be much worse. Grace was safe at home under Casey's watchful eye, and the Fassbender boat was locked safely in the NEI archives. So far, he was ahead in this game of cat and mouse.

By the time he reached home, he was feeling almost cheerful. When he walked through the doorway, Grace slammed into him like a charging rhino.

"Uncle Alec, you'll never guess what we did today!"

"Whoa. Slow down there." He placed his hands on her shoulders to halt her forward progress. "What did you do?"

"We made a snowman with all the snow in the backyard!"

He raised his brows. "All of it?"

"Almost all. Right down to the mud."

Casey walked in from the kitchen and smiled. "Her snowsuit is in the dryer."

Grace grabbed his hand and tugged. "Do you want to see him? He's almost as tall as Casey. We used a carrot for his nose."

"Okay, okay. I'll come out and take a look. Did you give him a name?"

Before she could answer, the doorbell rang. Alec glanced at Casey, who shrugged and shook her head. "Grace, why don't you go see if your snowsuit is dry enough to put back on while I answer the door."

He waited until Grace and Casey had left the room before pushing aside the edge of the curtain on the front door. On the other side of the glass stood his TA Maria. What was she doing here? He flipped on the porch light and opened the door.

"Maria, what can I do for you?"

She wet her lips. "I…uh…missed you in your office this morning."

He'd barely left his office all day. Maybe she'd seen his closed door and assumed he was out.

She slid the backpack offer her shoulder and unzipped the top. "I brought a present for Grace's birthday."

"Maria!" Grace ran toward the door with Casey hot on her heels.

Maria knelt with the package in one hand and held out her arms. Grace threw herself into the embrace with gusto. "You brought me a present!"

Maria gave her a squeeze. "Of course, I did. It's your birthday, isn't it?"

"Not any more. I'm already five."

"Oh. I guess I should take this back, then." With a solemn expression, Maria reached for the gift.

"Noooo!" Grace clutched the brightly-wrapped package to her chest.

"Then shall we open it?"

"Yes." Grace wriggled free, grabbed Maria's hand, and pulled her into the living room. She tore open the paper and squealed. "You got me a Princess Tia wig, just like I wanted!" She held up the long, curly black wig for Alec and Casey to admire.

"Very nice." *I wonder how long it will be before it ends up on that blasted monkey.*

"Would you like to try it on?" Casey asked, reaching for the box.

"Yes!"

While Casey helped settle the wig over Grace's blond hair, Maria straightened and turned to Alec. "Actually, Professor Bainbridge, I was wondering if Grace would like to go see that new animated movie about the family of lemurs tonight. I'd be happy to take her. I'm sure both you—" She shot a quick glance at Casey. "—and your nanny could use an evening off."

"Yes, yes, yes!" Grace jumped up and down, sending her new black curls flying.

Especially after the note today, Alec didn't want to let his niece out of his sight, but this was Maria. He'd trusted her to care for Grace since she was a toddler, and he'd never questioned the sincerity of her feelings for the child. "Aah…" He sent Casey an inquiring look.

She dipped her chin in an almost imperceptible nod then smiled. "That sounds like fun. Why don't we all go together?"

"Yay!" Grace whooped.

Casey turned her smile on Maria. "It's settled, then. We'll have a quick supper here then all go to the movie. What time does it start?"

The pretty brunette's expression went blank. "Uh…"

"That's okay," Alec said. "I'll check the theater schedule on my phone. Come in and take your coat off."

Maria's eyes darted from Alec to Grace and back. "I'm sorry, but I just remembered something I have to do."

Grace's lower lip quivered. "You mean we can't go to the movie tonight?"

Maria leaned down and touched Grace's cheek. "I'm sorry. We'll have to do it another time." She was out the door and down the front steps before Alec could respond.

A shuddery whimper drew his attention. When he glanced down, Grace squeezed her eyes tight to blink away the gathering tears, but a couple of small ones escaped and trickled down her smooth, soft cheeks.

His chest tightened. He'd always been a sucker for her tears, especially when she was trying so hard to be brave and grown-up. "You and Casey and I can still go to the movie."

Her face brightened, and she hugged his waist. "Thank you, thank you, thank you! I'm going to tell Balthazar!" And off she zoomed.

"Dinner will be ready in fifteen minutes," Casey called after her. She turned to Alec with a chuckle. "She lives life at warp speed, doesn't she?"

"Pretty much."

After a quick meal of grilled cheese sandwiches and tomato soup, they loaded into the Volvo for the short drive to the neighborhood movie theater, making it just in time for the seven o'clock show. Alec overruled Grace's choice of the front row, and they settled into seats mid-way back with Grace nestled between the two adults.

Alec leaned over, handed her the small, grotesquely expensive candy bar she'd talked him into buying at the concession stand, and whispered, "The movie lasts until after your usual bedtime. Do you think you can stay awake?"

"Of course, I can. Did you forget I'm five now?"

"Oh, yes. How silly of me." At her giggle, he draped an arm protectively across the back of her seat and settled in.

He wasn't a huge fan of animated movies, but even he had to admit this one was pretty cute. Grace kept her attention riveted to the screen, squeezing his hand tight when the youngest lemur was in peril. The couple of times Alec glanced at Casey, she seemed to be enjoying the show, too.

For the first few blocks of the drive home, Grace chattered nonstop about the movie, but by the time they pulled into the garage, she'd quieted, and her head lolled against the side of her car seat. She stirred briefly when Alec lifted her out of the car but dropped her head on his shoulder and was sound asleep again by the time they reached the back stoop. He waited while Casey unlocked the door then carried Grace up to bed. When he came back downstairs, he found Casey seated on the living room sofa with a steaming mug in her hand.

She gestured to another mug on a coaster on the coffee table with a smile. "Hot cider? I thought it might be a nice end to the evening."

"Thanks." Not fully trusting himself, he chose his leather armchair over the spot on the sofa beside her.

He picked up his mug and took a sip. Suddenly, the room felt uncomfortably warm. Maybe this wasn't the best idea. The lamplight softened and shaded her features, giving her a faintly seductive air and gilding the smooth flow of her hair. A man could get used to a sight like that.

Her lips curved. "It was a cute movie. Grace had fun tonight."

"So did I." As soon as the words left his mouth, he realized how true they were. The outing had been so normal, such a relief from the constant stress of the past few weeks. He hadn't thought about the note or the threat to Grace for hours.

"It's too bad Maria couldn't join us," Casey said.

A sense of unease he'd been suppressing all night wiggled to the forefront. Alec leaned forward, holding his mug in both hands, and rested his forearms on his thighs. Tilting his head, he pinned her with a questioning gaze. "Did Maria's behavior this evening seem odd to you?"

"I don't know her very well, but..."

"She stops by unexpectedly, asks to take Grace to the movie, and then suddenly remembers she has something else to do." He frowned.

"She certainly seemed edgy and distracted."

"She's a good student, a good TA, and I know she's always been fond of Grace." He straightened and took another sip from his mug. "I'm worried she may be having financial problems. Her family's from Cyprus, and I don't think they have much money. Graduate school can be tough for foreign students. I've been meaning to ask if there's anything I can do to help, but something always seems to come up. I'll make time tomorrow."

Casey finished her cider and rose, holding out one hand for Alec's empty mug. "I'm sorry the nanny cam didn't give us what we needed today. I'd really hoped..."

*The camera!* He'd completely forgotten to tell her.

"There's something else. I got another note today. It said *YOU'LL BE SORRY* in the same printing as the note in Grace's card."

"Where did you find it?"

"On my desk, after lunch."

"So, whoever it was came back." Excitement danced in her eyes.

"I assume so, although I suppose the hand on the door could have belonged to anyone."

Her brows pinched in disbelief. "Alec, come on. What are the chances the janitor would have opened your door a few inches without coming inside, then closed it? Besides, if the note was on your desk, the camera must have caught the perpetrator the second time."

He exhaled sharply. "I was so frustrated this morning, I forgot to put it back in place and reset it."

Her lips tightened. "We failed this time, but we'll get him. Based on the new note, I think he'll act again, and soon. We just have to be prepared."

"And how are we supposed to do that?" He clenched his teeth until his jaw ached. "This person has been ahead of us at every turn."

"We've managed to draw our adversary out. We know what he wants." Her voice was low, steady, and reassuring. "We have to be patient and keep doing what we've been doing. I'll keep Grace safe, and you watch everyone who shows any interest in the boat. One way or another, whoever is behind this is going to make another move."

She was right, but the wait was making him crazy.

She gave his arm a little squeeze then dropped her hand. "What did you do with the note?"

"I was so frustrated, I threw it in my desk drawer. I'll turn it over to the campus police in the morning."

ALISON HENDERSON

Crossing the room, she picked up his empty mug from the coffee table. "I don't know about you, but I'm about ready to call it a night."

"It's been a long day." He gave her a sheepish grin. "I hate to admit it, but those singing lemurs nearly lulled me to sleep a couple of times."

"Believe me, I understand. You go on up." She headed for the kitchen. "As soon as I rinse these, I'll be right behind you."

Alec hesitated, captivated by the gentle sway of her hips as she left the room. He was getting much too used to having this beautiful woman in his house. There was something dangerously normal about it. As he headed up the stairs, her words resounded in his head. "I'll be right behind you." He had a sudden vision of her following him up to the room they shared, to the bed they shared.

As he stood in the doorway of his bedroom, he scrubbed his face with his hand and blinked.

*Snap out of it. She's young and beautiful, with her whole life ahead of her – a life of her own choosing. She's here temporarily to protect Grace, not to fulfill your fantasies, you fool.*

The next morning, after breakfast, he kissed Grace on the head, and headed to work. He hung his coat on the back of his office door then checked the surveillance camera. After yesterday, he hadn't expected results, but that didn't prevent the brief pang of disappointment when the recording came up blank again. He left a message for the young cop who'd picked up the previous notes and the headless monkey, then phoned Maria. When she didn't answer, he left a message asking her to stop by as soon as she arrived.

He turned on his computer but, instead of jumping into a project, sat staring at the wallpaper of the pyramids at Giza as if he'd never seen them before.

*What now?*

He didn't want to miss the officer or Maria, so he couldn't go to the archives to work with the Fassbender boat, and he wouldn't feel comfortable bringing it to his office until the threat of theft was eliminated. His class notes were ready for the next three weeks, and he didn't have any other research projects pending. Out of habit, he opened his email and found two messages from his correspondents in Berlin that kept his mind occupied until a knock on his door interrupted.

Alec glanced up. "Come in."

Maria poked her head inside. "You wanted to see me?"

"Yes, if you've got a minute."

She hesitated then approached his desk.

"Have a seat." He gestured to the chair across the desk.

She sat on the edge of the chair and rested her hands in her lap as she twisted the end of her waist-length hair around one finger. "Is...is anything wrong?"

"I just wanted to make sure you're okay. I've been worried about you."

Maria dropped her gaze. "I'm sorry. I know I've let a few things slip." Her words spilled out with a nervous urgency.

Alec stopped her. "No, no. Your work is fine, but you haven't been yourself lately. You've seemed distracted, even worried."

When she didn't respond, he continued. "The final push to finish your dissertation is always stressful, but I wondered if there was anything else bothering you— money, perhaps, or finding a job? I'd like to help if I can."

When she glanced up, he noticed a tell-tale gleam of moisture in her dark eyes. "You've already done more than most advisers. You helped keep my research on track, read my chapters right away, and sent off all my letters of recommendation ahead of the deadlines. I couldn't ask for more."

He hated to see her in distress. In the years she'd been his teaching assistant, he'd come to respect Maria as a promising young scholar, not to mention the fact that she'd spent so much time with his niece, she almost felt like family. "Is it money problems? Graduate student stipends can be pretty skimpy, especially in the Humanities. I know your babysitting income is down since I hired a full-time nanny for Grace, but I'm sure I could ask around and find other faculty members who could use your services."

She sniffed almost imperceptibly. "That's very kind, but I think I'll make it. Money is tight, but I only have a few more months until graduation."

"If you're sure…"

"I'm sure." She pushed the chair back. "Thanks for offering, though. I'm sorry I've been distracted, and please tell your nanny I'm sorry for acting weird last night." She glanced at her watch. "If there's nothing else, I have someplace I need to be."

As she rose, Alec stood, too. "Okay. But let me know if anything changes. The offer stands."

She flashed a quick smile on her way out the door.

"Take care of yourself," he called after her, but the door shut before he finished.

He returned to his chair. He hadn't learned much, but at least he'd let her know he was paying attention and had offered to help.

Before he could decide what to do next, another knock sounded. He only hoped Fermin hadn't seen Maria leave and decided it was a good time to pay a visit. "Come in."

The door opened, and Officer Foster stepped in. "Professor Bainbridge?"

Alec motioned him in. "Thank you for coming."

The officer approached the desk. "Your message said you received another note. The perp seems to be picking up his pace."

"Yes." Alec opened his drawer and handed over the note. "This time, I found it on my desk. I thought you'd want to give it to the detective."

"Yes, sir." The young man produced a plastic evidence bag from his jacket pocket and slipped the note inside.

"I don't suppose the detective has come up with anything." Alec didn't expect good news. He'd almost given up hope of any lead panning out.

"No, but every piece of evidence helps establish a pattern."

"I hope so. Anyway, thanks again."

The young cop tipped his hat. "See you later, Professor."

*Only if you have good news, which I doubt.*

The officer left the door ajar, so Alec rose from his desk to close it. He was in no mood to deal with casual visitors. He glanced down the hall and saw two figures at the head of the stairs. Based on the long, dark hair and oversized black sweater, the woman with her back to him was Maria. All he could see of the second person, who appeared to be standing a step or two below her on the stairs, was a glimpse of shorter dark hair. Maria's rapid head movements suggested an animated conversation, and when she suddenly thrust her right arm forward in a forceful shove, a derisive masculine laugh followed. Maybe she was having boyfriend troubles. That might account for her recent moodiness and distraction. If so, Alec was afraid he couldn't be of much help.

Around three o'clock, his phone rang. He answered on the second ring, expecting it to be the call he'd been anticipating from a colleague at the Cairo Museum.

Instead, a childish voice greeted him. "Uncle Alec, you need to come home right now."

His heart plunged.

# CHAPTER TEN

Phone crammed against his ear, Alec shut down his computer and raced to grab his coat from the hook on the back of his office door. "What's wrong, Grace? Can you tell me what happened?"

"Balthazar has been bad." Sniffles clogged her voice.

Alec shrugged into his coat, changing ears. "What did he do?" He locked the door and ran down the hall.

"He got out."

He swore under his breath as he pictured the monkey on the loose in the neighborhood, swinging from the leafless trees and harassing passers-by on the sidewalk. He'd promised Tom Huerta they'd keep his furry companion safe. What if the evil little monster ran away and they couldn't find him? How was Alec going to tell his friend they'd lost Balthazar?

The well-oiled oak doors of the Institute opened smoothly as he pushed through and bounded down the steps. "Did you and Casey go outside to look for him?" Maybe he should call Animal Control.

"Why would we go outside?" Grace sounded puzzled.

"Grace, it's cold and snowy, and Balthazar is a tropical monkey. He could get hurt or sick if he's outside very long."

"Oh, he didn't get out of the house. He stole the key to his crate and let himself out."

He slowed his pace and took a deep breath. "Then he's fine."

"No, he's mad. He's yelling. I put him in his crate for a time-out and shut the door."

Alec halted, and a young man scurrying along the sidewalk behind him ran smack into his back. After regaining his balance, he closed his eyes and counted to three in his head. "Grace, if everyone is fine, why did you call me?"

"Casey isn't fine. She fell down the stairs when she was chasing Balthazar cuz he stole her stuff. I think she's hurt."

He muttered a curse under his breath. What if Casey had sprained her ankle or broken a bone? "Can you give her the phone so I can talk to her."

"She can't talk. She's sleeping."

His heart paused then gave a big thump. "Hang on. I'll be there in five minutes."

****

Casey awoke to Grace's face looming over hers from a distance of about three inches. The child's blurry, oversized features reminded her of an image from a horror movie. Casey blinked and moved her head.

*Ouch!*

She raised one hand and gingerly touched the back of her skull. Her fingers encountered a firm lump at the same moment her head screamed in pain. She jerked them back.

*What happened? Where am I?*

Keeping her head as still as possible, she glanced around and recognized the old-fashioned wallpaper in the Bainbridge's front hall. She was lying at a strange angle, and something long and hard dug into the flesh across the middle of her back. Exploring with her fingers, she determined she was lying near the bottom of the stairway across the first step while her head rested on the edge of the second.

"Are you awake now?"

She turned toward Grace's voice and winced. "I think so."

"I called Uncle Alec. He's coming home."

Slowly and carefully, Casey pushed herself up on her elbows. The action relieved the discomfort in her back but intensified the pain in her head. For a moment, she was afraid she might throw up. Before she could decide, a key rattled in the lock, and Alec burst through the door.

When she straightened her arms in an attempt to stand, he shouted, "Don't move!" He dropped his pack and knelt beside her, sliding one arm behind her shoulders. He turned to Grace. "Hand me the phone. I'm calling nine-one-one."

Casey struggled to sit up and raised a hand to her throbbing head. How much would an ambulance ride cost? Since she was no longer officially a student, she didn't even have her bare-bones student insurance anymore. "I'm sure there's no need for that. I...I'm okay...I think."

"You're not okay." Alec's voice was harsh and insistent. "You've probably got a concussion, and God knows what else."

"It's not that bad. I just slipped on the steps. Before we do anything drastic, I want to see if I can stand."

He grumbled but helped her to her feet, his arms bearing most of her weight. Gradually, he eased her weight down. "Does anything hurt?"

She tested and took stock. "Nothing's seems to be broken. I think I'm okay." She took a couple of tentative steps then swayed as a wave of wooziness rolled over her.

Alec wrapped one strong arm around her waist to keep her from falling. "I'm taking you to the Emergency Room. Now."

"But—" Her head was already starting to clear.

"No buts. Concussions can be serious. If your employer's Worker's Comp won't cover the visit, I will. It's my fault you fell."

"I don't know how you came up with that," she argued. "I'm the one who was supposed to be in charge when Balthazar escaped."

"And I'm the one who agreed to take that damned monkey in the first place."

"Uncle Alec, you said damn," Grace scolded.

"I'm sorry, but sometimes Balthazar can be very naughty. Where is he now?"

"He's still in his crate. I can hear him yelling."

"Good. Now, go put your coat on. I'm going to call Mrs. Greenberg to ask if you can stay at the Chiang's house while I take Casey to the hospital."

Ten minutes later, he pulled up in front of the Chiang's brownstone, and Casey waited in the car while he delivered Grace to the door. The housekeeper ushered her inside then waved at Casey. She managed a half-hearted wave in return.

Alec got back in the car and pulled away from the curb. "How're you feeling?"

"Not too bad. My head hurts, but otherwise I'm just a little bruised. It was as much a shock as anything else. I can't remember the last time I fell."

He glanced in the side mirror before changing lanes and signaling a left turn. "I never should have agreed to take that simian menace."

"You won't hear any argument from me, but Grace loves him, and he seems to reciprocate."

"Hmph." He slowed to turn into the Emergency entrance at the University Hospital. "You can tell me what happened while we wait. Since you're not shot, stabbed, or having a heart attack, it may be a while before we can get a doctor to examine you."

He pulled into the temporary patient parking area near the door then half-carried her to the Admission desk. When the clerk asked about insurance, Alec gave her his credit card. Casey tried to protest, but he silenced her. "This is my responsibility."

After she was seated as comfortably as possible in an orange, molded plastic chair in the overcrowded waiting room, he left to move the car to the main parking garage. While she waited for him to return, Casey watched the antics of an energetic toddler who was there with his mother and two sisters, one of whom had a kitchen towel wrapped around her hand. A few minutes later, an ambulance crew raced in, pushing an unconscious young man on a gurney and leaving a trail of large red blood drops across the speckled linoleum tile floor. They disappeared through the double swinging doors into the bowels of the building. The frenetic activity and cacophony of sounds, combined with the strong odor of pine-scented disinfectant, made Casey's head throb and her stomach squirm. She closed her eyes.

"Hey." A hand grasped her shoulder. "Are you feeling worse?"

She opened her eyes to see Alec bending over her. His cheeks were flushed, and the perfect golden waves of his hair looked like someone had taken an eggbeater to them. He must have run all the way from the parking garage. "Not really."

"Does your head hurt any less?"

She tried to smile, but it ended in a grimace. "Not really."

He straightened. "I'm going to check with a nurse to see how much longer it will be before they can see you."

She caught his sleeve with one hand. "Don't do that. They're busy this afternoon, and lots of the people here are in worse shape than I am."

He glanced around the room with a grunt of what might have been acknowledgement or possibly disgust, then settled into the chair next to her. Casey leaned her head against his shoulder. Her head ached, and she was so tired. What harm would it do to take a little rest? As he'd said, they might be waiting for hours. Her eyelids drifted down again.

A moment later, someone shook her.

"No sleeping."

He was starting to annoy her. "I wasn't sleeping."

"I may not know much about head injuries, but I've heard you're not supposed to let the injured person go to sleep."

"I'm tired."

He glanced at the big clock on the wall above the admission desk. "You probably need to eat. I'll see if I can find a vending machine."

Her stomach roiled at the thought. "There's nothing in a hospital vending machine that would stay down right now."

He twisted in his seat and started to rise. "You need something to keep you awake. How about a cup of tea or a cola?"

"How about you sit still and try to relax?"

"I can't relax in a hospital...ever. Some of the worst hours of my life have been spent in hospitals."

She reached for the hand resting on his knee and squeezed. "I'm sorry. Your mom?"

He nodded. "The last time she got sick I brought her to the hospital. Sara came, too. The doctors worked hard to save her, but they wouldn't let us see her for a long time—said we'd get in the way. It was probably true, but the waiting was agony."

His words reminded her how difficult his life had been compared to hers. "I'm so sorry." What else could she say?

"Thanks, but that was half a lifetime ago. Right now, I'm worried about you."

She shifted in her chair and sucked in a short breath when a deep ache flared across her hip and back. "I'll be fine. I just lost my footing on the top step while I was chasing Balthazar, trying to get my earrings and keys back."

"About that...what exactly happened?"

"Apparently he managed to unlock his kennel and escape."

Alec frowned. "But the key is always kept on the table across the room."

She shifted her weight again, mentally cursing the hard, plastic chairs. While easy to clean, they were also miserably uncomfortable, even in the best of circumstances. And no one in a hospital Emergency Room was in the best of circumstances. "One of us — and I can't be sure which — must have dropped it on the floor within reach after putting him back in his cage before lunch. Grace and I got busy, then the next thing I knew, that monkey sashayed into the kitchen with my keys in one hand and my grandmother's pearl earrings in the other."

"I warned you he likes shiny objects."

"When I tried to get them away from him, he danced around, staying just beyond my reach. I could swear he was laughing."

"He probably was. He's a nasty little bugger. I don't know how Tom puts up with him."

"Well, I plan to give him a piece of my mind when we get home. You should see the mess he made tossing my bedroom, looking for loot. It's a good thing I had my pistol unloaded and locked in my suitcase in the closet."

One corner of Alec's mouth twitched. Casey narrowed her eyes. "You think that's funny? I wasn't the only victim of his little crime spree. Wait until you see your room."

When his face clouded and he grumbled something about a furry hoodlum, she burst out laughing, then winced and rubbed the back of her head. "Ouch. I probably shouldn't have done that."

Before he could fuss any further, a nurse with a chart in her hand called out, "Casey Callahan!"

Alec insisted on helping her stand and kept a tight grip on her arm as they followed the woman back to a curtain-shrouded cubicle containing a bed and assorted medical equipment mounted to the wall.

"You can sit there, sir." The nurse pointed to another of the ubiquitous orange chairs. "The doctor will be in shortly." She pulled the curtain closed behind her when she left.

A few minutes later, a young Indian woman in scrubs and a lab coat entered and introduced herself as Dr. Bhardwaj. She asked Casey several questions, noting the answers on her chart. When the doctor prepared to examine her, Alec stood to leave.

Dr. Bhardwaj glanced at him with a smile. "You're welcome to stay while I examine your wife, sir."

A look of panic spread across Alec's face. "I...uh..."

Casey spoke up quickly. "He's not my husband. He's my employer."

"In that case..." The doctor gestured toward the opening in the curtains, and Alec scooted out.

Dr. Bhardwaj proceeded to examine Casey from head to toe and performed a series of memory and cognition tests. She made more notes on the chart as Casey put her clothes back on, then looked up with a satisfied smile. "It appears you have a mild concussion and some bruises, but nothing too serious. I don't believe a CT scan or MRI will be necessary."

"That's good news." Even though Alec had insisted on paying her medical bills, she hated to think what those tests would have cost.

"I'm going to let you go home now, but you have to promise to get plenty of rest, and someone will need to watch you closely for the next few days for any neurological symptoms or signs of altered mental status. Will that be a problem?"

Altered mental status? That sounded ominous. Would she be able to safely take care of Grace alone? Maybe she should ask Madelyn to send another agent for back-up for a day or two.

She shook her head, which only caused a mild ache. "No. I'm sure that can be arranged."

"Good. I'll send your employer back in, and he can take you home."

Alec must have been hovering somewhere nearby. A couple minutes later, he shoved the curtain aside. "The doc says you can go home." He grabbed Casey's arm as she swung her legs off the bed. "Hold on." He helped her rise slowly. "She also said someone has to check on you tonight."

She grabbed the bed rail when a brief wave of dizziness hit. "I'm worried about the next couple of days. I should probably call my boss to see if she can send over another agent to help out. You didn't hire a bodyguard so you could play nursemaid."

He held her coat while she slid her arms into the sleeves. "Don't give it a thought. I've got this. I promised to watch every move you make and haul you back here at the first sign of altered mental status."

Casey grimaced. "The doctor told you about that, did she?"

"Uh, huh." He steered her into the corridor. "And I'll make sure you don't exert yourself and get plenty of rest."

"That won't be easy. As you've said more than once, Grace is pretty lively."

"The car's this way." They headed toward a sign that read *Parking Garage*. "I've decided to take tomorrow off, then it'll be the weekend. By Monday, I'm sure you'll feel much better."

She hoped so but hated to make him alter his schedule, especially when he was in the middle of such a critical project. "I don't want you to miss work on my account."

He dismissed her concerns with an impatient shake of his head as they approached his SUV in the now-dark parking ramp. "It will do me good. I haven't taken a day off in ages, and the stress is making me crazy. For three days, we'll pretend none of this is happening. Besides, Grace will be thrilled."

"But the boat—" She stopped next to the passenger side.

Alec pushed his fob to unlock the door then opened it for her. "Will remain safely locked in the archives."

"And the thief?"

"Won't be able to do a thing with both of us at home. He's not likely to mount an armed invasion and try to kidnap Grace from under our noses." He closed the door then walked around to the driver's side.

While he started the car and backed out of the parking space, she considered his statement. He was probably right. So far, their adversary had shown no inclination toward violence, seeming content with vague threats and mutilated stuffed animals. His strategy appeared to rely solely on Alec's devotion to Grace. It wasn't a bad strategy, but she had to wonder if they were dealing with a hardened antiquities thief or a hopeful amateur.

Casey stared out the car window as they drove the few blocks from the hospital to the Chiang's house to pick up Grace. Streetlights and storefront signs glowed against the black sky. Dusk had come and gone while they'd waited in the Emergency Room. She glanced at the glowing clock on the dashboard. It was past eight. Carolyn would have fed Grace, but Alec must be starving. Her own stomach had settled to the point that she no longer suffered from active nausea, but she had no interest in food. Mostly, she just wanted to sleep. Closing her eyes, she leaned her head against the head rest.

"Hey."

She dragged her eyes open and blinked when a hand gave her shoulder a shake. "Huh...what?"

"You'll sleep better tonight if you can manage to stay awake a couple more hours." Alec pulled the car into an open spot on the street a couple doors from the Chiang's house, opened his door, and climbed out. "I'll be back in a minute with Grace."

He must have called Carolyn before they left the hospital, because Grace was waiting at the door, bundled and ready. She bounded down the walk, holding Alec's hand, and climbed into her car seat on her own. After he buckled her in, she leaned forward. "Are you better, Casey? Balthazar didn't mean for you to get hurt. It was an accident. I'm sure he's really sorry."

*I doubt it. That monkey's had it in for me since the day I arrived.*

She gingerly turned her head and smiled. "I'll be fine. I just have a little headache."

Grace settled back in her seat, seemingly satisfied. "Uncle Alec said he's going to stay home and play with me tomorrow."

"I'm sure you'll have lots of fun."

"I'm gonna wear my new explorer costume, and we're gonna hunt for lost treasure."

162

Casey had visions of the two of them turning the house upside down in their search for valuable "artifacts" and wondered if the Explorer-in-Chief also had plans to clean up afterwards. Right now, even the thought of putting her bedroom back to rights after Balthazar's looting mission made her head throb.

When they got home, Alec settled Casey on the living room sofa under the afghan and hustled Grace off to bed. She tried reading her book, but the words kept floating together, so she finally gave up and resorted to turning on the television. Alec came back downstairs then headed through the hall toward the kitchen at the back of the house. Soon after, the tinkling sounds of glass and metal and the aroma of melting butter wafted her way.

Minutes later he appeared carrying two plates and handed one to her. "I made us a couple of omelets." He set his plate on the coffee table. "I'll be back in a second with juice. I figured you shouldn't have coffee at this hour."

A perfectly delicate, mottled brown crust enveloped fluffy egg, with melted cheese oozing out in a couple of spots. It smelled like her mother's kitchen on a Sunday morning. "Thanks. You didn't need to go to so much trouble. I would have been happy with a couple pieces of toast."

"Well, I wouldn't, and besides, you deserve a hot meal after everything you've been through." He scooted her legs out of the way and sat beside her before picking up his plate.

"You're making too big a deal out of this. I fell down the stairs—that's all. I wasn't shot, stabbed, or blown up. I didn't even break anything." She took a bite. "This is delicious, by the way."

"It is a big deal. You have a concussion. And you're welcome, by the way." He shifted his attention to the actors on the screen. "*The Mummy*. Terrific! It's one of my favorite movies."

"Mine, too." She gave him a mischievous smile. "I never imagined I'd meet a real-life Egyptian archaeologist."

"This movie is one of the reasons I went into the field. I was a senior in high school the year it came out, and it made archaeology look like non-stop adventure—not to mention the perfect way to pick up hot chicks."

Casey laughed. "I have to confess the teenage me wouldn't have minded being an imperiled librarian if it meant riding off into the sunset with Brendan Fraser."

Alec snorted. "You girls are all the same. Only after one thing."

She grinned and popped a forkful of omelet into her mouth.

While they ate, they discussed the characters, marveled at the special effects, and Alec pointed out a few of the most glaring historical inaccuracies.

"I don't care," Casey insisted. "You can't ruin this movie with facts."

"I'm not trying to, I just—"

She waved her fork at him imperiously. "Enough. Your objections are making me tired." They both laughed.

Whether from the power of suggestion, the effects of a full stomach, or the culmination of the events of the day, her head began to droop the minute she set her empty plate on the coffee table. The lure of sleep was so strong, she felt like she'd been hypnotized into a trance and lacked the strength to break free.

After she'd jerked herself awake three or four times, Alec glanced at his watch then turned off the television. "Good girl. You made it until ten o'clock." He rose and reached for her hand. "Let's get you to bed."

She threw off the afghan and blinked a couple of times. "The movie's over."

He smiled and pulled her to stand. "Uh, huh."

When she leaned over to pick up the dirty dishes, he stopped her. "Leave those. I'll get them later."

"But—"

"You're going to bed—now." He led her to the stairs then followed her up, close enough to catch her if she stumbled.

As she approached her room, Casey groaned softly when she remembered the mess awaiting her. Oh, well. It would have to wait a few more hours. She didn't have the energy to deal with it tonight. She flipped the switch, and the lamp on the bedside table turned on, revealing a neat, tidy room. Where were the tipped-over toiletries on the dresser? The clothes strewn across the floor? She turned to Alec in confusion. "When...?"

"I did a quick damage-control sweep after I put Grace to bed. You'll want to put things away properly tomorrow, but at least you can find the bed tonight."

"Thank you. You didn't need to do that."

The expression in his eyes clouded. "Yes...I did. Now, you get ready for bed, and I'll be back to check on you after I clean up the kitchen."

As Casey stood at the bathroom sink washing her face, Alec was front and center in her thoughts. From the moment they'd met, she'd found him attractive—if a little intimidating—and had been surprised to discover his outward seriousness hid a dry sense of humor. She also appreciated his intelligence and admired his unquestioned devotion to Grace. But today she'd seen him in a new light, one that could have a profound effect on the rest of her life.

Alec was many things, but he was no actor, no matter how hard he tried to hide his emotions at times. He had been genuinely concerned about her injury. She'd seen it in his eyes, felt it in his touch.

He might be paying for her professional services, but from the start, they had felt more like partners than employer and employee. Most employers, once they were satisfied Casey wasn't seriously hurt, would have been content to have a replacement agent for a couple of days while she stayed home to recuperate. Not Alec. He'd driven her to the hospital, then sat with her for hours, keeping her company. He had taken charge of everything—including paying her bill—when she was weak, fuzzy-headed, and in pain. Then he'd brought her back to his house, where he insisted on taking care of her himself.

Based on what Carolyn Chiang had told her about his relationship with Sara and what she'd seen of his behavior toward Grace, Casey knew he had a highly developed sense of responsibility. But Sara and Grace were family. She was...what?

Her gaze fell on the three toothbrushes lined up in the porcelain toothbrush holder mounted to the tile wall—hers alongside Alec's and Grace's, as if it were the most natural thing in the world. As if it belonged. It seemed that in a matter of weeks, the family of two had become a family of three. How had that happened?

And what would happen once they discovered the identity of their adversary and eliminated the threat to Grace? Casey would leave, either to take the job in Boston or to continue her job hunt, and Alec and Grace would resume their normal routines. Whatever happened, she wouldn't be standing here, brushing her teeth in his sink much longer.

The thought sent waves of pressure pounding through her skull. She closed her eyes, braced her hands on the sides of the sink, and hung her head. If this job didn't wrap up soon, she didn't know how she could bear to leave them. It might already be too late. Was it possible she'd fallen in love in such a short time?

# CHAPTER ELEVEN

In an effort to let Casey sleep in on Friday, Alec set his alarm for fifteen minutes earlier than usual. He took a quick shower, threw on an old sweatshirt and a pair of jeans, and slipped into Grace's room before she awoke. He stood next to her bed for a couple of minutes, gazing down at her. Pale blond curls spread across her pink pillowcase in a riot of untidy ringlets. Someday she would probably fuss and fume about her hair, but he loved it. It reminded him of Sara's. Grace's rosy cheeks and lips were her mother's, too. Every time he looked at her, his heart contracted painfully, yet he loved her beyond measure.

He laid one hand on her shoulder. "Hey, sleepyhead, wake up."

The little girl stirred and mumbled but refused to open her eyes, so he bent down and whispered in her ear, "Chocolate chip pancakes."

Grace's eyes popped open.

"How would you like to go to Charley's for breakfast?"

"Like we used to?"

Guilt jabbed him in the ribs. It had been too long since he'd taken her out to breakfast. He'd allowed the busyness of life to gobble up what had once been a regular outing. "Yep. Just you and me, kiddo."

"Shouldn't we bring Casey?"

"After her accident yesterday, I think we should let her sleep. How fast can you get ready?"

She threw off her covers. "Really fast!"

He fed Balthazar and cleaned his cage while Grace dressed, and fifteen minutes later, they were walking hand-in-hand down the sidewalk toward their favorite breakfast joint. When they returned home an hour later, they found Casey sitting at the kitchen table, wrapped in her fuzzy blue robe, nursing a cup of coffee.

"We had chocolate chip pancakes!" Grace announced with glee.

Casey smiled, but the skin around her mouth appeared tight, as if she were gritting her teeth. "Did you? That sounds good."

"They're dee-licious!" Grace handed Alec her coat. "I'm going to visit Balthazar."

After she raced off, he turned his attention to Casey. Despite the extra sleep, she looked exhausted. Her cheeks were pale, and her eyes lacked their usual sparkle. "How's your head this morning?"

"It still hurts, but it's more like a dull ache today. The main problem is the brain fog. It sounds weird, but I feel like I'm detached from my body somehow—like I'm here, but I'm not."

"That sounds like a typical concussion. The doctor wants you to take it easy and get plenty of rest, and I'm going to make sure you follow her orders."

She gave him a wan smile. "I'd argue with you, but I don't have the energy."

"I'm sure your other bumps and bruises are sore today, too. Why don't you take a long soak in the tub? Grace and I will stay out of your way in the playroom."

"A spa day—just what I need." She sucked in a quick breath as she pushed up from the table. "I'm sorry to be so useless. Be sure to deduct this wasted time from your next Phoenix, Ltd. bill."

He reached for her elbow as she stood. "My bill is the least of my worries. Let me help you back upstairs."

Fortunately, she was much closer to her normal self the next morning. He still refused to let her resume her regular duties, but he was relieved when she started to push back. By Sunday, she insisted she was fully recovered, and he allowed her to help fix pasta for dinner. Monday morning, she was up early and beat him to the kitchen. Her easy smile and bustling energy convinced him he could safely leave her alone with Grace and go to work.

The day passed slowly. Since he'd been out of the office for several days, he half-expected to find another message on his desk, but there was nothing. Nor did he receive a phone call from his faceless nemesis. The museum director had sent another email asking for an update on his progress on the boat, but as much as he wanted to be finished and rid of the whole thing, Alec couldn't bring himself to work on it. He fiddled around, dealing with small issues and wondered how Casey was feeling. Several times he thought about calling her but decided against it.

By Wednesday, when he still hadn't heard from the SOB who was threatening them, he almost convinced himself he never would — that the whole ugly situation had simply disappeared. He spent much of the day in an email exchange with a colleague at the Metropolitan Museum in New York. He was so close to wrapping up his work on the boat, he could almost taste it. Only a few details remained to be confirmed. The director might not be happy with his conclusion, but at least the boat would no longer be Alec's problem.

The last rays of the setting sun streaked the darkening sky when he stepped out of the building. Here and there, windows glowed in the houses and apartments tucked between the academic and commercial buildings where the campus blended into the surrounding city. Streetlights and headlights illuminated the gathering gloom. The sidewalks teemed with students and staff heading home at the end of the work day, and slow-moving traffic choked the streets.

Alec cut across a small park adjacent to a school playground to get a break from the din. Despite a damp sting in the air and the scent of exhaust fumes, he enjoyed walking home, especially after a day spent cooped up in his office. Tonight, his body craved movement. Maybe he could talk Casey and Grace into a quick trip to the gym before dinner. His niece enjoyed the play area and often ran into a friend or two, and Casey seemed to have recovered enough to exercise safely if they kept it light.

She might already have started dinner. The image of her in front of the sink peeling carrots while Grace stood on an upturned milk crate beside her gave his heart a funny little squeeze. Casey was gentle, practical, highly competent, and distractingly pretty, but in truth he knew very little about her. It was time to change that.

He picked up his pace, darting across the intersection at the end of his block in front of a cab that had stopped to drop off a fare. As he neared the cozy blue Victorian, he slowed to sidestep the eight-year-old boy from next door who was trudging down the sidewalk, pulling his younger brother on a plastic saucer.

"Hello, boys," Alec said as he passed.

"Hi, Professor," the eldest replied, his words slow and drawn out with melodramatic fatigue.

Alec suppressed a laugh. "It's only a few more steps, James."

Heavy sigh. "I know."

Alec had the oddest urge to whistle as he opened his gate and climbed the front steps to the porch. Light glowed through the living room windows as he unlocked the front door and stepped inside, but something was off. Only the ticking of the antique mantel clock broke the silence. He unzipped his coat and stuffed his gloves in the pockets. Maybe Grace was upstairs playing with Balthazar. He headed toward the kitchen in the back of the house, sniffing the air for signs of cooking. Nothing. The kitchen was empty. Maybe they were both upstairs.

"I'm home," he called on his way up the stairs.

The only response was an angry shriek from Balthazar's room. Alec's gut knotted. Casey hadn't mentioned plans to be out this afternoon. He searched the second floor before going up to the playroom. Toys lay scattered across the floor. The knot tightened.

As a last resort, he checked the basement, but it was dark and silent.

Except for Balthazar, the house was empty.

He hadn't noticed anything unusual when he'd come in—no splintered wood or broken glass. The front door had been locked, and the alarm system was set to *At Home*, the way Casey kept it when she and Grace were home alone. But the spot on the counter where she usually kept her purse was empty.

Maybe they had walked to the store for some last-minute ingredient for dinner, although the kitchen showed no signs of meal prep. The thought turned Alec's worry to annoyance. It was nearly six o'clock and fully dark. This was Chicago, not Mayberry. If Casey needed something, she should have called him to pick it up or waited until he came home and could drive her. He pulled out his phone and hit her number, ready to lay into her the minute she answered.

"Hello?" Her voice seemed to hold a hint of amusement.

"Where are you?" he demanded, scowling out the window over the kitchen sink to the empty darkness beyond.

"Right behind you." Her voice came from over his shoulder, not through the phone.

He spun around to find Casey and Grace standing in the doorway with their coats on. Casey's lips twitched in a suppressed smile, but Grace laughed out loud.

"We fooled you, Uncle Alec!"

He forced himself to smile. "You sure did. Where have you been?"

Grace unzipped her purple parka. "We went to visit Sophia."

Casey took the little girl's coat. "Carolyn and I discussed some joint afternoon activities to keep the girls occupied until the doctor says Grace can go back to school."

Some of the tension in Alec's chest eased. Once again, Carolyn Chiang had his back. But he still wanted to discuss the matter of the improperly set alarm with Casey.

"That sounds great." He reached out and tousled Grace's fly-away hair. "Before you two get settled, I had an idea. Are you hungry?"

"Not really. Sophia and I ate lots of fruit snacks while we colored."

"How would you like to go to the gym and play for a while? Then we can stop at Sally's Diner on the way home."

Grace hugged his leg then started jumping up and down. "Yay!"

"I'll take that as a yes." He turned his attention to Casey. "Are you up for a trip to the gym?"

She glanced at Grace's expectant face and smiled. "Sure. I'd be happy to play with Grace while you work out."

Alec hesitated. "You're welcome to join me—we'll keep things low-key. Grace will be fine in the children's playroom. There's plenty of staff, and they're very safety-conscious."

Grace grabbed his hand and tugged. "I hope Latisha's there. She's my favorite. She dangles me by my feet!"

Uncertainty clouded Casey's brandy-colored eyes. "Are you sure? I really should stay with her."

"Latisha is the center on the university's women's basketball team. If she's working tonight, Grace will be in good hands."

Casey hesitated then shrugged. "Okay. You're the boss."

Ten minutes later, Alec parked in the garage next to the glistening new Rittenhouse Gymnasium and ushered Casey and Grace inside.

Latisha was indeed working in the children's playroom, and enveloped Grace in a giant hug when she raced in. "Hi, sport! Haven't seen you in a while."

"I'm glad to see you, too." She pointed to Casey. "This is Casey. She's my new nanny. I promised you'd show her and Uncle Alec how you make me walk on my hands."

The young woman grasped the child by the waist and easily flipped her upside down, holding her so her hands touched the ground. Grace's pale hair hung straight down, and her face reddened as she giggled. After a couple of seconds, Latisha flipped her right-side-up as deftly as catching a cross-court pass and set her on her feet. Grace giggled again.

"That does look like fun." Casey smiled, but the tiny lines between her brows suggested she still had misgivings about leaving Grace.

"She's going to be fine," Alec said.

Latisha placed a long-fingered hand atop Grace's small blond head. "Don't worry. Sport, here, and I are buddies. I'll keep a close eye on her."

Casey released a long, slow breath and smiled. "Thank you. Have fun, Grace."

"I will." Grace grabbed Latisha's hand. "Let's go jump rope!"

Alec directed Casey down the hall to the locker rooms. "I'll meet you at the desk and sign you in."

****

Casey grimaced at her reflection in the long mirror in the locker room. She'd pulled her hair into a short, bouncy ponytail before securing it with an elastic band. Her pale blue T-shirt had originally read *Nantucket* when she'd bought it years ago on vacation with her parents. Most of the lettering had since worn off, and it was a little too snug across her chest. Her black, capri-length yoga pants had lost some of their clinging power and were faded from too many washings.

When she'd packed for this assignment, she hadn't thought to include cute exercise clothes—not that her graduate student budget had allowed for extras like that. She frowned and gave her shirt a dissatisfied tug. Why had she agreed to come to the gym with Alec? Unfortunately, short of telling him she was feeling worse—which would have been a lie—there was no way to wiggle out of it at this point. Looking herself in the eye, she tightened her ponytail with a jerk and headed out to meet him.

As she'd expected, he was waiting in the hall. Something about his smile when he saw her lit a little fire deep in her abdomen, but she quickly tamped it down. Regardless of her feelings for him, he was her client, and this was not a date. But she couldn't help noticing the swell of muscle under his gray T-shirt and the latent strength in his rangy limbs. He clearly did more at the excavation site than stand around supervising the students and workmen.

His gaze flashed over her from head to foot and back. "Ready?"

"As I'll ever be."

He led the way to a row of ellipticals with two unoccupied machines on one end. "How about we try these at a nice, slow pace?"

"That sounds great." Her head felt fine, but the doctor probably wouldn't approve of a hard-core workout yet. Besides, she wasn't sure she could keep up with Alec even without a concussion. Between working part-time and trying to finish her dissertation, she hadn't found time to exercise in months. Not that she'd ever been any kind of gym rat.

Once they settled into a comfortable pace, Alec glanced over. "When I got home tonight, I noticed the alarm wasn't properly set." His voice rose over the din of the machines.

*The alarm?* Then she remembered. "It was Balthazar."

He shot her a skeptical look. "I'm surprised you let him out of the doghouse."

"Grace begged. And he did look contrite."

His brows shot up. "Contrite? Hah! I'm sure he's never experienced a moment of contrition in his life. Besides, that still doesn't explain the alarm. Balthazar's tricky, but he's never de-activated the alarm system before."

"No, it wasn't that. I had my purse on the counter because Grace and I were about to leave for the Chiangs'." She gritted her teeth at the memory. "That bleeping monkey jumped up and snatched my keys before I could react, then raced around the house shaking them and cackling at me."

"Tell me you didn't chase him."

"No." She shook her head, sending her ponytail swinging. "I'm not looking for trouble, but by the time Grace caught him and got the keys back, we were late, and I was so flustered, I guess I hit the wrong button and set the alarm to *At Home* instead of *Away*. It won't happen again."

For the next few minutes, they powered through the up-down, back-and-forth motion of the ellipticals in silence. Then Alec reached over and tapped her arm. "Lighten up. Are you still worried about leaving Grace in the children's playroom?"

Casey hadn't realized she'd been frowning. She relaxed her face into what she hoped was a calm, confident expression. Trying to match his pace on the machine was pointless and required a lot more concentration and effort than she was willing to admit. "No, you're right. I'm sure she's perfectly safe. Someone would have to be watching the house and then follow us here. I can't believe we're under twenty-four-hour surveillance."

By the end of the sentence, short, breathy pauses separated her words. *Rats.* All those weeks glued to a chair in the library had taken their toll.

He shot her a concerned glance and slowed his pace. "I don't think so, either. Our adversary doesn't appear to be that dedicated or well-organized."

She nodded and adjusted her pace to match.

He wiped his face with the towel he'd draped over the machine. "I forgot to tell you, I talked to Maria the other day."

"Oh? What did she say?"

"She's hasn't been feeling well, and she's been under a lot of financial pressure lately—the usual grad student stuff."

Casey understood financial pressure all too well. She pictured the pile of bills on the desk in her apartment and felt a bond of kinship with the embattled TA. It wasn't difficult to understand why the young woman might resent someone usurping even a small portion of her meager income.

"She said things are looking up," Alec continued, "and asked me to apologize for her behavior the night we went to the movie."

"That was strange, but I'm glad she's doing better."

He reached down and turned off his machine. "That's probably enough for today. We can try a more strenuous routine when you're fully recovered."

*Please, no!* "Sure."

She probably shouldn't have done as much as she did. Her limbs were as saggy and limp as warm Jell-O when she climbed off the elliptical. A few minutes later, standing in front of the locker room mirror, she could barely lift her arm high enough to drag a brush through her hair. Trying to keep up with Alec had been just plain stupid, and tomorrow she would pay.

She met him outside the locker rooms, and together they walked to the children's playroom. Alec didn't appear winded or tired. In fact, he looked even better than usual. His smile was relaxed, his deep blue eyes twinkled, and his hair curled in perfect golden waves, with only the tips still damp. It was so unfair.

The minute they stepped through the door, Grace dropped her red rubber playground ball and raced to greet them. "You'll never guess who came to see me!"

Alec frowned. "Someone came to see you here?"

"Uh, huh." She gave a vigorous nod. "It was Theo, Casey's old boyfriend from the zoo."

Casey's heartbeat stuttered. *What would Theo be doing here?*

"He stuck his head in the door and smiled at me, but Latisha made him go away."

Alec squatted and slid one arm around her narrow back. "Grace, it must have been someone who looked like Theo. He works at the zoo, and this gym is only for students and staff of the university. Theo wouldn't have been able to get in."

Her pale brows knit in the ominous scowl of a determined five-year-old. "I know who I saw. It was Theo."

Casey decided to intervene before the rumbling volcano blew. "I think it's time for dinner. What do you want to eat at Sally's tonight?"

Grace's frown dissolved. "A hamburger, with ketchup and mustard and lots of pickles. And ice cream for dessert!"

Alec pushed to his feet and shot Casey a grateful look. Then he smiled at Grace. "I think that can be arranged. Go get your coat."

Sally's Diner was a neighborhood institution, popular with both students and faculty families. The black-and-white checkerboard floor tiles, chrome-banded counter stools, and big, colorful jukebox against one wall gave it a fun, retro atmosphere.

As usual, the place was packed, but the hostess smiled broadly when they approached her podium and grabbed three menus. "Professor Bainbridge, Grace, it's so nice to see you. It's been a while."

"This is Casey," Grace said.

Casey smiled and nodded a greeting.

The hostess shot a quick, assessing glance around the room. "I've got a nice table in front of the windows. Follow me."

They trooped after her and waited while she fetched a booster seat. Alec grabbed Grace under the arms, hoisted her into the air, and swung her around before plopping her into her seat, eliciting a giggle. He and Casey studied their menus while Grace drew pictures with her finger in a small puddle of water on the Formica tabletop.

Alec leaned across the table toward Casey. "What looks good to you?"

She'd been to Sally's a number of times during her years at the university and usually tried to avoid the heavier, home-style meals. But tonight, after all the energy she'd expended at the gym, she felt no obligation to count calories. "I'm trying to decide between the meatloaf and the lasagna."

"That sounds—"

"Look, Uncle Alec," Grace interrupted, "there's Maria."

A few tables away, Maria sat deep in conversation with two other young women. Casey was a little surprised to see her since Alec had said her finances were tight. Sally's prices weren't cheap.

"Can I go say hi to her?" Grace was already wriggling out of her booster seat.

Alec pulled her chair back so she could hop down. "Okay, but just for a second. She's with her friends and is probably busy."

"Oh, she'll be happy to see me." Grace marched off toward Maria's table with an air of supreme confidence.

"It's good to be five," Casey observed with a smile.

"It's good to be Grace." A cloud descended across his features.

"What's the matter?"

"She deserves to be happy and safe. Every time I let myself forget some nutjob is threatening her, reality comes roaring back."

Casey reached across the table for his hand and gave it a squeeze. "I know. But everything's going to be all right."

His frown partially eased as he regarded her. "Grace seems fixated on the idea of this Theo being your boyfriend."

She managed a half-hearted smile. "She has the makings of a hopeless romantic."

Her comment didn't seem to appease him. "When you first came to us, you said you didn't have a boyfriend. I want to know why not. A woman like you should be able to have any man she wants."

*A woman like me?*

She lifted a shoulder in an attempt at a careless shrug. "You know how it is."

"No, I don't. I haven't had time for a relationship with a woman since Grace came to live with me, but you..."

His persistence was getting on her nerves. "You're not going to gracefully let this drop, are you?"

"No. I want to get to know you better."

She blew out a frustrated breath. "All right. Up until a couple of months ago, I was engaged."

"What happened?"

"We discovered we didn't suit each other."

"That sounds civilized and amicable."

She thought about the final confrontation, when Peter announced he was leaving. Alec was right. It had been civilized, lacking in drama—just like him, like their whole relationship. "Exactly."

"Do you miss him?"

"Not at all." And she didn't.

"That's good, I guess."

"It is. Now, smile. Here comes Grace. You don't want her to see you frowning."

Grace came back, munching a breadstick. "Maria gave this to me. She said I looked hungry."

Alec whisked her up and plopped her onto her booster seat as the waitress approached the table. "I hope you're still hungry for that hamburger."

"Of course, I am. I'm *starving*."

He laughed and placed his and Grace's orders, then deferred to Casey.

"I'll have the meatloaf." She handed her menu back to the waitress.

They had nearly finished their meal when Alec's phone buzzed, indicating he'd received a text message.

He glanced at it then frowned and picked it up. "It's from the alarm company." He kept his voice low, glancing at Grace, who was scooping the last soupy bit of ice cream from her bowl with her spoon. "A window has been broken at the house, and they've notified the police." He turned to his niece. "Eat that quickly. We have to go home."

Casey was already on her feet, pulling on her coat. She hurried around the table and helped Grace into her parka while Alec grabbed some bills from his wallet and stuffed them under the edge of his plate. He picked Grace up and strode out of the diner toward the car with Casey at his heels.

Less than ten minutes later, they pulled up in front of the house behind a police cruiser. Two officers, a man and a woman, were walking toward the front door. Alec turned off the car and half-turned to Casey.

"Watch Grace." He hopped out and ran up the concrete path to meet them.

"Why are there police at our house? What's going on?" Grace's voice wavered.

Casey undid her seat belt and swiveled to face the little girl in the back seat. "I'm not sure, but we'll wait here while your Uncle Alec talks to the officers."

Alec unlocked the front door and stepped aside to let the cops enter first. Lights came on, illuminating their figures as they moved through the house, room by room.

"I'm getting cold," a small voice complained.

"Me, too. I hope the police won't take much longer, but we can't go inside until they finish."

A couple of minutes later, all three trooped out of the house. The officers returned to their squad cars, and Alec climbed into the Volvo.

"Uncle Alec, I'm cold."

"We'll be inside in two minutes. Then you can have a hot bath and get right into bed." He started the car, drove around the end of the block to the alley behind the house, and pulled into the garage.

Casey resisted the urge to ask what the cops had found. She hoped it was just a malfunction in one of the new window sensors.

The little girl wrapped her arms tightly around his neck and buried her head against his shoulder as he carried her from the garage to the house. As soon as he unlocked the back door, she lifted her head and glanced around the kitchen. "Is it safe?"

"Would I bring you inside if it wasn't?"

"Why were the police here?"

"Because someone naughty threw a snowball and broke one of the windows in the dining room."

Grace wriggled against his grasp. "I want to see it." When he set her on the floor, she headed straight for the dining room. "I bet it was James from next door. He's *always* naughty."

Casey grabbed her hand and pulled her up short before she entered the room. "Hold on. You don't want to step on any of that." Shards of broken glass lay scattered across the wood floor in front of the window, and a large dark spot on the rug could have been from melted snow.

Alec squatted beside his niece and gave her hug. "You should run up and check on Balthazar. He's probably scared from the noise of the breaking glass and having policemen in the house."

Grace's brows shot up and her mouth rounded into an *O*. "I bet you're right!" She turned and ran from the room.

Casey had noticed something odd about the broken window and walked over for a closer look. "Look at this."

Alec joined her, peering over her shoulder.

She pointed to the lock. "It's unlocked."

He eased back. "The officers noticed that, too, and assumed it was jarred loose when the snowball hit the window."

She checked the hardware on the other windows in the room. It was old but so tight she could barely turn the latch. She doubted the impact from a snowball could have shaken it apart, no matter how hard it was thrown. "I'll call someone to replace the lock, as well as the glass, tomorrow morning. Do you have any plywood in the basement or garage we could use to cover the window tonight?"

Alec hesitated, as if taking a mental inventory. "I might. I'll check. I'm just relieved the incident turned out to be so minor."

She forced her lips into a smile. "Yes. We were lucky."

*Maybe.*

# CHAPTER TWELVE

*Waah! Waah! Waah! Waah!*

Casey bolted awake to a blaring din coming from the hallway. *What the...?* Her head pounded in rhythm with the deafening cacophony. Instinctively, she covered her ears. *Why won't someone stop that thing?* A couple of seconds later, she recognized the clamor of the fire alarm.

*Grace! Alec!*

She threw off the covers and ran into the hallway, her heart thundering, just as Alec emerged from Grace's room, clutching her small body against his T-shirt-clad chest. She couldn't see any flames, but oily, acrid-smelling smoke filled the open stairwell and corridor. Her throat tightened, and she coughed.

"Get some shoes on and grab our coats!" he shouted. "We'll meet you in the front yard."

The strobe light on the ceiling alarm flashed frantically, slicing through the darkness and half-blinding her as she fumbled in her darkened room before finding her workout shoes. She rammed her feet into them then hesitated, her brain bouncing between confusion and panic.

*What was I supposed to do next?*

*Alec and Grace are outside without coats. Go!*

Spurred into action, she sprinted back into the hall and down the stairs. She flung open the hall closet door, gathered an armful of coats, then burst out the front door and down the steps toward Alec and Grace, who huddled near the street.

Her breath sent short puffs of vapor into the frosty air like smoke signals. "Here." She thrust the wad of coats at Alec.

He pulled out Grace's purple parka and zipped her into it, snugging the hood around her head, before finding his own black wool jacket. Casey grabbed her down coat and zipped it up, grateful for the immediate warmth. In the distance, the oscillating sound of sirens caught her attention.

"Uncle Alec!" Grace glanced around frantically. "Balthazar! You have to get Balthazar!"

Alec knelt beside her and took both her hands. "Grace, we have to wait for the firefighters to check things out. We don't know if it's safe to go back in the house yet."

Tears rolled down her rounded cheeks. "You have to get him. He might die!"

Casey's heart contracted at the sight of Grace's genuine anguish. Balthazar might be a giant pain, but she couldn't just stand outside and let him succumb to smoke inhalation. She tapped Alec's shoulder. "I'll get him."

He pushed to his feet. "You'll do no such thing. If anyone's going back in there, it'll be me." He stared at the house. There were still no signs of flames, but smoke obscured the windows. He thrust Grace's hand into Casey's. "Take care of Grace. I'll be back in a second with the damned monkey."

He took off up the front walk, ran up the steps, then hesitated for a second before flinging the door open and disappearing inside. Casey felt a tug on her left hand and shifted her gaze to Grace.

The child sniffed loudly. "Is Uncle Alec going to be okay?" Her eyes swam with tears, and her voice wavered.

Casey squatted beside Grace and wrapped her in a big hug. "Oh, yes. Don't you worry. You know how big and strong your Uncle Alec is. Well, he's fast, too. He'll be back with Balthazar before you know it." She prayed it was true.

Her words were prophetic, because a split-second later the front door banged open, and Alec dashed out of the house with the monkey clinging to his coat with one front paw. The other had a death grip on Alec's right ear.

"Balthazar!" Grace opened her arms. The monkey immediately abandoned Alec and leapt to her, grinning while she nuzzled his furry cheek.

"I'm counting the minutes until Tom gets back from Costa Rica," Alec grumbled as he searched his pockets for gloves.

Casey couldn't help but smile at the picture he made, with his tousled blond curls and blue-and-white-striped pajama bottoms sticking out from under his coat. Both he and Grace wore snow boots he'd grabbed on his way out the door.

Two fire trucks, one a hook-and-ladder, rounded the corner at the end of the block and pulled up in front of the house. Their sirens faded, but the blue and white lights continued to flash.

Firefighters in full turn-out gear poured out of the trucks, and one who seemed to be in charge approached Alec. "Is everyone out of the house?"

"Yes."

"Do you know where the fire started?"

"No idea. I never actually saw any fire, just a lot of smoke."

The fireman nodded. "We'll check it out." He motioned to two others, who followed him up the walk and into the house.

Casey wasn't surprised when lights flipped on next door and across the street. The sirens and lights of the fire trucks would certainly have awakened the neighbors. And since the firefighters left the engines running, their steady, rhythmic rumble continued to disturb the peace of the normally quiet block.

She wiggled her toes inside her shoes and stomped her feet on the frozen sidewalk, wishing she'd thought to grab a pair of socks. By the time they were allowed back inside—or forced to find other shelter for the night—her feet would probably be numb.

Alec wrapped an arm around her shoulders and hugged her close against his chest as he bent his head near her ear. "It's going to be okay." Grace and Balthazar snuggled against his legs.

Casey nodded. "Yes." From the shelter of his embrace, she stared at the house as dark figures moved past the windows, illuminated by the swinging beams of flashlights. Even though her purse and most of her clothes were at risk inside, she felt oddly comforted, as if everything would be okay simply because Alec was beside her.

"Alec?"

He dropped his arm from Casey's shoulders and turned toward the voice.

A man she'd never seen before stood behind them wearing an overcoat over his pajamas and holding out a thermos.

"Holly made you some cocoa." He passed the thermos to Alec. "And I grabbed a few cups."

Alec accepted the stacked paper cups. "Thanks, Chris. And thank Holly for me." He tipped his head toward Casey. "This is Chris Bullock, our next-door neighbor. Chris, meet Casey, our new nanny." They exchanged a quick handshake before he continued. "You'd better get back inside. Holly will kill me if you freeze out here."

"She's worried about you, and especially Grace, being out in the cold. Do you want to come inside for a while?"

Grace nodded vigorously, which caused Balthazar to latch onto her hair with both front paws and shriek.

Alec grimaced. "We can't, not unless Holly wants a crazy monkey loose in her house. Besides, I need to wait here until I get some news from the firefighters."

"Any idea what happened?"

"None. I woke up to the alarm blaring and the house full of smoke."

Chris turned toward his own house, where a woman—presumably Holly—gestured at them through a front window. "I guess I'd better go. Just knock on the door if you need anything."

Alec clapped him on the back. "Thanks, buddy."

As Chris headed down the sidewalk toward his house, Casey noticed several figures milling around the edges of the light cast by the fire trucks. Other neighbors must have come to check out the commotion. She had poured cocoa into three paper cups and handed one to Alec when the front door of his blue Victorian banged shut.

The firefighters who had initially gone inside to assess the situation were making their way single file down the porch steps. Since they weren't running or shouting to the rest of their crew, maybe the situation wasn't as bad as it had first appeared. Casey crossed her fingers. She doubted there was a single hotel in the city of Chicago that would accept a monkey, even a well-behaved one, which Balthazar certainly wasn't.

The lead firefighter approached Alec as Casey handed a steaming cup of cocoa to Grace.

"How bad is it?" Alec shifted his weight from foot to foot.

"We checked the place from attic to cellar and didn't find any active fire. Since the heat sensors didn't turn up any hot spots, we opened the windows. If you set up a couple of fans, you should be able to clear the smoke in a few hours. It might be a little cold to go back in tonight, but—"

Suddenly, the siren on one of the trucks wailed. Someone in the cab must have bumped it by accident, because it ceased as abruptly as it had started, but the noise sent Balthazar into a frenzy. He screamed and jumped on top of Grace's head, causing her to spill cocoa down the front of her parka.

"Balthazar, you bad monkey!" She brushed at the front of her coat furiously.

Her movements further distressed the agitated monkey, who leapt to the ground, screeching like an outraged banshee. Alec made a move to grab him, but

Balthazar scampered out of reach and continued his cacophony.

"Balthazar, come here," Alec ordered.

The simian looked him directly in the eye then turned and ran straight into the crowd of onlookers gathered in the street. Occasional startled grunts and exclamations marked his progress as he darted between legs or up and over anyone in his path.

"Balthazar!" Grace dropped her empty cup on the sidewalk and raced after him.

It took Casey's stunned brain a couple of seconds to react, but the moment her legs received the signal, she took off after Grace at a dead run, scaling the hard-packed ridges of snow left at the curb by the plows. "Grace...stop!"

But the little girl didn't stop. She disappeared into the crowd in the street almost as easily as her quarry.

"Grace!"

Casey heard Alec's heavy boots hit the snow-packed pavement in a rapid, pounding beat a half-step behind her, and the harsh pants of his breath sounded in her ears. When they reached the huddled group of onlookers, the sea of startled neighbors parted to allow them through. She halted so suddenly he almost plowed into her back as she scanned the sidewalk and shadowy yards for signs of Grace or Balthazar.

"Grace!" Alec's voice held the seeds of panic.

Casey grabbed his hand and squeezed. "We'll find her." If only she felt as confident as she sounded.

Turning back toward the crowd, which was starting to break up, her gaze darted from figure to figure. *Where is she? She couldn't have gone far.*

"There!" Alec pointed toward two figures walking away from them, hand in hand, down the sidewalk, half-way to the corner.

He took off running with Casey in close pursuit. As they approached, the outline of a small child in a parka with the hood up became clearer, and she seemed to be holding something bulky against one shoulder. The other figure appeared to be an adult.

"Grace...stop!"

At Alec's shout, both figures halted in the pool of yellow light cast by the street light and turned. A fall of long black hair identified the taller one as Maria. She still clung to Grace's hand. The bundle in the child's other arm squirmed and squawked. Balthazar.

Seconds later, Alec and Casey reached them. Maria released Grace as Alec swept her into his arms, along with the monkey. As he hugged his niece tightly, Balthazar wriggled free and climbed onto his shoulders.

Casey leaned forward, resting her hands on her thighs as her breathing slowed. Adrenaline surged through her veins, accompanied by sweet relief. Whatever else happened tonight, at least Grace was safe. When she straightened, Balthazar met her gaze and bared his teeth in his trademark cheesy grin. She couldn't help herself—she grinned back. Despite his many faults, she was glad to see him unhurt.

Ignoring the monkey squatting an inch from his face, Alec kept a tight hold on Grace, as though he was afraid she might disappear again if they lost physical contact. "You scared me tonight, kiddo." He pressed a kiss to her cheek. "You know better than to run off like that."

"But Balthazar got scared and ran away. He might have gotten hurt, and you told me it's my job to keep him safe." Grace twisted in his arms to face her former babysitter. "Maria helped me catch him."

"I'm glad she helped, but it still wasn't smart for you to chase him in the dark."

Grace cocked her head, clearly unconvinced. "Uncle Alec, nothing bad would happen to me on our street. We live here."

He didn't respond. Instead, he turned his attention to his TA.

Maria was slowly edging backward. "I'd better get home now. See you later, Grace. I'm glad your monkey is safe."

"He's not—"

"Hold on, Maria." A frown creased Alec's brow. "How did you end up out here in the middle of the night?"

"I live around the corner in the next block." She waved an arm in the general direction of the intersection. "I was up late working and heard the sirens. I thought I'd better check it out."

"I didn't know you lived so close." Alec hesitated, and his eyes narrowed. "Where were you taking Grace? Why didn't you bring her home?"

The streetlight overhead cast strong shadows across Maria's face, partially concealing her expression. "I didn't see you, so I thought I should take her back to my apartment to get out of the cold. I was going to call you as soon as we got inside." She crossed her arms and glanced away. "It's getting pretty late. I should go now."

Alec tightened his hold on his niece, and his frown deepened. "I can't imagine why you thought it would be appropriate to take her to your apartment. We'll discuss this tomorrow."

With a nod, she bent her head, turned, and hurried off down the sidewalk.

As Maria rounded the corner and disappear into the darkness, Casey wondered if she was being overly suspicious. The sudden appearance of Alec's TA seemed a more than a remarkable coincidence. There were several low-rise apartment blocks on the next street, and judging from her own experience, students often stayed up all night working, but her decision to take Grace back to her apartment showed extremely poor judgement, at best.

When Alec hitched Grace higher to adjust his hold, Balthazar returned to his former position in the little girl's arms and tucked his head under her chin. Alec turned back toward the house and craned his head to see over the few remaining bystanders. "It looks like the trucks are getting ready to leave. We'd better get back. I want to hear what the firefighters found."

As they neared the house, a police cruiser pulled into a spot at the curb behind the last fire truck. Casey wondered who had called the police, and why. Had the firemen found something unexpected?

Alec approached the firefighter who'd spoken to him earlier. "I'm sorry I took off like that, but..." He tipped his head toward Grace and Balthazar.

The man had removed his helmet and replaced it with a black knit beanie. "I understand, sir." His warm breath sent billows of steam into the frosty air. "The scene around any fire can get pretty chaotic."

Grace began to squirm, so Alec set her on the ground, keeping one hand firmly planted on her shoulder. "You said you didn't find any fire."

"That's right. There were no signs of combustion."

"But the smoke…?"

Glancing over Alec's shoulder, he gave a short nod. Casey and Alec turned in tandem to see two uniformed police officers approaching. Although she hadn't spoken with them, they looked like the same pair who had taken the report about the broken window several hours earlier. The male was of medium height and solidly built. His female partner had a couple of inches on him and a tall, lean frame.

The fireman acknowledged them with a nod. "Good to see you, Hank, Liz. I'm glad you're here, so I only have to go through this once." He swung his gaze to include Alec and Casey. "Let's go inside. It might be a little warmer, and you can sit down. I think we've got most of the smoke cleared from the living room."

Alec led the way up the steps, with Casey and Grace trooping behind, followed by the fireman. The police officers brought up the rear.

The firefighter has been right—with both big windows open, the room was nearly as cold as outside, but at least the smoke had dissipated. Casey settled on the sofa with Grace and Balthazar and wrapped the big knitted afghan around the three of them, creating a toasty human and monkey burrito. Alec sat in his leather armchair.

The fireman said something to the officers that Casey couldn't hear, then turned to Casey and Alec. "You folks make yourselves as comfortable as you can. I need to show Hank and Liz a couple things, then we'll be back with you." The three headed down the hall toward the back of the house before their boot steps sounded on the basement stairs.

About five minutes later, they returned and filed into the living room. After glancing around to make sure he had everyone's attention, the firefighter held up what appeared to be a charred wad of aluminum foil. "Here's your culprit."

Alec peered at the odd item with brows pinched in a puzzled frown. "What is it?"

"A home-made smoke bomb. Potassium nitrate, sugar, and baking soda. Simple, but effective. Anybody who took chemistry in high school or has access to the Internet could make one. This one was a little more sophisticated—we found the remains of a rudimentary timer. It was on the floor, behind a couple of boxes, in a corner of the basement laundry room."

"Do you have any idea how long it was there?" Alec asked. "The doors were locked when we got home this evening."

"We can't be sure, but the type of timer we found has a maximum of twelve hours."

The female cop stepped forward. "My partner and I have a theory, Professor. We believe the bomb is likely related to the broken window we found earlier this evening."

Alec frowned. "But how? The window is in the dining room, not the basement, and no one bigger than that monkey—" He shot a quick glance at Balthazar, tucked into the blanket on Casey's lap. "—could have crawled through the opening. Even he would have been cut by the shards of broken glass, and there were no signs of blood anywhere."

The male officer answered. "Not if the perp reached through the broken glass to unlock the window."

Alec took a couple of steps back until he could see through the opening into the dining room. "That's true. We assumed the impact of the snowball—if that's what it was—had loosened the lock, but it could have been purposefully unlocked."

Officer Hank nodded. "We believe the window was broken in order to trigger the alarm system and disguise the fact that someone entered the house with the intent of placing the smoke bomb in the basement. They then exited through the same window without leaving any traces. When we arrived on the scene, we found the broken window, no signs of entry, and evidence of a probable snowball on the carpet."

"And they hid the smoke bomb where you would have been unlikely to find it when you searched the house."

The officer nodded again.

Alec tapped his forefinger against his upper lip. "That's plausible, but I have no idea why anyone would have done it. If it was to cover up a theft, I can't think of a purpose for the smoke bomb. Besides, nothing was missing when we searched the house." He paused. "Unless the purpose was simply to get us out of the house."

Officer Liz glanced up from the small notebook where she'd been scribbling. "You were away earlier this evening, Professor. Can you think of any reason someone would have wanted you out of the house again tonight?"

"Honestly, no. No one could have re-entered without being seen. The Fire Department responded immediately, and Ms. Callahan and I were right outside the whole time."

Officer Liz flipped her notebook shut. "I think we've done all we can here tonight." She reached inside her heavily-padded, dark blue nylon jacket and pulled out a business card. "We'll turn our information over to one of the detectives, but please call me if you think of anything else that might be useful."

Alec took the card. "I will, and thanks for helping us tonight...twice."

Her lips parted in a brief smile. "It's all part of the job, sir. We'll be in touch."

Her partner touched the brim of his hat, and both officers followed the firefighter out the front door.

Alec closed and locked the door behind them then returned to the living room. He ran one hand through his hair. "What a night."

From her spot on the sofa, draped in a monkey and a five-year-old, Casey nodded. "You're not kidding." She scooted back a couple of inches into a more upright position, shifting Grace in her arms. "She's asleep, but I'm not sure I'll ever sleep again."

Alec paced in front of the fireplace. "I know what you mean. I'm so wired, I feel like I've been pounding down triple espressos all night, and I have no idea what to do now."

"Well, I don't know about you, but I'm not too anxious to spend the rest of the night wide awake alone in my room. Maybe we could have a sort of slumber party in here." She sniffed the air. "I don't smell smoke anymore. I think we can safely close the windows on the first floor. With the furnace running, the fans should be able to direct the warm air up and out the upstairs windows like a chimney. Your heating bill will be ugly, but—"

"It will be well worth it. At any rate, it won't be as expensive as a hotel. You stay there while I close the windows and grab a couple more blankets. When I get back, I'll light the fireplace to help warm the room."

After he left, she eased Grace's limp body into a slightly more comfortable position. Who would have thought a sleeping child could produce so much dead weight? Her forty pounds felt more like four hundred.

Casey rested her head back against the pillow on the sofa and closed her eyes. Alec was right—it had been a hell of a night. Her brain was too tired to make sense of the events of the evening. All she registered was gratitude that Grace and Alec were safe, and the three of them were together. For the next few hours, that was all she needed. Morning would come soon enough.

# CHAPTER THIRTEEN

After closing the first-floor windows and checking the smoke situation on the second floor, Alec returned to the living room with an armful of blankets. "Casey." He kept his voice low so as not to disturb Grace.

When he got no response, he crossed in front the coffee table to get a better look and banged his knee in the process. "Damn it!" The word slipped out on a hiss. Casey lay back against the pillows in the corner, eyes closed and soft lips slightly parted. Faint breath sounds matched the slow rise and fall of her chest. Grace nestled against her, sound asleep, with Balthazar curled up in a tight ball atop her, his head tucked beneath her chin.

The sight brought a lump to Alec's throat. He might have traveled the globe to exotic places, done things others only dreamed of, but at this moment his whole world lay wrapped in that afghan.

Except for Balthazar. Grace might love him, but as far as Alec was concerned, Tom Huerta couldn't return a minute too soon to reclaim the little vermin. Balthazar was far more trouble than he was worth.

He checked the clock on the mantel—four o'clock. No wonder he felt like a pile of three-day-old camel dung. He glanced at Casey again and sighed. Since it didn't look like he was going to get to spend the next few hours cuddled up with her in front of the fire, he ought to try to get a little sleep. He dropped the wad of blankets he'd pulled from the upstairs linen cabinet onto a chair, selected a lightweight down comforter and draped it over the slumbering trio on the sofa. After flicking on the gas fireplace for a little added heat, he settled into his leather armchair, propped his feet on the coffee table, pulled the remaining two blankets over himself, and closed his eyes.

But sleep refused to come. He kept thinking about the broken window, the alarm, and the smoke bomb. It had to be connected to the threats against Grace and the demand for the Fassbinder boat, but he couldn't figure out how.

The next thing he knew, something landed on his chest, followed by a familiar shriek. When his eyelids scraped open like sandpaper across an open wound, he found himself face to face with Balthazar's trademark grin.

"Get off me, you hairy demon," he growled.

He made a move to brush him off, but the monkey evaded him and scampered to the floor. He paused briefly to stick out his tongue before racing toward the kitchen, where a glowing light and soft voices beckoned. Alec pushed himself upright with his arms. When he tried to lift his legs from the coffee table, they tangled in the blankets. He kicked free, stood, and stretched. His back was stiff, his neck howled, and his mouth tasted like he'd been licking rocks. Half-stupefied, he blinked and scrubbed one hand across his bristly jaw.

*How in the world did I manage to fall asleep like that?*

Through the front windows, the first rays of dawn painted the snow with a rosy glow. Passing headlights indicated neighbors up and on their way to jobs and school. Alec glanced at the mantel clock—it read seven-twenty-three. He stretched, wincing when his abused muscles fought back. He stumbled in the direction of the kitchen, but Casey met him with a cup in her hand before he reached the door.

She must have been up for a while. The ends of her hair were damp, her face was scrubbed clean of make-up, and she'd changed into her fluffy blue robe. And at that moment, he wanted nothing more than to scoop her up, carry her upstairs to his bed, and spend the next several hours with her wrapped in his arms.

"Here." She handed him the steaming cup. "Drink this. It will help."

He took the coffee and slugged down as much as he could without burning himself. "Thanks."

"Come into the kitchen. There's bread in the toaster, and I'm scrambling some eggs."

He trailed after her in the direction of the kitchen. "How long have you been up?"

"Not too long. Balthazar got fidgety and woke Grace, who in turn, woke me. The smoke was gone, so I closed the windows upstairs and planted the two of them in the kitchen with a bowl of cereal and a banana while I took a quick shower."

In the kitchen, Grace sat slumped with both elbows on the table and her spoon dangling from her fingers. In defiance of house rules, Balthazar sat in the chair next to her, nibbling a banana. Alec decided to let it slide. They'd all been through an ordeal, and he didn't have the inclination or energy to be a hardass at the moment.

He patted the top of Grace's head. "From the looks of these two, I think they'll both be ready for a nap soon."

Casey brought him a plate of eggs and toast. "A nap doesn't sound half bad. I think we could all use some rest. Can you stay home today?"

Alec took the plate to his usual spot. "I really want to wrap up my work on the boat. The sooner I no longer have any connection to it, the sooner this lunacy stops."

Grace lifted her head. "What's loo—nuh—cee, Uncle Alec?"

"Craziness. I think things have been a little crazy lately. Don't you?"

His niece pinched her brows and pursed her lips before giving a firm nod. She glanced at Casey, who stood by the stove, loading another plate with eggs. "I want Casey to stay, but I don't want any more policemen or firemen here, and I want to go back to school."

"We all want the same thing." *And I'm going to do everything I can to make it happen.*

By the time he'd finished breakfast and taken a long, hot shower, he felt almost human—or at least human enough to make it to lunchtime. He checked in on Grace, who was playing jungle adventurer with her stuffed animals and Balthazar in her room, then headed downstairs.

Casey met him at the door wearing faded blue jeans and a fuzzy raspberry sweater with puffy slippers on her feet. Her honey-blond hair was pulled back in a ponytail, but a few feathery wisps had slipped free to frame her face. The smudges under her eyes told the same story as the pair of fine lines that bracketed her mouth. Without make-up, she looked achingly vulnerable.

After he pulled on his coat, she handed him his backpack. "Go. Do what you need to do. But try to come home as early as you can. You look terrible."

"Thanks." *You don't. You look like the answer to a prayer.*

She tucked a loose lock of hair behind one ear. "I can't get that smoke bomb out of my head. It doesn't make sense except as a means to get us—especially Grace—out of the house."

"I know. And what the hell was Maria thinking, taking her away like that?"

Casey shook her head. "I can't imagine. I guess it's possible she was telling the truth. You said she's been under a lot of stress lately."

"That's no excuse. If she doesn't pull herself together, she'll never graduate."

"Maybe you can talk to her again today, but in the meantime, don't worry about the broken window. I'll get it fixed this morning."

He hesitated, his gaze drifting from her warm cognac eyes to her soft pink lips. He tried to remind himself why he shouldn't kiss her but couldn't come up with of a single reason. As her lips parted slightly, what was left of his rational mind melted.

He took a step forward, and she met him half-way, sliding into his arms as naturally as a long-time lover. When he lowered his head, she stretched up to meet him. This time, there was nothing tentative about his kiss. He poured himself into her. When she responded with a slight moan, he deepened the kiss, stroking one hand down the curve of her back.

After one final kiss, he eased back. "Casey—" The word came out more as a croak.

She pressed a finger to his lips with a hint of a smile. "Shh. There's plenty of time. Just go and come back."

A glow kindled inside him, blotting out his worries as it grew. He shook his head. *How does she know just what to say?*

Kissing her again for good measure, he shouldered his backpack and headed out the door. The crisp morning air filled his lungs, and his energy level rose with every step. By the time he reached his office at the NEI, he couldn't wait to dive back into the Fassbender boat project. The end was in sight. He had finished his research and reached his conclusion about the origin of the artifact. Once he completed the final report, he would be free.

He was so pumped, he decided to bring the object to his office one last time. Having it in front of him as he wrote would serve as both inspiration and closure. After hanging up his coat, he headed down to the archives.

A couple of hours later, Maria poked her head in his office. "Good morning, Professor. I wasn't sure you'd be in so early."

He beckoned her in. "I could say the same to you."

She lifted one delicate shoulder. "I'm used to it. You remember what grad school was like."

"I do. And that's something I wanted to talk to you about." He took a sip from the tepid cup of coffee on his desk and grimaced. "I know you're under a lot of pressure, but your behavior last night really disturbed me."

Moisture pooled in her dark brown eyes. "I'm so sorry." When she blinked, one tear broke free and rolled down the side of her nose. She dashed it away with the back of hand.

Alec hated to see her pain, but this was too important to let slide. "What were you thinking?"

"I love Grace. I don't want anything bad to happen to her." She sniffled, and two more tears coursed down her cheeks.

Her remorse seemed genuine, and she appeared to be on the verge of a crying jag. "I'm sure that's true. And I want you to remember my offer to help with any school-related problems. Now, what did you want to see me about?"

She sniffed again as her gaze slid to the boat. "I stopped by to see if you needed help with anything."

"I don't think so." He glanced at the handwritten pages strewn around the top of his desk. "I'm taking one last look at the boat while I organize my notes for my report to the director. I should be ready to start the final draft this afternoon."

She tipped her head toward the papers. "I could transcribe those for you if that would make it easier."

"Thanks, but I'd better stick with my tried-and-true method. For some reason writing longhand has always helped me think."

"Well, if there's anything I can do..."

"I'll let you know."

She turned and headed toward the door, but before she reached it the museum director appeared. Christophe Moreau was tall and lanky with a loose-limbed gait, a prominent beak of a nose, and small brown eyes that flashed intelligence. Prior to joining the Near Eastern Institute, he had been an assistant curator at the Louvre in Paris.

Alec rose as soon as he saw him. "Good morning, Director. Please come in."

Director Moreau ambled into the room. When he spotted the boat, his customary dour expression brightened. "Ah, I see you're working on our boat! I don't mean to interrupt. I just came to ask if you have an estimate for the completion of your work. The trustees are becoming most anxious."

Alec had barely opened his mouth to reply when Fermin LeBlanc swept in, dressed in a black and white silk houndstooth jacket with a red scarf around his neck.

*The man must have some kind of freaking internal radar!*

Alec clamped his jaws together to keep from blurting out the words on the tip of his tongue. He returned his attention to the director. "You can let them know I've finished my evaluation and expect to begin writing my report this afternoon. It should be ready for presentation in a few days."

Moreau straightened and gave him a broad smile. "Excellent! Can you share your conclusion with me? I must admit, I have also been most anxious."

"Yes, please," Fermin interjected. "We are all very anxious." His right hand fluttered in the air.

Alec ignored him. "Based on the existing evidence, it seems Ernest Fassbender was up to his old tricks again. I can state beyond a reasonable doubt that this boat was indeed looted from a provincial museum during the Arab Spring uprising in 2011, as claimed by the Egyptian government."

The director released a long, drawn-out breath. "I feared it was too good to be true."

Fermin's sharp gaze darted between the two other men. "That's a shame, Bainbridge. It's a striking piece and would have made an excellent addition to the museum's collection."

The director gave a Gallic shrug. "Ah, well, perhaps we can use the repatriation as a gesture of goodwill. I will speak with the university's Office of Public Affairs about releasing a statement to the press."

Fermin turned to Moreau. "So, now I suppose you'll have to send it back."

"Yes, as quickly as we can. I'll begin the arrangements immediately."

Fermin placed a hand on the director's arm and accompanied him to the door. "Perhaps I can assist. I have a number of useful contacts..." Their voices trailed off as they disappeared down the hall.

After the two men left, Maria lingered. "Are you disappointed, Professor? You've worked so hard to authenticate that artifact."

It was a reasonable question, but considering the circumstances, he could hardly wait to get the thing out of the building and on its way back to Cairo. Only then would he be able to draw a free breath again.

"It's a question of point of view," he replied. "I worked hard to make sure the university and the museum didn't claim ownership of an object illegally. I've done that, so I actually feel pretty good about the whole thing."

She hesitated for a moment before the intensity of her gaze eased into a quick smile as she turned to leave. "As long as you're fine with it. Remember, I'll be around if you need me."

A few hours later, his stomach growled, reminding him he hadn't eaten. He wasn't ready to return the boat to the archives yet and refused to consider leaving it unattended in his office, even for the ten minutes it would take to run down to the café and bring something back. Since Maria had offered to help, he asked her to bring him a sandwich and typed while he ate. With so much information to include, it would take a few days to complete the report. But if no one else interrupted him, he figured he should be able to finish the introductory section that afternoon.

The work went smoothly, and by three-thirty he had a satisfactory draft. He had just started to edit when an ear-splitting clamor almost knocked him off his chair.

*The fire alarm.*

The sound catapulted him back to the night before. Two fire alarms in less than twenty-four hours? Really??

Heart pounding from the sudden jolt, Alec shot a quick, harried glance around his office. Maybe it was an unannounced drill. If not, it was probably a false alarm. But what if it wasn't? The museum had a sophisticated fire suppression system in the galleries, and the rest of the building was equipped with sprinklers, but the water would ruin nearly everything it touched—especially his books.

An indistinct rumble of voices and the clatter of footsteps filled the hall as faculty members, students, and staff poured out of offices and classrooms and headed toward the stairs. Alec sniffed the air. There was no hint of smoke, but since the alarm was still ringing, he should probably evacuate. He could take his notes with him, but his first responsibility was the boat.

He grabbed the loose papers on his desk, folded them in half, and stuffed them into the inside pocket of his jacket. Then he carefully fitted the wooden boat into its protective case and carried it into the hall, where he joined the stream of people headed for the stairs. When they peeled off toward the exit, he continued down the staircase to the basement. The boat would be safe in the fireproof vault.

Only a row of low-level emergency lights lit the corridor leading to the archives. The blaring alarm and blinding strobe lights on the ceiling gave Alec a weird, pulsating sense of disorientation. He had just reached the heavy metal door when a voice rang out behind him.

"Professor! Professor Bainbridge!"

He turned and was surprised to see a dark-clad male figure sprinting down the hall toward him. As the man drew closer, Alec recognized Officer Foster, the campus cop who had taken his reports on the anonymous letters.

"Wait a minute, Professor."

Alec frowned. If there really was a fire, he needed to secure the artifact as quickly as possible, not stand around chatting. "What is it?"

The officer's chest rose and fell from the exertion of his run. "I saw you come down here. The fire department asked us to help evacuate the building. You need to leave...now."

Alec's annoyance surged into outright irritation. "I will, but I have something important to do first."

"Is that the boat?"

Alec's eyes narrowed, and he tightened his grip on the case. "It is."

Officer Foster reached toward him. "I'll take care of it. For your own safety, you need to leave now."

Alec took a step back. The cop's overzealous attitude was out of place. "The safest place for this artifact is in the vault, which is where I plan to put it, and I don't need any help. You should go clear the rest of the building."

The young man scowled and puffed out his chest like a gorilla trying to intimidate a rival. "Look, Professor, this isn't up for debate. I'm a police officer. You're going to give me that box and leave the building, as ordered."

He stood his ground. "Or what? Are you going to shoot me for my own safety?"

Foster hesitated a second then relaxed his stance and switched to a more conciliatory tone. "Relax, Professor. I'm just here to help. I don't want you to get hurt. Give me the boat, and I'll put it in the vault for you."

"You don't have the necessary security code."

The officer's eyes narrowed slightly. "You can give it to me."

"I'm not authorized to give it out."

They stood facing each other, eyes locked, for several seconds. Then Foster advanced, backing Alec up against the door of the vault. "Give me the boat."

He reached forward and made a grab for the case, but Alec held fast.

Suddenly, the clanging alarm went silent. A moment later, a woman appeared in the hallway.

A stern voice echoed down the now-silent corridor. "Officer, what are you doing?"

The young cop spun around, releasing his hold on the case so quickly Alec had to juggle it to keep his grip.

Nora Samuels marched toward them. "The Fire Department has determined there is no fire. It was a false alarm. You can return to your regular duties."

The officer rammed his hat tighter on his head, shot Alec a menacing look, then marched past Nora without a word.

She half-turned to watch him go before returning to face Alec. "That was strange."

He released a nervous laugh. "You have no idea. Your timing was perfect."

Her naturally thin lips tightened further. "He appeared to be trying to grab that box from you."

Alec shifted the heavy case in his arms. "This contains the Fassbender boat, and I think he intended to steal it. I need to report him immediately."

Nora stiffened. "I know the chief of the campus police. I'll call him as soon as I get back to my desk. I don't suppose you caught the officer's name?"

"Foster. He's been to my office before...several times." Another impossible coincidence.

She eyed the case. "Since there's no fire, I suppose you can safely take the boat back to your office."

Alec shook his head. "Oh, no. This is going into the vault, and it's going to stay there until the director arranges transport back to Cairo." He didn't need the physical artifact to write his report, and at this point, he wouldn't be sorry if he never saw it again.

Her brows rose. "You've finished your work with it?"

"I have. This boat definitely belongs to the Egyptians."

She seemed to dismiss the matter as closed. "I'm sure Director Moreau is disappointed, but it can't be helped." She started to leave then hesitated. "Do you need any assistance?"

"No thanks. I've got it."

Nora's gray head bobbed in a crisp nod. "Very well. I'll leave it to you and go back upstairs to inform the chief about that Officer Foster—if he's even a real officer." She strode off, her low heels clicking on the terrazzo floor.

Alec turned back to the vault and balanced the case on one arm while he typed the security code into the keypad with the other hand. When the lock clicked, he pulled the door open, casting one last glance down the hall to be sure he was alone. He set the case back in its proper position on the shelf and quickly left the vault. Only after the lock clicked into place again did he realize his heart was still racing like a cheetah on speed.

# CHAPTER FOURTEEN

When he reached the main floor, Alec joined the animated throng streaming back into the building after the aborted fire alarm. Around him, students chattered about their interrupted classes, but Alec barely heard them. His head buzzed with fatigue as the stress of the night before and the bizarre altercation in the basement caught up with him.

Back in his office, he removed the notes he'd stashed in his jacket pocket and spread them on his desk. After staring at them for several minutes, he gave up and slipped them into his desk drawer. No more work would be accomplished today. His brain refused to cooperate. Besides, it was getting dark, and all he could think about was how much he wanted to be home with Grace and Casey.

As he stood in the hall, locking his door, Fermin LeBlanc stepped out of his office next door, wearing his gray tweed topcoat and a black fedora. "Ah, Bainbridge. Calling it a day?"

"Yes. The fire alarm disrupted my train of thought, and I can't seem to get it back."

Fermin nodded as he turned his own key. "I understand what you mean, but we're very fortunate the alarm was false." He regarded Alec with an unreadable expression. "The consequences of a fire could be disastrous."

"True." Alec was in no mood for a prolonged discussion. He turned and walked toward the stairs, but Fermin caught up with him in a few steps.

"I understand you were in the archives when the alarm sounded."

Alec shot him a quick sideways glance. "Where did you hear that?" *And why do you care where I was?*

Fermin looked flustered. "I'm not sure. I believe I overheard a group of people talking in the lobby when we were allowed back inside...not that it matters, of course."

"Of course." Alec picked up his pace, almost tripping down the stairs in his rush to avoid further conversation. As he pushed through the front doors, he wondered when Fermin was eligible for his next sabbatical. A full year without his officious meddling would be heaven, and it couldn't come soon enough.

Fifteen minutes later, he climbed the steps and opened the front door, expecting to be pounced on by a fully-rested, five-year-old bundle of energy. Instead, the front hall was dark and empty except for a tantalizing aroma wafting in from the kitchen. He hung up his coat and dumped his backpack before following his nose to the kitchen.

A heavy Dutch oven simmering on the stove seemed to be the source of the mouth-watering smell. Casey stood at the counter, stirring something in a big ceramic bowl with a long wooden spoon. When he gave an appreciate sniff, she turned, her lips curving into a smile. "I'm glad you're home. Dinner will be ready early. After last night, I thought you might not make it through the whole day at work."

"Whatever you're cooking smells wonderful, so I'm not complaining, but you shouldn't have gone to so much trouble." He crossed the room until he stood behind her. As if acting of their own volition, his arms slipped around her waist and pulled her gently back against his chest. He dropped a light kiss on the top of her head. "Your night wasn't any more restful than mine."

When she relaxed against his body, his pulse quickened for a moment. Then she straightened without pulling free and returned to stirring what looked like some kind of sticky dough. "No, but after the window company replaced the broken glass this morning, Grace, Balthazar, and I took a nice long nap. They're upstairs in the playroom now."

Alec leaned forward and peered over her shoulder. "What are you making?"

"Just some quick soda bread to go with the stew."

"You spoil us."

She hesitated before giving the dough a couple of vigorous rounds with the spoon. "I enjoy it. I haven't had anyone to cook for in a long time."

"What about your fiancé?"

He cursed himself the second the words left his mouth, but Casey seemed unconcerned.

"Ex-fiancé. I didn't have much time to cook, and our schedules always seemed to be at odds. I had long hours in my lab and he usually worked late in his, so we rarely ate together."

"Was he a psychologist, too?"

She shook her head. "Physicist. A brilliant scientist, but you'd be hard-pressed to find anyone less interested in the workings of the human mind." She turned the dough out onto a baking sheet and began shaping it into a smooth, rounded oval.

"It sounds like you didn't have much in common."

"We had enough...for a while." She gave the loaf a final pat then faced him with one cocked brow. "Now, would you like to talk about one of your ex-girlfriends?"

He stepped back and raised both hands. "Message received. Subject being changed."

Baking sheet in hand, she stepped past him. "Good." She opened the oven door and slid the bread inside. "Why don't you go upstairs and ask Grace to start picking up. By the time she's washed and ready, dinner should be on the table."

Alec climbed the two flights of stairs to the playroom, where he found Grace and Balthazar playing her current favorite make-believe — Jungle Adventurer. Grace was wearing her pith helmet, while the monkey sported his veiled pink princess hat.

"He's a giant gorilla who's rescuing the hippo from the flooded river." She pointed at her stuffed hippo, who was wrapped in an old blue bath towel.

Alec gave a mental shrug. After the kind of day he'd had, he could see no reason why a heroic giant gorilla shouldn't wear a conical pink princess hat. "Casey says it almost time for dinner. Have you two had a good day?"

"Uh, huh."

Balthazar nodded vigorously and chittered.

"That's good, but it's time to pick up. Feed Balthazar and wash your hands. Dinner's almost ready."

After an excellent meal, Alec settled into his chair in the living room. Casey had offered to take over bath duty, and with only a minor twinge of guilt, he'd let her. Now, he was trying to read a new article by Director Moreau about the collection of Egyptian baboon statuary in the Louvre, but he kept dozing off. After jerking awake for the third time, he set the journal aside and rubbed his eyes.

"You should have gone to bed." Soft fingers lightly brushed the top of his head.

He opened his eyes to see Casey standing in front of him. Her dark-honey hair was piled loosely atop her head with a couple of damp locks hanging down. They must have come loose during Grace's bath. She wore a loose sweatshirt, snug jeans with a tiny tear across one knee, and fluffy blue slippers. She was the most beautiful woman he'd ever seen.

He reached for her hand and pulled her toward him until she stood between his knees. "Have I told you lately how glad I am you're here?"

Her mouth tipped up on one side. "So, you'll give my boss a positive report on my performance?"

"Glowing."

She gently withdrew her hand. "You should go to bed. Fatigue is making you loopy."

"Undoubtedly, but I need to talk to you first.

"Okay." She sat on the couch, kicked off her slippers, tucked her feet beneath her, and faced him expectantly.

"I had a very weird day." He proceeded to tell her about the fire alarm and his run-in with the campus cop.

Her brows drew together. She unfolded her legs and straightened. "A false fire alarm? After what happened last night?"

"A pretty unlikely coincidence."

She rose and began pacing. "To put it mildly. And you say you've seen the officer before?"

Alec nodded. "He's the one who took the initial report about the anonymous letter then picked up the subsequent notes and that damned stuffed monkey."

"Did he show any unusual interest in the boat?"

"He asked about the boat, but I didn't think much of it at the time. The boat is pretty cool. Everyone is interested in it. Even Fermin acts like he wants to play with it, and he understands its true value. Or at least he should." He shook his head and blew out a breath. "In retrospect, I guess I should have been more suspicious."

"At least the department secretary is taking the matter to the chief of the campus police. He might be tempted to blow the whole thing off, since the young man is one of their own, but I hope she doesn't let him."

Alec quirked one brow. "I have a feeling nobody blows Nora Samuels off."

"Good." Casey stopped pacing and faced him. Her features lifted as a smile illuminated her whole face. "You know what this means. This officer...Foster...could be the one behind the whole scheme. If the campus police can find enough evidence to arrest him, this whole crazy situation might end soon. You can stop worrying, and Grace will be able to go back to school."

*And then what?* Alec pushed up from his chair. "Nobody wants that more than I do, but finding evidence is going to be a problem. I turned everything over to him. Remember? What are the chances he gave them to the detective?"

Her expression clouded. "They could search his apartment. There might be incriminating evidence there."

"I doubt they could get a search warrant based solely on the man's behavior this afternoon. I'm sure he could come up with a plausible excuse."

"That's probably true, but at least we have a suspect now. If the police can't—or won't—go after him, we can try something else to draw him out. We're so close now, I can feel it. Can't you?"

Alec smiled. With her hair up, no make-up on, and vibrating with positive energy, she looked younger than ever. He hated to douse her enthusiasm with the icy water of reality, but they had to be realistic. He reached for her and drew her into a loose embrace. "Tomorrow I'll find out what kind of response Nora got from the chief, but even though it's killing me, we may have to continue to be patient." When her lips tightened rebelliously, he couldn't suppress a smile. "You're the one who's always telling me to be patient. It isn't so easy, is it?"

"No."

"Having you here is the only bright side. Would it be so terrible to continue to live with me and Grace a while longer?" Even in the low light from the lamp beside the sofa, he could see color rising in her cheeks.

"Not at all, but—"

222

He dropped his voice and tipped his head until his forehead touched hers. "We'll keep doing what we've been doing and make the best of the situation."

Her lips parted, and the tip of her tongue slipped along the bottom one. "The best...yes."

Time seemed to hold its breath as Alec closed the gap between their mouths. She smelled of bubble bath and baby shampoo and tasted like the chocolate chip cookies they'd had for dessert. No woman had ever aroused him more.

He tightened his grasp until her soft, sweatshirt-clad breasts pressed against his chest and felt a swift surge of raw masculine triumph when her hands clutched his back, pulling him closer. When he increased the pressure of his lips, her mouth opened with a satisfied murmur. Alec groaned and moved one hand to cup her rounded bottom.

Soon, however, a small voice of reason whispered in his ear to stop, that he was taking advantage of her. That she was off-limits as long as she worked for him. Only a supreme exercise of willpower compelled him to break the kiss, and when he did, she immediately nestled her head on his chest in the hollow beneath his chin. Her breath came in short, soft pants, warm against his neck.

He kissed her hair, inhaling the clean, warm scent of her. "We should stop."

"Probably." Her head bobbed in assent, but she made no move to pull away.

"Now is not the time."

"No." The word came out half-muffled by his shirt.

"When this is over..."

She nodded again. "Yes."

His arms tightened in a brief squeeze before releasing her. She drew back until her big brown eyes met his in an unblinking gaze.

Alec cleared his throat. "I...um...guess I'll go up to bed." He took a step back.

She reached out and placed a hand on his arm. "Alec, it's all going to be okay."

He smiled. For some reason, he believed her.

He was running late the next morning. He'd lain awake for hours, thinking about Officer Foster's bizarre behavior. The idea that the young campus cop was the mastermind behind an elaborate extortion plot to steal a highly valuable antiquity was so improbable as to be absurd. Which made him think someone must have paid the man. Whatever the reason, Alec wanted to make sure Foster never set foot in the NEI again.

As soon as he arrived at the Institute, he hurried straight to Nora Samuels office. Her door was closed, so he knocked, waited, and knocked again, but there was no answer. A quick glance at his watch told him it was nearly ten o'clock. His agitation ratcheted up. Where was she? He made his way upstairs but couldn't settle into any work. He scanned the notes for his afternoon seminar three times without reading them then rose and roamed around his office, stopping occasionally to stare out the window.

An hour later, he returned to Nora's office. This time found her tapping away at the computer on her desk.

She peered up at him over the top of her purple-framed glasses. "Good morning, Professor. What can I do for you?"

"I need to know what you learned," he blurted out.

One salt-and-pepper brow arched higher. "About—?"

"That cop...yesterday. You were going to speak to your friend the chief."

She rolled her chair back from her desk and swiveled to face him. "I spoke to him yesterday then stopped by to see him first thing this morning. He was quite interested in what I had to say."

"That's a good first step, I guess."

Nora's expression assumed a hint of I-know-something-you-don't superiority. "It seems your Officer Foster has disappeared."

*Damn.* He had hoped the man wouldn't run, even though he had basically been caught red-handed.

Nora's chin bobbed in a crisp nod. "He failed to clock out yesterday afternoon. When he also failed to report for work this morning, the sergeant sent an officer to check his apartment. He wasn't there, and apparently no one has seen him since yesterday morning."

Alec wasn't sure how to take the news. Part of him wanted to believe the threats to Grace and the Fassbender boat had disappeared along with Foster, but a more cautious voice warned him not to get too comfortable. Things were seldom what they seemed, and until the man was apprehended and questioned, his part in the scheme was still uncertain. "I assume they're going to keep looking for him."

Nora shook her head. "As the chief pointed out, they have no grounds. There's no evidence of an actual crime having been committed. If Foster returns, they'll question him, of course, but otherwise..." She raised her shoulders in what was probably intended to be a casual shrug, but her sharp-eyed glance never wavered. "Unless you have additional, more concrete information."

"No." He'd handed over every bit of physical evidence to the likely perpetrator of the plot. *What an idiot.*

After leaving Nora's office, he stopped by the café to pick up a double espresso and a chicken sandwich, hoping the combination of caffeine and protein might jar his brain from its funk, and carried them up to his office. By the time his afternoon graduate seminar wrapped up, he was feeling better. There was nothing like a rousing argument over the proper dating of Old Kingdom potsherds to get the juices flowing.

He settled into his desk chair and pulled out his notes on the boat with renewed energy. He figured he had two solid days' work left on the final report. If he stayed focused, he should be able to complete it and deliver it to the director's desk by Saturday afternoon. Then he could wash his hands of the whole damned thing. The Fassbender boat and its disposition would be the director's responsibility.

His logical inner voice suggested it wouldn't matter who was technically in charge of the boat—as long as it was still at the NEI, the threat remained—but he banished the thought. It felt too good to believe the nightmare was nearly over.

The next couple of days passed smoothly and productively. According to Nora's inside information, the campus police still hadn't seen or heard from the missing officer. Based on his behavior at the NEI and subsequent disappearance, they'd concluded that he'd left town after experiencing some kind of mental breakdown.

Alec was inclined to agree. The entire atmosphere around the Institute seemed to have changed, as if the cloud of threat that had hovered over it for weeks had lifted. Colors seemed brighter, there was a hint of spring in the air, and the students seemed livelier. He found himself smiling at his colleagues more often. Even Fermin LeBlanc was less annoying that usual.

At two-thirty Saturday afternoon, he finished the final read-through of his authentication report on the Fassbender boat with satisfaction. He was proud of the result. It was thorough, scholarly, and indisputable. He signed his name to the bottom with an uncustomary flourish, clipped it into a binder, and carried it to Director Moreau's office with a spring in his step.

On his walk home, he was briefly tempted to splash in the puddles from the melting snow that covered the sidewalks. He felt as free as a hawk soaring over the golden desert sands after months in captivity. He couldn't wait to get home and celebrate. He might not be able to share his relief with Grace, but Casey would understand. Maybe he could take her out to dinner—just the two of them—like a real date. The closer he got to home, the better the idea sounded.

By the time he opened the front door, he was ready to scoop her up and sweep her off her feet. But only hollow silence greeted him when he stepped inside. His mood deflated as hung his coat in the hall closet. It was Saturday so they had probably gone to the Chiangs.

From somewhere overhead, a muffed voice caught his ear, followed by a high-pitched giggle. He turned and headed up the stairs. When he reached the second floor, the sound of footsteps above drew him up another flight to the playroom. When he peeked through the open doorway, he saw Casey holding Grace on her lap while Balthazar amused himself with a pile of oddly-shaped plastic blocks in the corner. Alec hesitated in the hall for a couple of minutes, listening to her read a lively book about a baby's adventures in the big city, using a different voice for each character. The scene kindled a warm glow deep inside.

Casey looked up from the book with a smile that sent tiny bursts of electricity to every nerve ending in his body. "Hi."

"Hi." More determined than ever to put his plan in motion, he approached and squatted beside them. "Say, Grace, you haven't seen Sophia for a few days. How would you like me to call her mom and see if you could have dinner with them and stay and play for a while tonight?"

His niece sighed. "That would be fun, but I can't."

"Why not?"

"We already called them after lunch, and Sophia has stripped throat."

*Strep,* Casey mouthed above the child's head.

"Oh, that's too bad." Alec's mind raced for another solution. "Maybe Maria could come babysit for a couple of hours this evening. You two haven't played together for a long time." After their recent conversation, he was sure his TA would be on her best behavior.

"Yes!" Grace bounced on Casey's lap then stilled. "But what will you and Casey do?"

"I thought we might go out to dinner at a grown-up place, someplace you wouldn't like. We might even eat fish."

"Fish! Eww!!" The little girl crinkled her face into a grotesque mask.

He pushed to his feet. "Great. I'll call Maria and see if she's available."

Casey scooted the child off her lap with a pat. "Grace, you stay here and play with Balthazar. I need to talk to your Uncle Alec for a few minutes." She rose and followed him to the door. As soon as they were out of earshot, she whispered, "What do you think you're doing?"

He continued down the stairs, with Casey a half-step behind. "What? I want to take you out for a nice dinner. You deserve it. We both deserve it."

She stopped at the second-floor landing but kept her voice low. "That may be, but I'm being paid to do a job here, and that job is to ensure Grace's safety. How am I supposed to protect her if I'm sitting with you in some fancy restaurant?"

"She'll be perfectly safe. Nothing's going to happen."

"You can't know that," she insisted.

"Look, there has been no sign of that rogue cop for days, and nothing suspicious has happened since he took off. The boat is safely locked in the NEI archive vault, and I delivered my report this afternoon. I'm finished. Done. It's over." He put his hands on her shoulders and drew her a step closer. "I just want to have some time alone with you outside the house. Is that so terrible?"

For a moment, she refused to meet his gaze. When she finally looked up, a mix of emotions warred in her eyes. "No, but at least let me try to arrange for a replacement agent from Phoenix."

"That would guarantee a scene from Grace. She wouldn't be at all happy about being left with a stranger, especially when she's been promised an evening with Maria. We might as well stay home."

"Then maybe we should." Casey pressed her lips together in a tight line.

He tugged her closer still. "Everything will be fine. I let Maria know, in no uncertain terms, that her behavior the night of the smoke bomb was out of line. She'll be thrilled to be asked to babysit again, and the money will really help her out. Grace will be happy. I'll be happy." He bent his head until a mere breath separated them. "You might even be happy, if you'll just relax." He pressed a soft, lingering kiss on her rebellious lips. "Come on. What do you say?"

# CHAPTER FIFTEEN

With Alec's lips on hers, Casey struggled to remember his question. And it didn't help when he began to kiss his way across her cheek.

"Say yes," he murmured, his warm breath tickling her ear.

*Yes, what? Oh, wait. Dinner. Yes.*

After spending every waking moment with her young charge for weeks, leaving Grace with her former babysitter felt like dereliction of duty, even though Alec was convinced she'd be safe. Casey wanted to believe the kidnapping threat had ended with the disappearance of the strange young policeman, but it had only been a few days. Could they safely make that assumption?

"The restaurant is only a few blocks away. We'll be gone a couple of hours, at most." From the seductive tone of his voice, you'd think he was offering her a weekend in Paris.

Her resolve wavered. "Well...maybe—"

t

"Great!" Alec planted a big, smacking kiss on her mouth then grinned. "I'll call Maria then make reservations at Luigi's." Whistling tunelessly under his breath, he headed toward his study, leaving Casey standing in the hall, trying to figure out what to do next.

Luigi's, with its dark paneled walls, cushy red carpet, and intimate private dining rooms, was the most expensive restaurant in the neighborhood. It was where high-ranking faculty took guests they wanted to impress, where the university president entertained visiting dignitaries. What on earth was she going to wear?

She hurried into her bedroom and began rifling through the clothes she'd brought, knowing she wouldn't find anything suitable. Black slacks and a fuzzy pink sweater Peter had given her for Valentine's Day two years ago were the best she could come up with. Sagging, she sat on the bed and tried to picture the wardrobe that remained in her apartment. She had a muted gray plaid interview suit, but it was showing its age and was too prim and business-like for a Saturday night dinner at a fancy restaurant. There was that little black knit dress she'd bought for the faculty cocktail party several years ago. It had been a bit snug across the hips the last time she'd tried it on, but that was months ago. Was there a chance it would fit now? It was worth a try. She'd have to make a quick trip across campus to her apartment, but she certainly didn't have time to go shopping for a new dress before dinner.

When the doorbell rang at six-thirty to signal Maria's arrival, Casey was still standing in front of the old-fashioned mirror above the dressing table in her bedroom. She'd done her best with her hair and was reasonably pleased with her version of the carefully messy up-dos she'd seen in magazines. Her main concern was the black cocktail dress. Bending first one way, then the other, she craned her neck to see as much of herself as possible. She smoothed the fabric over her hips and twisted to peer over her right shoulder into the mirror. The dress was fitted across the hips, but the cross-gather in the middle kept it from being unacceptably tight. The keyhole neckline was likely to distract Alec's attention, at any rate. She'd forgotten how much cleavage it displayed.

His deep voice echoed up the stairwell, followed by a feminine laugh and the sound of childish chatter. Time to go. The dress would have to do.

She grabbed the small black bag she'd picked up at her apartment along with the dress and headed for the stairs. As she made her way down, she kept a firm grip on the handrail. She couldn't remember the last time she'd worn heels, and with her nerves on edge, the last thing she needed was to take a tumble and end up on the floor at Alec's feet.

When she approached the foyer where Alec was standing with Maria, he glanced up. The overhead light glinted off the dark blond waves of his hair, and his navy suit darkened his eyes to deep azure. She realized she'd never seen him in a suit before. They might be headed to the highest-rated restaurant in the neighborhood, but he looked yummier than anything on Luigi's menu. Her traitorous inner voice suggested maybe they didn't need to go out at all. Maybe he could just pay Maria and send her home.

While Alec finished his instructions about keeping the doors locked, not leaving the house, and where to find the ready-to-heat leftovers for dinner, Grace bounced up and down, tugging on Maria's hand and begging her to come upstairs to play dress-up.

"Well, that about wraps it up," he said as he shrugged into his coat. "We'll be back before nine." He swept his niece up in a big hug. "You be good, kiddo."

Grace wriggled until he set her down. "Uncle Alec, you know I'm *always* good."

"So be extra good. And don't let Balthazar cause any trouble. We'll be back soon."

"Not too soon!" She dragged Maria toward the stairs.

"She seems happy to see Maria," Casey said as they walked toward the back door. "I think she's glad to have someone different to play with. I'm afraid I've gotten pretty boring."

Alec locked the door behind them then grasped her elbow and guided her down the concrete steps, even though most of the snow and ice had melted. "There's nothing boring about you. Grace just isn't used to spending so much time at home."

"Maybe I should plan a couple of outings for next week. The Shedd Aquarium has wonderful exhibits for children, although it's pricey."

He opened the garage door and helped her into the car before backing down the short driveway into the alley. "I think it's time she went back to school."

Casey's immediate reaction was, *is that safe?* A weight settled into her chest. *If the threat to Grace really is over, my job here is finished.*

Her practical inner voice spoke up. *And just in time. Remember your interview in Boston on Tuesday.*

*The interview. Yes.* She couldn't believe the date had arrived so quickly. So much had happened since she'd received the email from the Wiseman Institute, she'd nearly forgotten it. And the job that had seemed like a godsend in January had lost some of its luster since Alec and Grace had come into her life. Her stomach contracted in a squishy, unsettled sensation at the thought of leaving them.

The restaurant had a small parking lot in the back, pocked with rapidly freezing puddles. Alec parked in the last space then came around to help Casey out. When he opened the car door, she swung around and shot a quick glance at the ground before stepping out. Light from the security lights attached to the utility poles glittered on the surface of a huge black puddle.

He reached for her hand with a grimace. "I'm sorry about that. I should have dropped you off in front."

"Then I would have been forced to climb over the remnants of the pile left by the snow plows. I can make it." As she extended one leg, trying to figure out how to leap over the puddle, her dress rode half-way up her thighs. So much for making an elegant exit.

"Give me your other hand."

She did, and a second later she stood on solid pavement, high and dry. In one smooth, quick movement, he had pulled her out of the car and over the puddle without getting so much as a drop of water on her shoes. For a man who didn't have much free time to work out, he was deceptively strong. She tugged her skirt back into place. "Um…thanks."

He leaned over and shoved the door shut behind her. "If we want to keep your shoes dry, I should probably carry you inside."

Her stomach did a flip-flop at the image before she registered the twinkle in his eye and the wicked tilt to his grin. She lifted her chin. "That won't be necessary. I'll watch my step."

He chuckled and took her arm. "Have it your way, but the offer stands."

She made it into the restaurant without a mishap and managed to maintain an appropriate air of sophistication while the maître d' led them to a table for two, tucked into a dark, romantic alcove. But when he placed the heavy, leather-bound menu in her hands, her inner foodie squealed with glee. How would she be able to choose among the mouth-watering offerings? After much discussion, she and Alec settled on a starter of Fettuccine Alfredo with shaved truffles; sea bass with tomatoes, capers, and olives; and tiramisu for dessert. Alec ordered a bottle of Italian sparkling water for himself, while Casey selected a glass of the house rosé and did her best to ignore the astounding prices of everything.

After the waiter left with their order, reality crept back in. The whole dinner had an air of finality that sucked much of the pleasure from the experience.

She toyed with her glass, keeping her gaze on her fingers. "This restaurant is lovely, but you didn't need to bring me here."

"I didn't need to, but I wanted to." He wrapped his hand around hers to still its nervous movement. "The whole situation with Grace and the boat has been a living nightmare. Your help is the main reason I haven't cracked under the pressure."

When she glanced up, heat burned in his cool blue gaze. "You would never crack. You always have everything under control."

Alec's brows shot up. "Hardly. I was about ready to chuck it all in, pack Grace in the car, and head for the wilds of Montana."

The image made Casey smile. "You were not. As I recall, the day I walked into your office, you were mad enough to start knocking heads together."

His expression sobered again. "You'll never know how grateful I am for that day. You moved in and quietly took control. You brought stability to the chaos and made it possible for me to finish my work on that cursed boat."

Heat flared in her cheeks. She hoped the candlelight was low enough to disguise her blush. She'd only been doing her job, but to hear Alec talk, one would think she'd single handedly thwarted the would-be kidnapper's plan. Before she could think of a suitable response, the waiter appeared with their appetizer.

*Saved by the fettuccine.*

The food was amazing, and by the time the waiter cleared their main course dishes, Casey was questioning the wisdom of dessert—even tiramisu, one of her favorites. She needn't have worried. When it arrived, the fluffy custard flavored with espresso and dusted with cocoa powder melted in her mouth, taking up very little room in her stomach.

After six or seven bites, she set her fork on her plate and sighed. "That was heaven. Thank you."

Alec scooped up the remaining bite. "The pleasure was mine, believe me. I love watching a woman enjoy good food."

Her lips curved in a smile. "I love to cook, and I love to eat. I'm not going to lie."

In the candlelight, his eyes were so dark, only a hint of blue showed. "That's another thing I love about you. You say what you mean and mean what you say. No games."

"An offshoot of being a psychologist. I've seen the price of emotional dishonesty."

He shook his head "No. It's deeper than that. It's the essence of you."

"You've only known me a few weeks."

"That can be enough, especially given the intensity of those weeks."

She couldn't disagree. Living in the same house and dealing with an unending series of threats and crises together did tend to speed up the process of getting to know another person.

That thought led her to the big question that had been looming over her all day. Drawing a deep breath, she blurted out, "Do you really think it's over?"

"I hope so."

"What would make you sure?"

He pondered a moment. "Once the boat is out of the NEI and on its way back to Egypt, the thieves have nothing to gain by threatening Grace."

"When do you think that might happen?" Her pulse skittered. The tiramisu must have had more caffeine than she realized.

"Another week or two." His gaze sharpened, and a pair of creases appeared between his brows. "Casey, are you worried about your job? You sound like you think I might send you packing tomorrow."

*I will be packing tomorrow. And if they offer me the job at the clinic in Boston, I'd be a fool not to seriously consider it.*

She kept her voice and expression casually professional, despite a growing sense of loss that threatened to choke her. "One way or another, you won't be needing me much longer."

"What I need might surprise you." Although his voice was low, steely determination rang in his tone.

"But the threat to Grace—"

He reached for her hand. "We'll talk about it later." He signaled to the waiter to bring the check.

Alec kept a firm grip on her elbow as they walked back to the car but made no further jokes about carrying her. In fact, he said very little on the short drive home. Casey spent most of the drive sneaking sideways glances at his stern profile and trying to figure out what she might have said to upset him. She hadn't told him about Boston. For all he knew, even after she left his house, she'd only be a few blocks away.

When they arrived home, he unlocked the back door and stepped aside to allow her to enter first. The kitchen was dark, but a glow from the living room illuminated the hallway, accompanied by the muffled sounds of the television. Alec followed her to the living room, where they found Maria sitting on the sofa watching some kind of reality TV competition.

As soon as they stepped into the arched opening, she switched off the TV and sprang up with a startled, almost guilty expression. "Did you enjoy dinner?"

Alec glanced at Casey. "It was very nice." He pulled off his gloves and unbuttoned his coat to reach for his wallet. "Was Grace any trouble?"

"Not at all." Maria picked up her red coat from the back of the leather armchair and slipped it on, flipping her hair over the back. "She ate a reasonable amount of dinner and took a bath without protest."

Alec handed her a couple of folded bills. "I appreciate you coming on such short notice. I'll run you home in the car."

She pulled her gloves from a front pocket and tucked the money in their place. "That's not necessary. I live around the corner—remember? Besides, it's not that late."

"Are you sure?"

She paused with her hand on the door knob. "I'll be fine, but thanks."

"Okay. I'll see you at the office on Monday."

She gave him a brief, tight smile then let herself out, and Alec locked the door behind her.

A small voice called down from upstairs. "Uncle Alec, is that you?"

"Uh, oh. It sounds like someone's still awake." He hung his coat in the closet before taking Casey's. "I'll go up and check on her."

"I'm right behind you. I want to change out of this dress."

He paused on the second step, turned, and let his gaze drift appreciatively down her figure before returning to her face. "Don't feel you have to change on my account. It's a great dress—I should have told you earlier."

Her cheeks heated. He'd noticed. "Um...thanks."

He turned back and continued up the stairs. With a firm grip on the bannister, she followed, relieved to have him in front of her rather than behind. There was no way she was going to make it up gracefully in high heels and the tight little black dress he admired so much.

When Alec headed for Grace's room, Casey followed, lingering in the hall outside the door while he sat on his niece's bed in the room lit only by the faint glow of the monkey nightlight.

He reached out to ruffle her hair. "Why aren't you asleep, kiddo?"

"My mind is too busy."

The statement was so *Grace*, Casey had to suppress a laugh.

"Did you have fun with Maria?" Alec asked.

"Yes, for a while, but then she was crying."

"Why was she crying? Did something bad happen?"

"She was helping me put on my pajamas after my bath, and she got a call on her phone. First, she was yelling, but then she started crying." Grace's words tumbled out in a cascade. "I think she had a fight with her boyfriend."

"That's too bad, but I'm sure she'll be fine. Now, it's time for you to go to sleep."

But Grace wasn't finished. "Uncle Alec, she called him Theo. I bet he's the movie-star guy from the zoo who used to be Casey's boyfriend."

"Chicago's a big city. I'm sure there's more than one man in town named Theo."

Grace remained unconvinced. "Maybe, but I think he's the same one."

"And I think you have an overactive imagination." Alec straightened her comforter. "Now, it's time for you to settle your busy mind and go to sleep." He rose then leaned down to kiss her forehead. "Good night."

"Good night," she announced with vigor, before rolling onto her side to face the wall.

Casey was still in the hall when Alec stepped out and closed the door with a soft click. "What do you think?" she asked in a whisper.

He steered her away from the door. "About what?"

"About Grace's insistence that Maria's boyfriend is Theo from the zoo."

He raised one brow, but his eyes twinkled. "Why, are you jealous?"

She gave his shoulder a light shove. "I'm just saying, Theo's not a very common name."

He shrugged. "True, and I suppose it's possible, but that would be an amazing coincidence. And even if it were the same guy, I'm not sure what difference that would make."

Casey tried to think of any potential implications of the connection, but her brain stumbled. Where was that caffeine buzz from the tiramisu when she needed it? "I feel like there might be a problem here, but I'm not sure what it is."

Alec dropped a quick kiss on her lips. "Don't you start overthinking it, too. That's just asking for trouble."

"That's my nature—and my job."

"I'm giving you permission to take a night off. Why don't you change your dress and meet me downstairs? I'll make us some coffee."

She stepped back, away from temptation. "That sounds good." She headed toward her bedroom.

"Unless you need help with your zipper." He looked adorably hopeful.

"Shows how much you know. This dress doesn't even have a zipper." With a smile, she closed the door, cutting off his soft chuckle.

She peeled off the black dress and hung it in the closet before grabbing a pair of jeans. Trading her stockings for a pair of thick, warm socks, she pulled a dark gray sweater over her head, destroying the remnants of her carefully casual hairdo. She removed the pins and covered elastic band, then bent over and gave her head a good shake. When she straightened, her hair fell in a loose mass over her shoulders.

Staring at the mirror, she gave herself a mental prod. She'd procrastinated as long as she could. It was time to go down and re-join Alec. A swarm of butterflies seemed to be doing the Samba in her stomach. She couldn't understand why she was so nervous. As he'd pointed out earlier, they knew each other pretty well.

The problem was his mixed signals. What was she supposed to think?

Her inner therapist reminded her that just because she had decided she was in love with Alec didn't mean he felt the same way. The attraction was clearly mutual, but how sharp was the line between inappropriate behavior and an acceptable personal relationship? Where was it drawn, and who was responsible for drawing it?

No wonder her head hurt.

She grimaced at herself in the mirror. Maybe she should take Alec's advice and give herself a night off from worrying.

She found him in the kitchen, pouring coffee into a pair of mugs. He had removed his jacket and tie, unbuttoned his collar, and rolled the cuffs of his blue dress shirt a couple of turns, exposing tanned forearms. He might not be every woman's dream of the ideal man, but he was a perfect match for hers.

He turned and smiled. "You look more comfortable." He handed her one of the mugs. "Let's go into the living room."

Casey gave the steaming brew an appreciative sniff. "Thanks."

She set her mug on the coffee table then settled on one end of the sofa. To her surprise, Alec sat beside her instead of in his usual leather chair and casually draped his arm across the back, a scant inch from her shoulders.

Gazing at his chiseled profile, she fought the urge to tell him about the possible job in Boston. It still felt presumptive and premature. What if she didn't get it, or decided not to take it?

She leaned forward, picked up her coffee and blew across the top. "I've been meaning to ask you something."

"Um, hmm." His eyes glinted over the rim of his mug as he took a sip.

"I need to take a few days off at the beginning of the week to take care of some personal business. I hope that's all right."

He hesitated, an expectant look on his face. When she didn't elaborate, disappointment crept in. "Of course."

"I'm sure my boss can send over a temporary replacement."

"I think Grace and I can manage on our own for a couple of days."

She took a long sip, then set her coffee down. Something else had been worrying her all evening. "I had an idea I'd like you to consider. If you decide it's safe for Grace to return to school but aren't ready to terminate my contract, I think I should go with her. She might think it's strange, but I wouldn't feel right dropping her off alone."

"I had the same thought. I'll call the director Monday morning. Maybe her teacher could use a classroom aide for a couple of weeks."

*A couple of weeks. Then, depending on how things go, I might never see either of them again.* A lump the size of a grapefruit suddenly formed in her throat.

He reached out and stroked his forefinger lightly down her cheek and jaw. "Hey, what's the matter? You look like someone died."

*Because that's how it feels.* She raised her chin and met his gaze.

"This isn't the end, you know." His voice was as warm and velvety as melted chocolate.

"You said yourself, as soon as the boat leaves the Institute, your problem is over. Grace will no longer need a bodyguard. You won't need me anymore."

"I don't believe I said I wouldn't need you anymore."

An uncharacteristic flame of temper flared. "Stop teasing me, or whatever it is you're doing. This situation is…difficult. I've grown very attached to Grace over the past few weeks."

"Just to Grace?"

She hesitated. "No." The word shoved its way out, small and grudging.

"Good." Alec shifted on the sofa until he faced her squarely. "Because we've grown attached to you, too." He hesitated, as if struggling with some internal question, then lifted his chin. "Casey, there are some things we need to talk about — things I need to say."

Her internal butterflies cranked the pace of their Samba from lively to frenetic. "Go ahead." It was all she could do to keep the flutter from her voice.

He reached for her hand and stroked her palm with his thumb. "I can't wait for the day I no longer need you to protect Grace, but that doesn't mean I want you out of our lives."

The butterflies went wild, losing all sense of rhythm. "Wh...what are you suggesting? That I leave Phoenix and stay on here as Grace's nanny?"

He frowned. "No. Although I'm sure she'd love it, that wouldn't be fair to you. I doubt you spent all those years of hard work and all that money getting a PhD to become a full-time nanny."

"As much as I love Grace, I have to admit it wasn't on my list of potential career choices."

*Tell him about the job.*

*Not yet.*

A glint of humor sparked in his eyes. "I assume being a professional bodyguard didn't make the list, either."

She gave a little laugh. "No. It's way too stressful."

He was quiet for a moment, shifting his gaze to their joined hands, while his thumb continued to draw slow circles. "When this job is over, you'll have important decisions to make—decisions Grace and I can't be part of." His voice was soft, almost as if he were talking to himself.

*Tell him. Now!*

She opened her mouth, but before she could speak his head snapped up, and his grasp on her hand tightened. "God, I'm awful at this." He glanced away. When he faced her again, his expression was hopeful, with an endearing hint of vulnerability. "What I'm trying to say is I know you'll be leaving us as soon as the threat to Grace no longer exists, but there's no reason that has to be the end of our relationship. In fact, it could be the beginning of something new, something better, if you're willing." He searched her eyes. "Casey, I think I'm falling in love with you."

Somehow, she managed to keep her voice calm, although her heart was pounding so hard she could feel her pulse in her fingertips. "You're saying you'd like to keep seeing me after my job here ends and find out where that takes us."

The tension left his shoulders and jaw, and he smiled. "Yes. Exactly." He cleared his throat. "You can't have missed the fact that I'm attracted to you—I haven't done a very good job hiding it—but the timing has been all wrong. There's been Grace to consider, and my position as your semi-employer…"

"I understand." She did and loved him all the more for understanding. In some ways, he'd just made her decision about the Boston job more complicated, but in other ways he'd made it easier.

"I can't—" he began.

"We shouldn't—" Their words overlapped.

"When this is all over—"

"Yes." She breathed her assent as much as voiced it.

"It's been a long day. We should probably turn in."

She untucked her legs and rose, still holding his hand. "Probably."

He stood, too, drawing her into his arms. Brushing a kiss across her lips, he murmured, "You know what I want."

The firm solidity of his body left little doubt in her mind. "Mmm, hmm."

He kissed her again, slowly and thoroughly then rested his forehead against hers. "Soon."

"But not tonight."

When they eased apart, he took her hand and led her up the stairs. At the top, they stood facing each other for several long moments before reluctantly heading for their separate rooms.

Three hours later, Casey was awakened by the insistent ringing of the doorbell.

# CHAPTER SIXTEEN

Heart pounding, Casey grabbed her phone and checked the time. Two twenty-one. Who could be ringing the doorbell at two o'clock in the morning?

She clambered out of bed and threw her robe over the loose yoga pants and long-sleeved tee she wore to sleep. As she shoved her feet into her workout shoes, she grabbed her phone and slipped it into the pocket of her robe. Regardless of who was at the door, the situation was unusual, and it was always a good idea to have access to back-up.

Half-way down the hall, she realized it might also be a good idea to have access to her firearm before opening the door at this hour. Before she could act, Alec emerged from his room, rubbing his tousled hair and scowling.

"Stay here with Grace," Casey whispered as she passed him. "I'll see who it is."

His scowl deepened. "Like hell."

He charged ahead and reached the door first. When he peered out, his brow furrowed in a sharp frown. "What the—it's Maria." After turning off the alarm system, he unlocked the door.

His TA stood shivering on the porch, clutching herself with arms across her chest. Distress shone in her dark eyes. "I'm so sorry to disturb you, Professor." Her voice broke on the last word, and she looked away. "I left my purse here earlier, and I need my keys to get into my apartment."

"Your keys? It's two in the morning. Where have you been for the past four hours?" He had taken a step back to let her in when suddenly she flew through the open door and slammed into his chest. As he grabbed her shoulders to steady them both, a tall man stepped into the foyer.

Casey sucked in a sharp breath and grabbed the bannister. She couldn't believe her eyes. It was Theo. But instead of smiling flirtatiously the way he had that afternoon at the zoo, he was brandishing a small black automatic pistol. And her gun was upstairs.

Alec pushed Maria aside and faced the intruder. "What the hell are you doing here?"

Theo growled and swung the weapon toward him.

"No!" Maria screamed.

Alec raised his left arm to block the blow, but the gun clipped him in the temple and he sank to the floor with a low groan. Without pausing to think, Casey rushed to his side. When she knelt and slid one arm behind his back, he groaned again and leaned his injured head against her shoulder.

Theo waved her away with the gun. "Get away from him." He motioned her and Maria toward the living room. "Over there. Both of you."

She was slow to react. Her brain felt like it was wrapped in cotton batting. Shock and confusion brought her thought process to a momentary standstill. She shifted Alec's weight so she could check his head. A small rivulet of blood trickled from his temple.

The sight of his blood sent a surge of energy coursing through her body, kicking her brain back into high gear. Sliding her hand down his arm, she felt for the pulse in his wrist. It was strong and regular.

"Get up," Theo ordered again.

She eased away and stood.

Maria clutched Casey's sleeve. "I'm sorry. He made me do it. You have to believe me." A tear slid from the corner of one eye, and her voice wavered.

Casey had trouble mustering sympathy for the young woman. Her distress appeared genuine, but she might simply be a good actress. Either way, she was responsible for bringing this man into Alec's home.

Alec groaned again then raised a hand to the side of his head and winced.

Theo pulled a pair of handcuffs from his back pocket and tossed them to Maria while keeping his gun pointed at Casey. "Put those on him. Behind his back."

Maria sniffed hard as she picked up the cuffs. She knelt beside Alec and moved his arms behind his back. After snapping the cuffs closed, she bent her head near his and whispered, "I'm so sorry, Professor."

Keeping the gun trained on the women, Theo reached down with his left hand and grabbed Alec by the shoulder. He jerked him to his feet and pushed him into the living room.

Alec stumbled against the back of the sofa and groaned. "If you want money, I—"

"Oh, I want money, Professor, but a lot more than you have here." Theo shoved him against the wall. "Sit down and stay there." Alec sank awkwardly to the floor. Theo turned to the women standing together in the front hall and waved his gun. "Maria, get in here."

She glanced at Casey and hesitantly obeyed. Anxious to keep a close eye on Alec, Casey followed.

Theo grabbed Maria's arm and pulled her to stand in front of Alec. "Watch him. If either of you moves, I'll shoot you both." Then he pointed the gun at Casey. "Where's the girl?"

Her heart skittered in her chest. This was more than a simple robbery. He wanted Grace.

"No!" Alec's bellow echoed through the house. He pushed back against the wall and struggled to his feet.

Theo strode back in, thrust Maria aside, and swung the gun toward Alec's head again. It connected with a resounding *clunk*, and he collapsed to the floor like a popped balloon. "Shut up and don't move," Theo growled. He grabbed Casey's arm. "I assume Grace is upstairs in bed. Let's go."

As he marched her up the stairs, she wracked her brain for ways to keep him from finding the little girl and cursed herself for not taking the time to go back for her Sig when the doorbell rang.

When they reached the upstairs hall, he shot a quick look around. Three doors stood open and two were closed—Balthazar's and Grace's. "Grace! Grace, come out here!"

"No!" Casey shouted.

Theo gave her a rough shake. "Shut up. Unless you want me to knock you out, too."

Before he could make good on his threat, Grace's door opened, and the little girl appeared, dressed in footed pink flannel pajamas and rubbing her eyes. "What's going on? Where's Uncle Alec?"

"Downstairs. We're going down to see him." Theo moved toward Grace, but Casey resisted, jerking hard against his grasp. He lost his balance for a second and swore violently.

Grace narrowed her eyes at him and plunked her fists on her hips. "Theo, stop that. You're hurting Casey. And why are you here? You made Maria cry tonight. I know it was you." Her gaze moved to the pistol in his hand, and her jaw sagged. "You have a gun!" She threw back her head and yelled at the top of lungs, "Uncle Alec!"

A muffled reply sounded from the first floor. "Grace!"

The tightness around Casey's heart eased a fraction. At least Alec was alive and conscious. Suddenly, wild shrieking and chattering sounded behind the remaining closed door.

Theo tensed and spun toward it, pistol aimed and ready. "What the hell is that?"

Grace headed toward the door. "That's Balthazar."

"What's Balthazar, a hyena?"

"He's a monkey, and you've upset him." When she opened the door, the din filled the hall.

Theo recoiled. "My God, that thing must be some kind of monster. Shut the damned door and get over here."

The little girl hesitated and glanced at Casey with a question in her eyes.

Casey had a sudden thought. *Why not throw a literal monkey wrench into the situation?* She might be able to twist the ensuing chaos to her advantage. She tipped her head toward the room. "Give him the key, Grace. It will quiet him down."

Grace's eyes widened, then she nodded and disappeared inside the room.

"Get back here!" Theo yelled.

The shrieking ceased, and Grace reappeared. The child ran to her, and Casey enfolded her in an embrace.

"I did it," Grace whispered.

"Good girl." Casey hugged the child's quivering body tighter. "Don't worry. It'll be okay."

Theo gave her a hard shove. "You two get downstairs."

"What's happening?" Grace's voice was small and scared as they descended the steps.

"I don't know." Casey swiveled her head to face their assailant. "Theo wants something, but he won't tell us what."

"You'll find out soon enough."

When they reached the foyer, he motioned them into the living room, where Maria hovered over Alec. The blood from the small cut on his forehead had trickled down in front of his ear and partially dried. He glared at Theo. "You're going to pay for this, I promise."

"No, Professor, you're going to pay."

"Why are you doing this? What exactly do you want?"

Theo gave a short laugh. "I thought you would have figured it out by now. I want the boat, and you're going to get it for me."

Casey stared at him. *The boat? What the —*

Alec glanced at Casey. "Meet Officer Foster, the missing campus cop who took the reports and the notes threatening Grace—also your admirer from the zoo and Maria's so-called boyfriend."

"He is not my boyfriend," Maria declared. "His real name is Theo Fotopoulos. He's a thief and a criminal."

"Then why did you bring him here tonight?"

Tears glinted in her eyes, but her stiff posture suggested fury rather than fear. "They made me. I never would have helped him, but his filthy uncle is holding my sister hostage at home in Cyprus. He threatened to kill her unless I help this one—" She jerked her head in Theo's direction. "—get the boat."

"But why involve Grace?"

"That was the uncle's idea. To force you to cooperate. I tried to warn you to be careful after Theo tried to take her from school."

"You're the one who put that note on my desk?"

Maria nodded then shot an angry glance at Theo. "He was furious when he found out about it. Then, he decided to use the idea to his advantage and made me write the others."

The last pieces of the puzzle that had been floating in Casey's mind snapped into place. "And, of course, the police never saw any of the evidence."

Theo's lips curled in a smirk. "That's right."

Even sitting on the floor with his arms cuffed behind his back, Alec's taut posture radiated fury. "You must have thought it was pretty funny."

Theo snorted. "Oh, I did, Professor. You think you're so smart, but you had no idea."

"And the break-in here?"

Theo nodded. "With assistance from the ever-helpful Maria."

"I didn't know what he was going to do," Maria insisted. "I swear."

Alec spit out a guttural Arabic phrase that Casey didn't understand and didn't want to. Throwing his weight backward, he banged the metal cuffs against the wall. "How do you expect me to get the boat for you if I'm handcuffed in my own living room?"

Theo straightened and puffed his chest, basking in his control over the situation. "Here's what's going to happen." He waved the pistol at Casey and Grace. "Maria, get over here with these two." She warily crossed the room and stood beside them. "Good. Now, pay attention, Professor." He pulled a small key from his pocket. "This is the key to the handcuffs. I'm going to leave it on this table." Keeping his gaze on Alec and the gun pointed toward the women, he set the key on the coffee table about ten feet from Alec. "After we leave, you can come over here and unlock the cuffs."

"But they're behind my back."

"You're supposed to be a smart man. Figure it out. By the time you do, we'll be long gone. As soon as you're free, go straight to the Institute. Get the boat, leave it in the Egyptian gallery of the museum, and return here. When I have the boat and am safely away, I'll call you with instructions about where to find these three."

Alec shook his head fiercely. "I'll get you the damned boat, but leave them here."

"You're in no position to negotiate, Professor. They're coming with me, and if you don't do exactly as I say, you'll never see them alive again."

Grace clutched Casey's leg and began to cry. Casey picked her up and kissed her hair, fury building inside her. There was no way she would let this lowlife hurt the child.

"Don't touch them!" A ribbon of fear wove through Alec's hoarse shout.

Theo laughed and waved his pistol. "You have no say in this."

Grace's crying became louder. As Casey tried to soothe her, a blur of movement on the stairs caught her eye. Suddenly, Balthazar flew into the living room with a shriek, leapt onto Theo's outstretched arm, and sank his teeth into his wrist.

The gunman loosed a blood-curdling scream and swung his arm wildly, trying to dislodge his assailant. Suddenly, a shot exploded from his gun. Chunks of plaster rained down from the ceiling, and the gun clattered to the floor. Balthazar jumped down and ran toward Grace with a macabre grin showing blood-stained teeth and discolored fur around his mouth. Sensing this might be her only chance, Casey made a lunge for the pistol. But before she could reach it, Theo bent and snatched it up, waving it in a wide arc.

"If you try something like that again, I'll kill you all."

She stood her ground, positioning herself in front of Grace. "You do, and you'll never get the boat."

A stream of angry-sounding but incomprehensible words flowed from his lips as he wrapped his left hand around his right wrist, trying to staunch the blood that ran through his fingers and dripped onto the carpet. His chest heaved as he glared at Maria, who cowered against the wall near Alec. "Get me something for this. Now!"

She shot a nervous glance around the room.

Beside her, Alec shifted position with a grunt. "Towel. In the kitchen."

After she ran from the room, Theo turned to Casey, his handsome features twisted in pain as blood continued to drip from his hand. "I'm going to kill that freaking demon!"

Tiny monkey fingers dug into the flesh above her knee as Balthazar hid behind her leg. She shook him loose and ordered, "Go!" in a harsh whisper.

He must have understood, because he scuttled back upstairs with the speed of a highly motivated cockroach. Theo crossed the hall in two large steps, seemingly bent on carrying out his threat.

Balthazar could be a royal pain, but Grace loved him, and he had just demonstrated his own brand of loyalty to the family. Casey couldn't allow Theo to catch him.

"Hey!" She grabbed his sleeve as he passed. "Do you want that boat, or not? You've got a pretty elaborate plan, and the longer you drag this out, the greater the risk to everyone, including you. I'm sure you'd prefer to be long gone by the time the museum opens in a few hours."

He jerked free of her grasp but stopped and turned. "You're right."

Maria appeared at his side clutching a pale-yellow kitchen towel. With a guttural expletive, he held out his mangled wrist, and she wrapped the towel around twice, tying it in a clumsy knot. He rotated his forearm and opened and closed his fist. A couple of dark spots appeared on the towel, but nothing dripped on the floor. "I guess that will have to do for now. You two, come with me." He clamped his bloody hand on Casey's shoulder and pushed her and Grace toward the front door with a nod to Maria. "Let's go."

As he reached the door, Theo twisted his head toward Alec, who still sat on the floor in the living room. "Remember what I said, Professor. As soon as you free yourself, go straight to the archives, get the boat, and leave it on the bench in the Egyptian gallery. Once you have returned here, wait for my call. If I see any police, you won't like the outcome. Got it?"

Alec nodded, fury blazing in his eyes. "I've got it. But remember this, Fotopoulos—if you hurt them, I'll make you pay."

Theo gave a short, ugly laugh. "You don't frighten me, Professor. You forget who's holding the gun." He pushed Casey and Grace toward the open doorway, motioned for Maria to go ahead of him, and followed the trio out the door.

When the blast of cold air struck them, Grace shivered. Casey picked the child up and held her tighter against her chest. "It's freezing outside. Let me grab our coats."

"You won't need them where we're going. Now, get to the car."

She cast one last look at Alec over her shoulder before stepping onto the porch. He was conscious and alert—and mad as hell. The cut on his head had stopped bleeding, but she worried the two hard blows to the temple might have caused hidden damage. He needed a doctor. Leaving him felt like tearing her heart in two, but the only thing she could do now was protect his niece at all costs. Her fingers brushed the flat shape of the phone in her pocket. If she could find a way to escape Theo's presence for a moment, she would call for help.

The cold outside air brought an instant chill to the bare skin of her ankles and penetrated the thin fabric of her pants below the edge of her robe. When they reached the small black sedan parked at the curb, Theo ordered Casey and Grace into the back seat and Maria into the front. He climbed in, started the car, then handed her his pistol.

*His hold over her must be strong, if he feels safe giving her his gun.*

"Keep it aimed at them," he ordered as he pulled away from the curb. "And don't try anything, or I'll kill you first."

He drove slowly down the street, presumably to avoid attracting the attention of anyone who might be awake at this hour. The other houses on the block were dark, but the streetlight illuminated the gaps between the cars parked at the curb like a slow-moving strobe. When a flash of movement caught Casey's eye, she turned her head and squinted. It looked like...no, it couldn't be...but it was. The small, wiry figure of a monkey with its tail curled high scampered down the sidewalk, keeping pace with the car. Balthazar stared into her eyes and bared his lips in a familiar grin. The furry little menace was following them.

# CHAPTER SEVENTEEN

As Theo rolled through the quiet streets toward the center of campus, Casey cuddled Grace and tried to figure out the best way to call for help. With Maria leaning over the back of the seat, aiming a gun straight at her, it wouldn't be easy.

They cruised past the Gothic-styled Student Center toward the cluster of dorms that surrounded the central quad and main library. Here occasional small groups of students dotted the sidewalks. It might be after three in the morning, but it was Saturday night on a college campus, and not everyone was ready to call it a night.

Her internal antennae went up when Theo pulled into an open space at the curb in front of the old gymnasium.

Grace tugged at the sleeve of her robe. "What's happening?"

"I don't know." Casey made no attempt to keep her voice low. She wanted an answer, too.

"Shut up and get out of the car. All of you." Theo opened his door and climbed out, closing the door with a soft click. Maria hesitated a couple of seconds, then lowered the pistol and got out of the car. She opened the back door and whispered, "Come on."

When Casey stepped out, her foot sank into a puddle of frozen slush so deep it oozed over the top of her shoe. "Shi--oot!"

Theo uttered an ominous growl. "Quiet. Not a sound from any of you." He rounded the car, snatched the gun from Maria's hand, and held it low, aimed at Casey's middle. "Get the girl out. Now."

She leaned in and lifted Grace, taking care to keep the child well above the lingering snow piles. As she closed the car door, a short, sharp squeak caught her attention. It didn't sound like a door hinge. She cast a quick glance around and spotted a pair of glowing eyes under the bumper of the car parked in front of them. When she started to turn, the squeak sounded again and white teeth flashed.

*Balthazar.* He'd followed them all the way from Alec's house. Was he simply curious, or was he cooking up some kind of devious plan?

Theo grabbed her upper arm and gave her a rough shove. "This way." He gestured toward a narrow concrete walk leading to a side door of the gym.

Casey turned her head to see if Balthazar was still hiding under the car, but he had disappeared. Then she checked to see if anyone was close enough to help if she called out, but the block was deserted. A short white security pole topped by a blue light beckoned from across the street. If she could reach it and push the button, it would summon the campus police. If she were alone, she might take the chance, but burdened by Grace, she had no choice except to comply with Theo's orders and watch for another opportunity to escape. Running wasn't an option with a gun leveled on her.

When they reached the door, he pulled a heavily-loaded key chain from his jeans' pocket—one of the perks of being a campus cop, even a bogus one—selected a key, and fit it into the lock. A branch from one of the small evergreen shrubs bordering the walk brushed her leg as she followed Maria through the door. When she glanced down, a small, familiar face grinned at her from inside the bush.

*Whatever that monkey's up to, he's on his own. I've got more pressing concerns at the moment.* She shook her head and continued inside.

The old gym building was dark and deserted. Grace clung to her like a frightened octopus, her arms and legs wrapped around Casey like tentacles.

The door opened into a narrow stairwell lit only by a glowing red *Exit* sign mounted to the pale-yellow tile. With no idea which way to go, Casey and Maria halted on the landing just inside. Theo followed them in and eased the door closed. No alarm had sounded, leading her to wonder if he'd disabled the system in advance.

He poked the muzzle of his pistol in Casey's back. "Go down. Two flights."

She gripped the metal railing with her free hand and eased down the dark stairs that disappeared into the bowels of the building. It was much warmer inside, but she couldn't suppress a shiver. Even if she got an opportunity to call for help, would she be able to get cell service in this subterranean cavern?

When they reached the bottom, he directed them to a narrow passageway lit by dim service lights attached to the rounded concrete ceiling every ten feet or so.

Grace buried her face in Casey's shoulder and tightened her grip around her neck. "I'm scared." Her small voice wavered with unmistakable fear.

Casey stroked her head. "I know. But you're doing a great job being brave."

"I don't want to be brave anymore. I want to go home. I want Uncle Alec."

*Has Alec managed to free himself? Has he called the police, or is he following Theo's instructions?*

"No talking." A sharp poke in the shoulder blade accompanied Theo's hissed command.

As she walked, she shifted her attention to their surroundings. Any detail she was able to remember might help the authorities locate them later. She refused to consider that they might be truly helpless and at this dirtbag's mercy.

They seemed to be in some kind of utility tunnel. It was much warmer now, possibly thanks to the collection of large pipes running the length of the tunnel, attached to the ceiling. She was even beginning to sweat a little under her thick robe. She shifted Grace's weight to her right arm and casually brushed one of the pipes with her left hand.

Jerking her hand back, she sucked in a harsh breath. The pipe was burning hot. No wonder the corridor was warm. They might as well be inside a radiator. The university's original heating system relied on a central boiler plant to send steam to most of the older buildings. She remembered a couple of notices from the Facilities Department during past winters when the system had to be shut down due to maintenance issues. This must be one of the main steam tunnels that ran between buildings on the main campus.

Casey tried to estimate the direction and distance they'd walked but soon became disoriented in the narrow, winding tunnel. Even her sense of time seemed distorted. Had it been five minutes or fifteen? They could be on the other side of campus for all she knew.

"Stop." Theo poked her again with his pistol.

She and Maria halted next to a gray metal door fitted into one side of the tunnel. Theo withdrew the wad of keys from his pocket again and unlocked the door. He pulled it open then reached inside and flipped a switch. A bare overhead bulb came on, illuminating a room about the size of a large closet that appeared to contain maintenance and janitorial supplies. "Get in."

Maria obeyed, but Casey hesitated in the doorway. She had no idea what he had planned for them, and once she and Grace were inside, there was no way out except the door.

A hard shove in the back solved her dilemma. She stumbled forward but regained her footing in time to avoid dropping Grace. Theo followed them in, locking the door behind himself. As her gaze darted around the tiny space, the walls seemed to move closer, closing in until there was barely enough air to breathe. Her heart hammered in her chest. She licked her dry lips and swallowed hard.

*Keep a cool head*, her stern inner voice ordered. *Think. You're responsible for this child. You have to keep her safe and get her out.*

She drew a slow deep breath. Her head cleared, and the blind panic receded. She slid Grace from her hip to the floor, tucking the child into a corner, then gave her a quick hug and whispered in her ear, "Everything's going to be okay. Stay brave."

When she straightened, she moved between the little girl and Theo. "Why have you brought us here? What do you intend to do with us?"

"I brought you here to sit and wait, so you might as well make yourselves comfortable." He gestured toward a stack of cardboard boxes that claimed to contain refills for institutional paper towel dispensers. "If the professor does what I told him, you might not be here too long. If not—" He shrugged. "—who knows?"

Maria stiffened. "You aren't going to leave me here, too, are you? That wasn't part of the deal."

"You'll do whatever I tell you. There was no *deal*."

"There certainly was! I help you, and your uncle releases my sister."

"She's not my concern. I'm here to get the boat, and as soon as I have it, I'll be on the first plane to Cyprus."

"But what about my sister?" Tears welled in her eyes, and her voice rose in outrage.

He shrugged. "When I hand over the boat and collect my money, I'm done. Your sister is Uncle Cyril's problem."

Maria's face flamed, and her breathing became irregular. Fearing the consequences of an overt breakdown, Casey stepped in to distract Theo. "What exactly does your uncle plan to do with the boat?"

"Uncle Cyril runs a thriving *personal shopping* business in antiquities. Several months ago, he received an order from a private collector for the Fassbender boat. He called his contact in Chicago and arranged for me to pick it up. I'll get a nice, fat slice of the commission as a finder's fee when I hand it over."

"After all I've done, I demand to speak to your uncle about my sister." Maria's voice wavered on the edge of hysteria.

"You're in no position to demand anything. Although, I have to admit, you were a big help." He gave a short, ugly laugh. "In fact, you were so helpful, it won't be much of a leap for the police to decide you were a full partner, maybe even the mastermind." His tone and smile made it clear he enjoyed taunting her with her unwilling complicity.

Maria's taut body shook. "You piece of−" With a scream of frustration, the petite woman launched herself at her tormenter. He pushed her away with a derisive snort, but she kept coming, her arms flailing in ineffective fury.

Casey edged away from Grace. This was the opportunity she'd been waiting for. Maria might not be doing Theo any real damage, but she had engaged his full attention. Keeping her back to the wall, Casey edged slowly around the small room. A few more steps and she'd be behind him.

She was still a couple of feet away when Maria landed a chance blow on Theo's injured wrist. His angry bellow of pain reverberated off the concrete block walls. A split second later, he backhanded her with enough force to send her flying into a metal shelving unit loaded with old paint cans and plastic jugs filled with chemicals. She crashed to the ground, along with half the contents of the shelf. Her sharp yelp was cut off when her head hit the concrete floor with a sickening thud.

A couple of seconds ticked by in silence while Theo stood frozen, staring at her motionless, crumpled body. From beneath her dark hair, a small puddle of blood emerged.

Casey's stomach turned over.

Then Maria gave a low moan and moved one arm. When Theo took a step towards her, Casey tensed. *Now!*

She surged forward and drove a hard kick into the back of his knee. With a grunt of surprise, he toppled forward, dropping the pistol. It skittered away, just beyond his reach. Casey lunged for the gun.

Before she could grab it, Grace jumped in. Pulling a broom from a bucket next to the door, she hit Theo in the head with the handle. "You hurt Maria! I hate you!"

He raised his left arm to block the blows while he snagged his gun with his right hand. With a curse, he yanked the broom from Grace's hands, flung it aside, and staggered to his feet. He faced them, his features contorted by rage. "You're both as crazy as that freaking monkey!"

Casey shoved Grace behind her back. Theo looked like a man over the edge. His black eyes burned with fury, and he was waving the pistol in wild, sweeping motions. If it went off—accidentally or on purpose—within the tight confines of the storage closet, any of them might be killed or seriously injured.

He continued his rant. "Why couldn't you just do as you're told? I never wanted to hurt you. I just want the boat."

The situation was deteriorating rapidly. A few more minutes, and Theo might convince himself his only option was to kill them all. Offering one hand in a conciliatory gesture, she kept her voice low and non-threatening. "It's not too late. Nothing has changed. You can still get the boat. I'm sure Professor Bainbridge has freed himself and is at the Near Eastern Institute right now."

Theo's glance bounced around the room as if he needed an outlet for his agitation while his brain tried to focus. "Yeah, you might be right. I've got to get over there."

He pushed past her and opened the door. A second after he slammed the door, Casey heard a soft click as he locked them in.

She was trapped in an underground storage room with a badly injured woman and frightened child. Then she remembered the phone in her pocket, and her pulse surged. With a quick prayer, she pulled it out and stared at it for a second, willing it to work, then swore softly.

No signal.

**\*\*\*\***

Alec winced as the metal handcuffs bit into the flesh of his wrists, and cursed Theo for the hundredth time. Why did the bastard have to cuff his hands behind his back? Did he really expect him to be able to free himself and get to the NEI sometime this week?

Unlocking the cuffs would have been hard enough if they'd been in front. Holding the tiny key in his fingers and searching for a hole he could neither see nor feel was nearly impossible. After dropping the key for the second time, he'd figured out it was a lot easier if he sat on the coffee table. That way he could feel around until he found the key without having to crawl on his knees on the floor to pick it up.

He cast another nervous glance at the clock on the mantel. Theo had been gone with Casey, Grace, and Maria for almost half an hour. Hopefully he hadn't taken them far.

The key dropped to the table with a soft metallic ring...again. *Son of a—* Why couldn't he open the freaking handcuffs?

He held the key pinched between his thumb and forefinger. His eyes were closed in concentration, as he tried again to fit it into the tiny hole.

When a soft creak sounded from the front door, his eyes popped open, and his heart paused before responding with a big thump. Was Theo back? Maybe one of the neighbors had noticed something wrong and called the police. But there were no footsteps, no voices. Only a faint skittering sound, like the rustle of dry leaves.

Suddenly Balthazar appeared in front of him and began bouncing up and down and chattering excitedly. The monkey's agitation honed Alec's already razor-sharp nerves. He rattled the handcuffs as his frustration escalated.

At the clinking sound of the metal links, Balthazar stilled and cocked his head. Alec rattled the cuffs again. The monkey had already proven adept at opening the lock on his cage. Was there a chance he might be able to unlock the cuffs?

With a gleeful cackle, Balthazar hopped up on the coffee table. Alec waved the key behind his back, hoping to attract the monkey's attention. A second later, he felt the brush of the monkey's fingers as Balthazar plucked the key from his hand.

He held his hands as still as he could. "Put it in the lock, just like your cage," he encouraged. "You can do it."

Small, furry paws brushed his hands, and the metal key scraped against the cuffs. After what was probably no more a minute, he was rewarded by a soft click. The cuffs released, and he threw them to the floor. Balthazar jumped up and down on the coffee table, celebrating his feat.

Alec swept him up. "Thanks for that. You're on the road to redeeming yourself."

The monkey answered with a spate of excited chittering.

"Yeah, yeah. I get it. You did a great job. You're the hero. But I've got to find Casey and Grace, so it's time for you to go back in your cage."

The monkey wriggled free and ran to the door.

Alec darted after him. "Come back here. I don't have time to chase you now."

Balthazar eluded him and ran out onto the front porch, still rattling away in monkey-speak.

Alec blew out a frustrated breath. "Look, I've got to get some clothes on. If you're not back inside in two minutes, you're on your own." When the monkey stared at him and blinked, he shrugged. "Have it your way."

He turned and loped up the stairs two at a time. While he dragged on jeans, heavy socks, and a sweatshirt, his mind was on the women and Grace. *Where could Theo have taken them?* He grabbed his phone and keys off the dresser and headed back toward the stairs. When he passed Casey's room, he paused. *Her gun. I might need her gun.*

She kept it unloaded and locked in her suitcase, along with the ammunition. But first he had to find the key. A quick scan of the room located her purse. He dumped the contents on the bed and snatched up the keys, then hauled the suitcase from the floor of the closet, unlocked it, grabbed her pistol and the loaded clip, and headed downstairs.

Balthazar was still on the front porch when Alec stepped outside, zipping his parka. He stowed the gun in his pocket and eyed the monkey. "Last chance to spend the rest of the night in a nice warm house, bud. What do you say?"

Balthazar shrieked and ran half-way down the front walk, where he stopped, turned, and shrieked again.

Alec turned and locked the door. "Okay. If you freeze, it's your own fault."

He started down the walk then realized he had no idea where he was going, no plan. He pulled out his phone to call the police, then he thought of Casey's employer, Madelyn Li. It might be three in the morning, but he felt certain she would want to know her employee had been kidnapped. Besides, as a former FBI special agent, Ms. Li would be much better equipped to deal with this situation that he was. He searched the phone for the agency number.

Balthazar waited at the front gate, but when Alec stopped, he squawked, ran back, and yanked on the leg of Alec's jeans.

Alec tried to shake him loose. "Knock it off. I've got to make a call." The monkey held his death grip on the denim and continued to chatter. "Shut up. Just because you unlocked the cuffs doesn't mean you're in charge here."

Balthazar refused to be quiet, so Alec ignored him. He found the number, dialed, and got the agency answering machine. With no other options, he left a message, along with his number, and disconnected.

*Now what? Oh, yeah, the police.*

He'd only gotten as far as the *nine* when Balthazar's wild frenzy became too loud to ignore. Alec scowled at the frantic monkey. "Will you shut up, you little maniac! I'm trying to get us some help."

Balthazar released him, ran a couple of feet toward the street, then turned and shrieked again. When Alec didn't move, he raced back, pulled on Alec's pant leg again, then ran back toward the gate.

*What the – ?* Alec's scowl deepened. "Are you trying to tell me something? Do you have some idea where he took them?"

The monkey screeched, ran out the gate onto the sidewalk, and screeched again.

Alec strode after him. "Okay, I'm coming, but you'd better not be yanking my chain."

Balthazar scampered down the sidewalk, heading toward campus with Alec in close pursuit. He stayed about eight feet ahead and seemed to know exactly where he was going. As they turned the second corner, Alec's phone went off in his pocket.

He pulled it out. "Yes?"

"Professor Bainbridge, this is Madelyn Li." She sounded wide awake and in full professional mode.

Keeping his eyes on Balthazar, he filled her in on what had happened, as quickly and concisely as possible.

"And you say you're following a monkey?" Her voice was skeptical.

"Yes. I believe he may have followed the abductor's car."

There was a pause, then he heard her talking to someone in the background before coming back on the line. "Excuse me. I've asked my husband to reach out to my contact at the FBI. We're on our way now. I assume you've called the police."

"Not yet. I was about to."

"I'll notify them. Are you in a car?"

Alec hurried toward Balthazar, who had stopped a half-block ahead. "No. On foot."

"Okay. Please stay on the line if you can and keep me updated as to your location. It will make it easier to connect once we reach the university."

He heard a muted thud like a car door slamming, then Madelyn's voice came back with a different, breathier tone, as if there were some level of interference. She must have switched to Bluetooth in the car. "No traffic to speak of on Lake Shore Drive at this hour. We're about fifteen minutes out."

He continued to follow Balthazar toward the center of campus, updating Madelyn on his location at every intersection. The monkey had stopped his chatter. He seemed focused and intent as he raced down the sidewalks, stopping occasionally to check that Alec was still behind him but never allowing him to catch up. When they reached the old gymnasium, he scampered to the side door and began chittering wildly.

Alec halted, his breath coming in short pants. "What is it? Are they in there?"

Balthazar responded by jumping up and swinging from the door handle.

Madelyn's distant voice sounded from the phone in his hand. "Professor Bainbridge, we've just passed the Near Eastern Institute. Where are you now?"

He raised the phone to his ear. "About a block away. At the side door of the old gym, corner of Fifty-Sixth and University."

"Hold on. Campus police are nearly there. The Chicago PD and a pair of agents from the Bureau are on their way, too. We'll be with you in a couple of minutes."

Alec's pulse pounded in his ears, and his muscles twitched. Despite Madelyn's instructions, he couldn't *hold on* another second. Balthazar released the door handle and dropped to the concrete walk. With a sudden burst of chatter, he launched himself at Alec's chest, clinging to his coat and vocalizing wildly.

Alec muttered a curse as he pried the tiny fingers loose, but Balthazar refused to get down. The monkey scrambled nimbly over Alec's shoulder onto his back, where he attached himself like a wad of gum and released another boisterous barrage.

Alec turned his head, casting a determined glance over his shoulder. "You're right. We're not waiting. They'll find us. We're going in."

# CHAPTER EIGHTEEN

Alec tested the handle and breathed a swift sigh of relief when it depressed easily. He pulled the heavy metal door open slowly, expecting an alarm to start clanging. When nothing happened, he stepped inside into a stairwell.

*Which way now? Up or down?*

Balthazar was no help. He remained on Alec's back, muttering to himself but giving no direction. Alec analyzed the situation for a couple of seconds. The main floor contained the actual gymnasium, and the second level had an elevated running track, but the basements of these old buildings were often rabbit warrens of small rooms—perfect for hiding hostages. Unfortunately, that meant they were equally difficult to search. Down it was.

He took the stairs to the basement two at a time with Balthazar clinging to his back. When he reached the bottom, he was confronted by a closed door and two passageways. One hall was dark, but a string of low wattage ceiling lights lit the other, so he chose it.

The narrow, tile-lined tunnel seemed to go on forever, and he had to bend to keep from banging his head on the collection of pipes overhead. Instinct urged him to call out to Grace and Casey, but Theo might still be with them. Although Alec had Casey's pistol in his pocket, he decided it would be smarter to retain the element of surprise. While part of him relished the idea of a showdown, any confrontation could put the captives at risk.

Miraculously, Balthazar remained silent as Alec picked his way down the tunnel as quietly as possible, stopping every twenty feet or so to listen for voices or other sounds that might indicate the presence of his quarry. After he'd gone about a hundred feet, a faint, metallic banging caught his attention. He paused and held his breath. When the noise sounded again, he followed it down the dimly lit corridor. After he'd gone another twenty feet, the clanging grew louder and was joined by the muffled sound of voices calling for help.

He abandoned any thought of stealth and sprinted down the tunnel. With every pounding step, the noise grew louder and more distinct. He spotted a door up ahead and ran toward it.

"Help! Help!"

Even through the heavy metal, he recognized Casey's voice.

"Uncle Alec!"

Balthazar screeched in response to Grace's cry.

Alec banged on the door with his fist. "Hang on! I'm here!"

"Theo locked us in and took the key," Casey called out.

ALISON HENDERSON

He cast a frantic glance around the yellow-tiled tunnel. He had Casey's gun, but he wasn't about to fire with the most important people in the world on the other side of the door. Then he spotted a fire extinguisher attached to the wall several feet away. Next to it, a glass-fronted cabinet held a red fire axe. He expected to have to break the glass, but when he tried the door it was unlocked. The axe came free with one hard jerk.

He turned his head to the monkey literally on his back. "Time to get down, bud. I can't swing this thing with you there."

Balthazar cocked his head twice then released Alec and leapt to the floor. He positioned himself a few feet from the door and settled into a tense crouch, ready to spring into action.

Alec hefted the axe in both hands and eyed the lock. "Stand back!"

The first blow glanced off the door a couple of inches above the knob, sending reverberations through his hands and arms, almost causing him to drop the axe. He shook his arms and shoulders then raised the axe again. This time the blade hit the knob square-on, shearing it off. He tossed the axe aside and shouted, "Push hard!"

After a couple of blows from the other side, the door swung open, and Casey and Grace stood in the opening. Grace was in tears. He rushed in and swept them both up, one in each arm. He squeezed Grace and pressed a smacking kiss against her salty cheek. "I'm so glad to see you, kiddo."

Her arms tightened as she pressed her face against his neck. "I was scared."

"Me, too, but everything's all right now." He hugged her again before setting her down.

Balthazar had joined them, and as soon as Grace's feet touched the ground, he chortled and leapt into her arms. She grinned and gave an answering squeal.

Alec turned to Casey, who had stepped back from his embrace, and ran a quick glance from her head to her feet and back. "Are you okay?"

"I'm better now, but—" She turned toward the prone figure on the floor. "—I'm afraid Maria is seriously injured. We need an ambulance right away."

His TA lay on the concrete floor, eyes closed and unmoving. At the sight of the blood pooled beneath her head, he sucked in a quick breath. While he stared, Maria stirred and moaned.

Casey knelt beside the injured woman and smoothed her hair from her forehead. "We need to get help for her, and I couldn't get a phone connection down here."

"I'll try mine." He pulled his phone from his jeans' pocket. No signal. "I'll have to go outside to call." He squeezed her shoulder. "Stay with her."

Casey nodded, her eyes worried. "Hurry. Theo did this to her. Regardless of her role in his scheme, she's a victim, too."

The moment Alec stepped out of the storeroom, a female voice called out from back down the tunnel, "Professor!" and several dark figures with flashlights broke into a jog. As they drew nearer, he recognized Madelyn Li, the owner of Phoenix, Ltd. A tall, dark-haired man accompanied her, and two campus police officers followed close on their heels.

Madelyn drew up beside him, slightly out of breath. "You were supposed to wait."

"I couldn't."

She ignored his response and leaned to the side to peer around him into the supply room. "A couple of my former colleagues from the FBI are almost here, as well as a CPD squad car, but the situation appears to be under control."

Casey stepped into view and took Grace's free hand. "We're both fine."

"Good." Madelyn gestured to the tall man beside her. "This is my husband Carter Devlin, and these are Officers Harrison and Muldoon." Carter shook Casey and Alec's hands, and the officers nodded in acknowledgement.

Casey turned and gestured toward the woman lying on the floor. "I'm afraid Professor Bainbridge's teaching assistant needs medical assistance right away."

Maria moaned. Her eyes fluttered open, and she struggled to speak. "What...oooo."

The younger of the two cops, Officer Harrison, pushed past the others and knelt beside her. "Don't move, miss. We're getting help for you." He reached for his radio and relayed the details to the dispatcher then disconnected. "An ambulance from University Hospital should be here within five minutes."

"Theo hurt Maria."

The adults turned in unison at the sound of the small voice. Grace clung to Casey's hand with Balthazar draped around her like a security blanket.

"I hit him with a stick." She met Alec's gaze with defiance. "And I'm not sorry."

His heart twisted at the thought of his baby being forced into a situation where she felt she had to defend herself or her friends. He squatted beside her and caressed her hair. "You have nothing to be sorry for. Theo did some bad things."

Grace's soft little brows tightened in a frown. "At the zoo I thought he was nice, but he's not."

Alec sighed. If he'd had his way, she wouldn't have had to learn that particular lesson at the tender age of five. "I'm afraid people aren't always who they seem to be. Sometimes they pretend."

"You mean Theo was just pretending to be nice, and really he was mean all along?"

He nodded. "But you don't have to worry about him anymore." He straightened to face Madelyn and Officer Muldoon. "Does she?" His tone suggested it wasn't a question.

The solid, middle-aged cop spoke directly to Grace in a reassuring voice. "We're here to make sure nobody has to worry about Theo Fotopoulos ever again."

Grace bounced her chin in a decisive nod. "Good."

The officer turned to Alec and pulled a notepad and pen from his inside jacket pocket. "Ms. Li gave us a brief description of the events, but we'll need the details of everything that happened tonight from you and Ms. Callahan."

"Can't that wait?" Alec's sharp question belied his growing agitation. Grace and Casey might be safe, but the nightmare wasn't over. "I'm supposed to get the Fassbender boat and leave it in one of the museum galleries at the NEI."

The cop regarded him with a frown. "What do this kidnapping and assault have to do with a boat?"

"It's complicated, but the Fassbender boat is a valuable ancient Egyptian artifact. Fotopoulos intends to steal it, and if I don't bring it to the museum on time, he'll disappear and we may not get another opportunity to catch him."

Muldoon didn't appear convinced. "If he wants it bad enough, he'll wait."

"We can't be sure of that. It's got to be what...four o'clock already? If I don't show up with the boat, Theo will figure he's missed his chance and take off."

Before he could make his case further, voices sounded in the hall, and a team of paramedics, male and female, appeared with a stretcher. Alec picked up Grace and Balthazar and stepped into the corridor — along with Casey, Muldoon, and Madelyn — to give the EMTs room to assess their patient, while Officer Harrison stayed with Maria.

Casey gripped his arm. "You go." Her voice was low, laced with an undercurrent of urgency. "I'll stay here with Grace and give Officer Muldoon his statement."

"Are you sure?"

She nodded.

"I have to see this through to the end. After what Theo did to us, I can't let him get away."

Her fingers tightened in a reassuring squeeze. "I know, and we'll be fine. Go do what you have to do, and don't worry about us. I want to be sure Maria is going to be all right."

He hesitated then transferred Grace, along with Balthazar, into Casey's arms. He was torn between an overwhelming desire to never let either of them out of his sight again and his need to see Theo brought to justice.

As she settled the little girl on one hip, anxiety flashed in Casey's eyes. "Alec, promise me you'll be careful. The man's armed, and he's hanging by a thread."

He leaned in for a quick, hard kiss and murmured, "I promise." Then he turned and sprinted down the tunnel toward the exit.

Rapid footsteps pounded the floor behind him, and Madelyn's voice echoed through the corridor. "Don't worry. We'll go with him. I'll have the FBI and CPD meet us at the Institute."

Madelyn and Carter caught up with him at the gymnasium side door. When Alec charged ahead down the walk, she grabbed his sleeve. "Hold on. We need a plan."

He jerked free and increased his pace to a jog. "My plan is to catch Fotopoulos with the boat and make sure he pays for everything he's done."

Despite her shorter legs, Madelyn matched his pace. "We'll need to coordinate with the FBI and the CPD officers when we reach the Institute and determine who has jurisdiction."

"I don't care who arrests him, as long as he leaves the building in handcuffs." He glanced both ways across the empty intersection and sprinted across the street.

The NEI loomed ahead on the next corner, its ivy-covered stone foreboding in the pre-dawn gloom. Streetlights provided regular bursts of yellow light down the length of the street, but the bulk of the building receded into shadow.

When they reached the front steps, Madelyn stopped. "Before we go inside, I need to know what you're planning to do."

He nodded, his mind churning. "I'll go in alone while you two wait here for backup — the police or FBI, whoever shows up first. I'll go downstairs, pick up the boat, and take it to the drop-off point. Theo should be in the building by now, but he won't show himself until he sees the boat. If help arrives in the next ten minutes, meet me in the corridor outside the Egyptian gallery. It's through the large double bronze doors in the main foyer."

"My FBI contact texted me while we were on our way here. They're only a couple of blocks away. We'll find your location." Madelyn reached into her bag, pulled out a small, high-powered flashlight, and handed it to him. "You'd better take this."

He accepted it without comment. At least he'd grabbed Casey's gun. He hoped he wouldn't need it, but he refused to be caught helpless again.

Alec bounded up the front steps, pulled his keys from his pocket, and unlocked one of the front doors. It swung open easily and silently on well-oiled hinges.

The large, two-story lobby was dark and silent. As Alec had expected, Theo must have disabled the alarm system. Light from the street lamps outside shone through the leaded-glass windows, casting oblong patterns across the speckled terrazzo floor. A few emergency lights provided the only interior illumination.

Now that he was alone, he made no effort to hide his presence as he walked down the main stairs to the basement. He wanted Theo to know he had arrived and was on his way to get the boat, as directed. Knowing he was so close to achieving his goal would help keep the man's attention focused.

When Alec reached the lower level hallway, he switched on the flashlight. As he headed for the door to the archives, he strained his ears for any sound. Just because Theo had instructed him to leave the boat in the museum gallery didn't mean the thief intended to follow his own plan. He could just as easily jump Alec the moment he unlocked the door, snatch the boat, and run.

It took three tries to get the combination of the lock right. He shouldn't be nervous — Grace and Casey were out of danger — but he was. The Fassbender boat was a rare and beautiful artifact, and he didn't want to risk it being damaged or destroyed, but he also didn't want Theo to get away unpunished.

As the lock clicked open, he shot one last glance over his shoulder. Seeing no sign of anyone, he opened the door, slipped inside, and locked it behind him. He followed the flashlight's beam to the location on the shelves where the boat rested.

As he viewed the bulky, custom-made container, trying to figure out how to carry both it and the flashlight, an idea struck him. Theo hadn't said anything about removing the boat from the case. If he saw the box sitting on the bench in the museum gallery, he'd have no reason to question whether the boat was inside.

Alec removed the boat, set it gingerly on the shelf, and hefted the empty case. Confident in his plan, he locked the archive and strode down the hall toward the stairs.

When he reached the main foyer, he headed directly for the doors that led to the interior galleries of the museum. The doors swung open silently despite their weight. Up ahead he spotted several shadows in the corridor outside the entrance to the Egyptian gallery.

When he stopped outside the gallery, the shadows detached from the wall. Two stony-faced men had joined Madelyn and Carter. Since they were wearing business suits at four o'clock on a Sunday morning, they had to be from the Bureau.

Alec drew a deep breath and squared his shoulders before going in. *This is it. We're going to catch this bastard and end the nightmare once and for all.*

Carrying the box in front of him, he walked through the entrance and into the gallery. He hoped to draw Theo's attention and allow the others to slip into the room unnoticed. Although he held the flashlight in one hand, enough ambient city light filtered through the large domed skylight to make it unnecessary.

The hairs on the back of his neck prickled as he passed between the glass-encased, elaborately painted, Middle Kingdom sarcophagus and the towering, four-thousand-year-old, polished stone statue of a lesser pharaoh. Was Theo watching?

Alec hesitated when he reached the long wooden bench at the center of the gallery. The museum was as silent as its ancient inhabitants. He glanced around, but no movement caught his eye. After setting the box on the bench, he turned and walked out the way he'd come. When he reached the doorway, he edged into the shadows behind a case filled with carved sandstone sculptures of baboons. There was nothing to do now but wait.

****

"I'm tired. I want to get Uncle Alec and go home." Grace rubbed her eyes with her fist.

Casey rotated her head and rolled her shoulders. "I know. Me, too."

The paramedics had assessed Maria before bundling her off to the hospital with Officer Harrison in attendance. Despite the fact that her head wound had nearly stopped bleeding, she needed to be evaluated for a possible skull fracture and concussion. Casey took some comfort in the fact that by the time they left, the young woman was fully conscious and talking.

When a cracking voice came over the Officer Muldoon's shoulder radio, he pushed the button to reply then listened to the response. After signing off, he flipped his notebook shut. "I've got enough information for now. You and Professor Bainbridge can stop by the station later and give a complete statement to one of the detectives. I need to get over to the NEI to meet a couple of CPD squad cars. Campus dispatch is sending a courtesy vehicle to meet us there and drive you home."

"I want Uncle Alec." Grace's demand had changed from plaintive to insistent.

Casey understood. She wanted Alec, too. She wanted him safe and whole and out of danger. "I know. But he's doing something very important, and we have to wait until he finishes and comes home."

Muldoon held the door open for them. "Let's go." He shot a wary glance at Balthazar, who bared his teeth and nestled against Grace's chest. "But I'm not having that crazy monkey in my car."

Casey bit back a sharp retort. *That 'crazy' monkey is the only reason you found us.* Instead, she nodded and forced a tight smile. "Of course not."

"But—" Grace started to object.

She leaned close to the child's ear. "Shh. Everything will be all right. Trust me. He found us before, remember? Now, put him down."

Grace's forehead scrunched in a mutinous frown, but she loosened her hold.

"Balthazar, down." When Casey stared the monkey in the eye and pointed to the floor, he hopped down.

As they followed Officer Muldoon down the hall toward the exit, she glanced over her shoulder and crooked a finger. The monkey scampered after them. When they reached the door to the building, she checked again and spotted a pair of round, primate eyes staring at her from the shadowed stairwell. Still carrying Grace, she pushed through the door, holding it open a second longer than necessary, and a small, dark shape darted through behind her and into the shrubbery.

When they reached the patrol car parked at the curb, the officer opened the back door for her and Grace then closed it with a sold *thunk* and went around to climb in the driver's side. While Casey settled Grace and buckled her seatbelt, she spotted Balthazar crouched on the sidewalk and gave the little girl a nudge. Grace's eyes widened as soon as she saw him, but Casey placed a warning finger to her lips. Grace responded with a solemn nod. Muldoon started the engine, and they set off on the short drive to the Near Eastern Institute with the monkey in close pursuit. When they pulled up in front of the building, two other police cars were idling near the front entrance, their blue lights flashing.

Muldoon opened his door then twisted in his seat to face Casey, his stolid features set in a stern expression. "Stay in the car. Your ride will be here in a few minutes."

When she nodded, he grunted and heaved himself out, slamming the door as if to reinforce his command.

Grace wriggled in her seat. "Do we have to stay out here? I'm cold, and I want to see Uncle Alec."

"We'll be warm as soon as we get home. In the meantime, you can snuggle inside my robe." She reached across and unbuckled the child's seatbelt.

Instead of climbing onto Casey's lap, Grace stood and looked out the front windshield at the three uniformed officers huddled together in conversation on the sidewalk. Because it was a campus police car instead of a city patrol car, there was no barrier between the front and back seats, giving her a good view. Suddenly, she leaned forward and pointed. "Look, there's Balthazar!"

The monkey had tucked himself into a shadowed corner near the front steps.

The three officers finished their conversation and broke up, with two headed around the side of the building while Muldoon made his way toward the main door. When he opened the door, the monkey raced after him and darted inside, his tail disappearing just as the door closed.

Grace jumped up and down in alarm. "We have to get him!" Without warning, she scooted into the front seat and grabbed the door handle.

"No!" Casey made a grab for her. "Grace, stop!"

But the child was too quick. In a split second she was out the car door and running up the steps.

In a panic, Casey flicked open the latch on her seatbelt and reached for the door handle, but the panel her fingers touched was smooth. Her pulse shot up. Of course. She was in the back seat of a cop car. The only way out was over the seat and out the front door.

She grabbed the back of the seat and scrambled over. Seconds later, she hit the pavement running just as Grace pulled the big oak door open. Casey raced up the steps, but when she stepped inside the cavernous foyer, there was no sign of the child.

A soft sound echoed across the vaulted stone space as a pair of large bronze doors closed. She ran to them and pulled them open. A few yards ahead, two small figures walked down the dim passageway, hand in hand.

Unconcerned about the slapping sound of her sneakers against the hard floor, Casey sprinted up and grabbed Grace's free hand. "What do you think you're doing?" Her furious whisper echoed through the empty hall.

"I had to get Balthazar." The monkey grinned at the sound of his name.

"We have to leave. Come on."

"But Uncle Alec is in there." Grace pointed to a large open doorway.

The first thing Casey saw when she glanced into the room was a monumental statue of the jackal-headed god Anubis. Of course, Grace would know the location of the Egyptian Gallery. She practically grew up at the Institute.

From where they stood, she had an unobstructed view between the glass-fronted display cases and dark, hulking statues to a large oblong box sitting on the bench in the center of the gallery. It must be the Fassbender boat. Apparently, Theo hadn't shown up yet.

The light filtering through the skylight cast deep shadows around each structure in the gallery. Were Alec, Madelyn, and the others hiding somewhere inside? If so, no hint of sound or movement gave away their positions. Wherever they were, Casey needed to find a safe hiding place. She couldn't risk Theo finding her and Grace in the hall. She gave the little girl's hand a warning squeeze then guided her into the room. They inched their way around the perimeter in the dark until she found a spot where she could watch the bench unseen and settled in to wait.

A few minutes later, a male figure materialized from the gloom deep in the gallery. She recognized Theo's build and gait as he made his way to the bench and picked up the box. The bloody kitchen towel was still wrapped around his right wrist. He hoisted the crate under his left arm and turned to leave.

Before he took a second step, Alec's voice echoed through the hall. "Put the box down."

# CHAPTER NINETEEN

Casey held her breath as Alec emerged from behind a monumental stele carved with hieroglyphs, followed by Madelyn and her husband. Where were the FBI agents and the cops?

With long, firm steps Alec strode toward Theo while the other two held back, blocking the way to the main exit from the gallery. "You're not going anywhere."

Her pulse shot up when she realized he was holding her gun. He must have gotten it from her suitcase before coming after them.

Theo's lip curled, and he released a short laugh. "You are not going to shoot me, Professor. Now, get out of my way. I have a plane to catch."

Alec took a step forward and raised his weapon. "You underestimate me. There's no way I'm letting you walk out of here after what you've done to my family, not to mention Maria."

Theo snorted. "She was a tool, that's all."

A deep growl emerged from Alec's throat as he took another step. Theo pulled his pistol from his jacket pocket with his injured hand and pointed it at Alec. "Back up or I'll shoot. I swear." His voice rose with each word.

"Drop your weapons, both of you." Officer Muldoon emerged from behind a display case with his service revolver drawn.

As Alec bent to set his pistol on the floor, Theo surged forward, slamming the heavy wooden container into his shoulder and knocking him to his knees.

"Uncle Alec!" Grace jerked her hand from Casey's and ran toward her uncle. Casey raced after her.

Theo shoved past them and was on his way toward the gallery entrance and freedom when a small figure flew out of the darkness and landed on the back of his head with a blood-curdling shriek. He dropped the box and waved his arms wildly, trying to dislodge the attacker, but Balthazar evaded him. He clung to the man's shoulders with his back paws, cackling with glee as he grabbed both of Theo's ears with strong fingers and gave them a violent twist.

"Aaagh! Get this monster off me!" Gun still in hand, Theo continued to bat at the monkey in a frantic effort to free himself.

Casey shot a quick glance around the room. Alec sat on the floor holding Grace, and Muldoon had stooped to pick up his discarded weapon. Madelyn and Carter were advancing cautiously, but she was closest to the fracas.

This needed to end, and it needed to end now.

Theo was still thrashing around in incoherent rage with the vengeful primate clinging to his head when she ran up behind him and shoved him hard in the middle of his back, toppling him forward. As soon as his knees hit the ground, the pistol clattered to the floor and Balthazar hopped off.

Officer Muldoon reached them a split second later, snatched up the gun, and shoved Theo to the floor face-first. In one practiced movement, he pulled the handcuffs from his belt and clapped them on his suspect before hauling him to his feet. Balthazar stood beside him, bouncing up and down and pumping both fists in the air like a victorious prizefighter.

With Theo in custody, Casey had turned to rejoin Alec and Grace when the overhead lights flared, and Fermin LeBlanc strolled into the gallery. Despite the hour, he was impeccable in black trousers and a black-and-white tweed jacket, accented by a maroon cashmere scarf. In deference to the weather, he also wore black leather gloves and a black fedora.

Alec pushed to his feet with an annoyed frown. "Fermin, what on earth are you doing here at four in the morning?"

A condescending smile appeared on the man's face as his right hand slipped into his jacket pocket and emerged holding a shiny silver automatic pistol. "I've come to finish what this fool—" He waved the pistol in Theo's general direction. "—could not."

"What? You mean—"

Fermin's smile became oilier. "That's right. You didn't really believe he could design and execute such a complex plan on his own, did you?"

Theo tugged against his restraints. "Hey—"

"Shut up," Fermin snapped. "I'm sorry I let your uncle talk me into using my connections at the university to get you a position on the campus police force. He'll be very disappointed when I tell him about your performance."

"But I—"

"Not another word." Fermin dismissed his co-conspirator and aimed his gun at the center of Alec's chest. "Now, Bainbridge, you are going to bring me the boat, then I'll be out of here, and you can all get on with your lives."

"Sounds good to me." Alec smiled and started toward the box, which lay on its side on the floor near Theo and Muldoon. He stooped to scoop up the box before heading back to Fermin.

As he passed Officer Muldoon, the cop raised an arm to block his way.

"It's all right, officer. Trust me."

A glanced passed between them, and Muldoon dropped his arm.

Alec marched up to Fermin and thrust the box toward him with a smile. "Here you go."

Fermin reached for it with his left hand. He bobbled the case a couple of times while trying to keep the gun trained on Alec, but ultimately managed to get a satisfactory grip. "Thank you, Bainbridge. I'll be going now."

"Professor," Theo raised his wrists and rattled the cuffs.

Fermin dismissed him with a short laugh. "I'm afraid you'll be staying right where you are."

"After everything I've done, you've got to take me with you." Theo's tone became more urgent. "Do you know what they'll to do to me?"

"Nothing more than you deserve. You are a thief and a kidnapper, after all." Fermin edged toward the broad gallery entrance, keeping his weapon trained on the group inside.

"My uncle will kill you!" Theo bellowed in rage.

"Of course, he won't, you silly boy. You might be family, but this is business. He'll pay me enough for this boat to retire comfortably to a nice little island with no extradition treaty."

"Not so fast, Professor." A short, sturdy, female figure stepped into the arched opening, flanked by two men in suits.

"Nora?" Alec's voice rose in stark incredulity.

Casey peered at the men beside the NEI secretary. In unison, they pushed aside their jackets and grasped the butts of official-looking firearms.

Fermin curled his upper lip in a snarl and waved his pistol. "I don't know who you think you are, or what you're doing here, but get out of my way."

Nora produced a black leather ID holder and flashed her credentials. "I'm Nora Samuels with the FBI Art Theft Program, and these are Special Agents O'Rourke and Gustafson of the Chicago Field Office. What have you got there, Professor LeBlanc?"

Fermin shot a nervous glance between the agents, who filled the entranceway, as his weapon wavered. "You know very well what I have. Now step aside, or I'll smash this box, destroying the Fassbender boat and creating an international incident."

"You're not going to do that." Nora's gaze remained calm, but steely.

"I will if you push me too far!" But instead of advancing, Fermin retreated a step.

"I don't think so, Professor." Officer Muldoon, who had approached silently from behind, reached forward and jerked the gun from his hand.

As soon as he was disarmed, Nora and the agents marched forward and seized the box before slapping a pair of handcuffs on Fermin.

"Wait a minute." Alec approached Nora. "Before you take him away, I want him to get a good look inside. After all, he destroyed his life to steal it." He took the case and opened it, holding it in front of Fermin's face.

Stunned silence greeted the sight of the empty box.

"Where is the Fassbender boat?" Nora's brusque question demanded an immediate response.

"Safely locked in the archives where it belongs." Alec's voice held a note of triumph as he narrowed his gaze on Fermin. "You didn't really think I would turn a valuable antiquity over to an extortionist and thief, did you? Especially one who wasn't smart enough to make sure he had the real thing." He shook the empty case under Fermin's nose. "This is what you threatened my family for, you weasel. Nothing."

Faced with the extent of his failure, the dapper little man deflated, becoming visibly smaller and more pathetic. The pair of FBI agents each took an arm and hauled him out of the exhibit hall.

As Casey stared after them, the last flicker of her nervous energy winked out. Her limbs felt both leaden and weightless at the same time. It was over. Their long, terrifying ordeal was finally over. When she swayed, an arm came around her middle to steady her, and she melted against Alec's side. Grace had wrapped herself around his leg, and Balthazar clung to her.

Nora Samuels approached Alec with a look of satisfied determination. "I'm sorry to have kept you in the dark, Professor Bainbridge, but it was necessary for the success of the operation."

He stiffened. "What exactly was this *operation?*"

"Our team has had its eye on Fermin LeBlanc for several months. He was suspected of being the primary U.S. contact for a major antiquities smuggler and middleman located in Cyprus."

"That must have been the uncle Theo mentioned."

Nora nodded. "Shortly after Ernest Fassbender bequeathed his boat to the NEI, we received information from INTERPOL indicating Cyril Fotopoulos had an order for it from a shadowy Middle Eastern collector. I was assigned to prevent that transfer from occurring."

"You could have told me upfront. I would have taken extra precautions."

"It would have been inappropriate and potentially dangerous to have shared the details of the operation with a civilian."

"Dangerous!" He snorted. "It's hard to believe it could have been any more dangerous than leaving me in the dark. Tell me, was endangering my family part of your operation?"

"No." She dropped her gaze to her sensible black sneakers before lifting her chin to face his angry glare. "Absolutely not. If I'd had any indication—" Her expression softened when she glanced at Grace. "We had no idea he would go to such lengths."

"You clearly didn't know your man."

"Clearly not. And that's regrettable. I apologize on behalf of the Bureau."

Alec ran his free hand through his hair and blew out a frustrated breath. "All I want to do now is take my family home."

When he tightened his grip on Casey's waist, her heart did a little flip-flop.

Madelyn and Carter had been watching from the sidelines, but now she stepped forward and offered her hand. "Special Agent Samuels, we haven't met, but I'm Madelyn Li, formerly with the Bureau and now owner of Phoenix, Ltd. Personal Protection Agency. I'm Ms. Callahan's employer."

Nora shook her hand with a brisk nod of acknowledgement. "The Special-Agent-In-Charge of the local field office mentioned you."

"My clients have been through a horrible experience tonight, and I'd like to take them home. I'm sure you'll want to speak with them further, but there will be plenty of time for that after they've rested."

"Of course." Nora offered her hand to Alec. "I apologize again, Professor, for everything you and your niece have been through. We'll be in touch."

He hesitated for a moment then accepted her hand. "Give us a couple of days, if you can."

"I'm sure that will be fine. We have quite a few questions for Mr. Fotopoulos and Professor LeBlanc first."

As Nora left to talk to Officer Muldoon, who still held Theo by the arm, Madelyn turned to Alec. "Our car is right outside."

He hefted Grace onto one hip and guided Casey with the other arm out of the gallery, through the lobby, and out the main door to the black Town Car parked at the curb. Carter unlocked the car, and he and Madelyn climbed into the front seat, leaving Alec to load his crew into the back.

Grace stirred on his shoulder. "That's the zoo car."

Casey smiled and rubbed her back. "Yes, it is. Didn't we have fun with the penguins that day?" She slid into the back seat and reached for the child. Alec handed Grace to her before climbing in. Balthazar clung tight, refusing to be separated from his best friend.

As Casey fussed with her seatbelt, Grace crossed her arms. "I wish we'd never gone to the zoo. That's where we met Theo, and he's mean."

"He is mean," Casey agreed. "But you don't have to worry about him anymore. You'll never see him again."

Grace snuggled against Casey's soft robe. "Thank goodness."

By the time they arrived home, both she and the monkey were sound asleep. Alec maneuvered them both out of the car and carried them up the walk to the front door, while Casey paused for a quick word with her boss.

Madelyn smiled. "Good work, Callahan."

Was it? Casey had her doubts. True, they were all safe and the criminals were in custody, but Grace had been through a terrifying experience.

Madelyn shot her a shrewd glance. "Stop it. Your client is unharmed. You did your job."

"I did my best."

"You did all anyone could have done." Madelyn's voice was firm.

"Not by myself."

"How many cases have you helped with since you joined Phoenix, Ltd.?"

Casey did a quick accounting in her mind. "Maybe half a dozen."

"And did any single agent handle the entire job alone?"

"No."

"We back each other up. That's what we do. And we bring in outside help when we need it. Now go inside and get some sleep—unless you'd prefer to be dropped at your own apartment."

"No. Everything I need is here." As soon as the words left her mouth, she recognized the truth of them.

"Good. We'll talk in a couple of days." The window glided up as the dark car pulled away from the curb.

Casey dragged herself up the front steps. She felt hollow. The job was over, and she would be on a flight to Boston Monday morning. Whether she got the job at the Wiseman Institute or not, she would be leaving Alec and Grace.

She closed the front door and locked it behind her. Soft footsteps sounded overhead. Alec must be putting Grace to bed. Although the sky had already started to lighten, the soft pillow and fluffy comforter waiting upstairs called to her like a siren. Her eyes burned, and her back and shoulders ached. After the events of the past few hours, the need to sleep was overwhelming.

She climbed the stairs as quietly as she could but was too tired to put much energy into the effort. At the top she found Alec waiting for her.

"Grace and Balthazar are sound asleep in her bed." His raspy whisper sent a tiny sizzle up her spine. "I didn't have the heart to separate them."

When his arm came around her, she snuggled against his side, pressing her cheek to the soft fabric of his sweatshirt. "I never would have believed it, but that psycho little monkey really came through."

"He loves Grace."

"We all do." *And I love you, too.*

Alec sighed and drew her closer, wrapping his other arm around her and resting his chin on her head. "Yes."

They stood together in the early morning gloom as the antique mantel clock in the living room ticked off the seconds with rhythmic clicks. Finally, he loosened his hold. "We should try to get some sleep."

Casey eased back and nodded. She'd felt so warm, so comforted in his embrace, she was surprised she hadn't dozed off standing up.

He reached for her hand and took a step toward his bedroom. "Come with me."

Something in the back of her mind resisted, but her thoughts were too jumbled to determine exactly what.

"We're both exhausted. Right now, I just need to hold you," he said. "We'll deal with everything else later."

*Later.* That sounded good. She raised her chin. His dark blue eyes appeared almost black in the dim light of the hall, and the deep hollows around them spoke of worry and fatigue. She raised one hand to the swollen cut on his forehead left by the butt of Theo's pistol. "Yes."

In all the time she'd worked for him, she'd never been in his bedroom. The covers on the oversized, dark wooden sleigh bed were still askew from his abrupt departure several hours earlier. He grabbed the edge of the quilt and tossed it back then turned to her and slowly untied the belt of her robe. Casey never looked away as she shrugged it to the floor and stepped out of her shoes. She shivered and felt her nipples peak beneath the thin knit of her long-sleeved t-shirt.

He stroked one hand over the curve of her shoulder. "Get in. You're getting chilled."

She slid beneath the covers and huddled on the far side of the bed while he yanked off his shoes and shed his clothes.

When he turned to face her, he was wearing only his boxers. "Is this all right? My pajamas are around here somewhere, but I'm not sure I have enough energy to hunt for them."

Faint glimmers of dawn tipped the waves of his hair with burnished gold, and shadows defined the rounded planes of his shoulders, upper arms, and chest. He was much more than all right.

She nodded.

When he climbed into bed and pulled the covers over them, she went to him as naturally as if they'd slept together for years, tucking her head into the curve of his neck and shoulder. He smelled of warm man, earthy but not pungent, a smell all his own.

He adjusted his hold and pressed a kiss to her hair. "Sleep now."

And she did.

Sometime later she awoke with a start to thin sunlight filtering through the window. Her heart jumped.

*What time is it? Grace could be up and in here any second!*

Beside her Alec stirred and mumbled something unintelligible. His hair was tousled, and tawny stubble darkened his chin and jaw. The temptation to curl back up beside him nearly overwhelmed her. She beat it back and sat up. "I've got to go."

He blinked a couple of times and focused on her face. "Where?"

She threw back the covers on her side. "To my own room. What would Grace think if she saw me here?"

He cast a quick glance at the alarm clock on his nightstand, and his hand snaked out and grasped her wrist. "It's just past seven. She was unconscious when I put her to bed. She'll be out for a couple more hours, at least. Besides, she wouldn't think anything of it. She's precocious, but not *that* precocious."

"I don't know."

"Come here." He pulled her toward him gently, but relentlessly. He rolled onto his side and brought one hand up to smooth an errant lock of hair from her face.

Casey tensed. *I must look like an extra from a zombie movie.*

Alec stroked her cheek as his sculpted lips curved in a smile that turned her insides to jelly. "You're beautiful."

She remained silent, searching his eyes for unspoken truth.

"It almost killed me when Theo took you and Grace away. You have no idea."

"I felt the same, leaving you bleeding and helpless."

"I didn't know when, or if, I would see either of you again." Remembered pain lent a rough edge to his voice.

She leaned forward and pressed a soft kiss against his mouth. "We're all safe and together now."

When a tiny voice asked, *but for how long,* she brushed it aside.

"Yes." The husky quality of his voice spoke less of pain and more of something primal and urgent. One big, warm hand glided up her thigh, across her hipbone and ribs, to settle on the mound of her breast. "This feels so good. You feel so good." He kissed her with a dizzying thoroughness then drew back. "I know we said we'd wait until the threat was over and the situation resolved to figure out what to do about this attraction between us."

She gazed into his eyes, trying to untangle the tumultuous emotions there. "I sense a *but*."

"No *buts*. I've decided. I want you. Now, later, whenever you're ready." His expression softened into a rueful smile. "Although if it's going to be later, you'd better get back to your own bed as fast as you can. I'm not a kid—I can wait—but every man has his limits." He moved against her leg to demonstrate how close that limit was.

Casey couldn't help but smile back. She'd made her decision, too—weeks ago if she was honest with herself. "I don't see any reason to wait. Grace is safe, and Theo is no longer a threat to anyone. We're both adults. We know what we're doing."

She hoped it was true.

A sound that was a cross between a groan of relief and a growl of excitement rumbled in Alec's throat before he crushed her against his chest and smothered her with a flurry of kisses. Seconds later, her t-shirt and bottoms disappeared into the depths of the bed.

Back in his arms, she closed her eyes and let her remaining senses take over. The solid muscles of his upper arm and shoulder felt smooth and warm beneath her fingertips. The skin at the hollow of his neck carried a faint tang of salt. His breath tickled her ear, accompanied by murmurs of discovery and delight.

Soon she was too caught up in the maelstrom of sensations to separate one from another. When the storm broke, every nerve ending in her body flared, like a cloud of fireflies all lighting up at once. Then bliss as she drifted into deep, satisfied comfort.

She turned her head with a sigh and smiled. "That was astounding."

His answering smile contained a hint of amusement. "Not necessarily the word I would have chosen, but it was, wasn't it?"

"I could stay here all day." She snuggled back against his side and pillowed her face on the firm muscle of his chest.

Alec's arm came around her in a natural response. "That's fine with me."

"But we shouldn't." Her breath stirred the smattering of dark gold hair on his chest.

"Probably not."

"Maybe we could sleep, though. Just for a little while."

A chuckle rumbled under her ear. "At this point, I don't see how we could avoid it."

Her last conscious perception was the feel of his lips on her forehead.

# CHAPTER TWENTY

"Uncle Alec, where's Casey?"

Casey bolted awake from a sound sleep, her pulse pounding. *Grace!* Grateful that Alec slept on the side of the bed nearest the door, she dove beneath the covers.

He mumbled and stirred before pushing up on one elbow. "Hi, kiddo. How are you feeling?"

"I'm okay." Although muffled by the quilt, Grace sounded like her usual matter-of-fact self.

Casey felt frantically around the foot of the bed for her pajamas. Alec might be confident his niece had no inkling of the birds and the bees, but Grace was an astute child, and Casey didn't relish the idea of answering tricky questions while sitting in his bed stark naked.

"Balthazar and I are hungry, and Casey isn't in her room. Do you know where she is?"

"Uh..."

*Hah! Found them!* Still hidden by the covers, she wriggled into her t-shirt and sleep pants.

"Um...she's in here." He sounded uncertain.

Casey popped her head out and peered over Alec's bare shoulder at the little girl standing beside the bed, holding Balthazar's hand. The monkey bared his teeth.

"Good morning, Grace." Her heart was racing and she was sure her face was as red as a baboon's behind, but she pasted on a big smile.

Grace hopped up on the bed, right onto Alec's stomach. He flinched and groaned in surprise then wrestled her down, making smacking sounds against her neck while Balthazar jumped up and down, chattering.

Grace giggled and sat up. Pushing her hair out of her eyes, she peered at Casey with puzzlement. "I'm hungry. Why are you in Uncle Alec's bed?"

Casey sent Alec a panicked look.

He smiled and ruffled Grace's hair. "She was cold. You two were out for a long time last night in your pajamas without your coats."

"But I wasn't too cold to sleep."

"You had Balthazar to keep you warm."

Grace pondered his explanation for a moment then nodded. "That's true. He's warm because of his fur. Anyway, we're both ready for breakfast." The monkey hopped down, and she followed.

Casey scooted out of bed. "Let me get my robe, and we'll go make pancakes. How would that be?"

"Tee-rrific! And can we have bacon?"

"We can have bacon."

"What about Balthazar?"

"He can have whatever he wants. After last night, he deserves it."

The monkey chortled his approval and ran out of the room.

As Casey stepped through the door, she turned to Alec and mouthed, *thank you*.

Amusement lit his eyes. "Anytime."

After breakfast—which was more like brunch—and long, hot showers for everyone, Alec called the hospital to check on Maria. Casey was snuggled on the living room sofa with Grace and Balthazar, reading a picture book when he strolled in.

She paused and scanned his face. "How is she?"

He sank into his leather armchair. "Holding her own. The doctor said she had a small depressed skull fracture with a blood clot and concussion, but most of the bleeding we saw was from a laceration to the scalp. She'll be in the hospital several days, but at this point they expect a full recovery."

"That's good." Another ounce of residual tension melted away. It was amazing how restorative a little good news, a couple hours sleep, a hot shower, and a bout of mind-blowing, early morning sex could be.

"The police want to speak to her as soon as the doctor gives the okay."

"Do you think she'll face charges?"

"Probably, but I would expect some leniency on the part of the court, based on the circumstances."

Casey nodded. "I hope so. I don't suppose anyone's heard anything about her sister."

"I had a text from Nora. She said Interpol had coordinated with the police in Cyprus to rescue the sister and arrest Theo's uncle."

Grace wriggled and sat up, her brows pinched in a ferocious scowl. "I'm glad the police arrested Theo. He was so mean to Maria. I hate him. I'm glad Balthazar bit him."

Casey leaned down and hugged her. "I'm glad, too."

By three o'clock, Grace was beginning to droop. Casey settled the child on her bed with her favorite CD to "rest." The little girl was asleep before the second song. Casey then headed to find Alec. With her flight only a few hours away, she couldn't put off telling him any longer.

She found him downstairs on the sofa with his feet propped up on the coffee table, watching a basketball game on television, with an open book upside down on his lap. She brushed his feet aside, picked up the remote, and switched off the TV before taking a seat beside him.

"Hey, I was watching that, and the Bulls were only up by three!"

"I need to talk to you."

His expression became wary. "Okay."

This wasn't going to be easy. She might as well dive in and get it over with. "I'm leaving in the morning."

He surged forward, knocking the book to the floor. "Leaving? What are you talking about?"

"I have a job interview in Boston on Tuesday."

Color rose in his cheeks as his eyes narrowed. "When did this happen?"

She glanced down at her hands. "I had an initial video interview a couple of months ago, before graduation, and they recently contacted me to come for a final in-person interview."

"And you didn't think to mention it before now?"

The accusation in his tone, combined with her own twinge of guilt for not telling him sooner, sparked a burst of resentment. "What would have been the point? The Wiseman Institute is a world-renowned adolescent treatment center. I don't even know if they'll offer me the job."

Alec waved one hand with a dismissive snort. "They will. You're wonderful with children."

"Thank you."

"And if they do, I assume you'll take it."

His even tone belied the hurt in his eyes. Her heart tightened. "If they offer me the job, I'll have a decision to make."

"How long will you be gone?"

"Only until Wednesday evening. Then I can pack up the rest of my things and go back to my apartment."

He settled back against the sofa, his features stony.

She reached forward and took his hand. "Alec, we both knew this day would come. The job you hired me for is over. Grace no longer needs protection. We can't go on like we have been and pretend nothing has changed. You have your life, and I need to figure out what to do with mine."

His expression warmed as his thumb stroked the soft flesh on the inside of her wrist, sending tiny thrills up her arm. "We still have things to work out between us. What about this morning?"

Heat rose up her neck into her cheeks, and she glanced down at their joined hands. "Like I said, it was astounding."

"How about we go upstairs, and I'll see if I can do better than *astounding*." He tugged her toward him.

She resisted and withdrew her hand with a rueful smile. "I'm not sure the thinking you're doing right now involves your brain."

"And you're relying on yours too much," he countered. "Why not give yourself time for a little R & R? You can decide what you want to do with your life as easily here as in your apartment."

She wondered if he had any idea how seductive his offer was. Probably. She pushed to her feet. "No, I really can't."

"What am I supposed to tell Grace?"

"Tell her the truth. She can go back to school tomorrow and won't need a nanny anymore."

"She needs you for a lot more than that, and so do I."

Her eyes suddenly smarted with incipient tears. "Stop it. You're making this very hard."

"I'm just telling the truth. You've come to mean a lot more to both of us than a bodyguard or nanny."

What was he trying to say? Her natural caution hesitated to read too much into his words. She needed time and space to sort it out. "I'm too tired to have this conversation now. We can discuss it more when I get back."

"Count on it." Alec picked up his book from the floor then straightened. "When do you leave?"

"First thing in the morning. I've called for a cab."

"From here?"

"Yes. My luggage and most of my clothes are here, so it didn't make sense to go home."

Home. Funny, she hadn't thought of her apartment as home in weeks. Alec's cozy blue Queen Anne with its creaky floorboards and old-fashioned kitchen felt more like home than that dark, stuffy little box ever had.

At dinner, Alec told Grace that Dr. Allen had called to say she would be able to go back to preschool the next day. She was thrilled and spent the rest of the meal talking about seeing her friends again and doing all the things she'd missed. He made no mention of what would happen with Casey, and his niece didn't ask. After saying a long, drawn-out good night to Balthazar, she insisted that Casey help her choose the perfect outfit to celebrate the occasion and settled on a pink-flowered tunic and red leggings because they were "happy colors."

After she settled Grace in bed and turned out the light, Casey stood in the doorway for several minutes, watching her sleep. She had spent every waking moment for several weeks caring for this beautiful, challenging, smart, and creative little bundle of energy. If Grace were gone from her life, the hole would be unfathomable.

And then there was Alec. He'd been sharp and prickly at their first meeting, but she couldn't blame him—he'd just received the letter threatening his niece. The more time they spent together, the more she saw the brilliant, serious, funny, brave man beneath his professorial persona. He might experience fear, but never for himself, only for those he loved. And there was no boundary he wouldn't breach, no limit he wouldn't exceed to protect them from harm. How could she not love him?

But did he love her? Or was he still reacting to the danger and excitement of their recent ordeal? She couldn't be sure. She'd been wrong about a man's feelings before.

Alec met her in the hall as she headed to her room. "What time do you leave in the morning?" He kept his voice low so as not to disturb Grace.

"I have an early flight. The taxi arrives at six o'clock."

"I guess you'd better turn in then."

A whisper of disappointment fluttered through her when he didn't suggest she spend the night with him. "I guess so. I still need to pack."

"When do you get home Wednesday? I'll pick you up."

"The plane is due to land around four o'clock in the afternoon, but I don't want you to fight the traffic. I'll grab a cab at the airport. With luck, I should be here around six."

"We'll be waiting."

Staring into the deep blue depths of his eyes, she believed him.

When he reached for her and pulled her to him, she didn't resist.

"While you're away, I want you to think about what we could have, think about this." He raised his hands to frame her face, and his breath warmed her lips.

His mouth captured hers gently at first, with soft, almost tentative nips, melting the cold lumps of self-doubt and indecision. After a couple of seconds, frustration pushed her to increase the pressure. He responded instantly. With a groan, his hands dropped from her face, and his arms wrapped around her back, crushing her against his chest. Amid breathless kisses, she clung to him as if her life depended on it.

She protested wordlessly when he eased his hold, but he disentangled himself and stepped back. "You should get some sleep now. I'll see you in the morning before you leave." With a quick kiss on the forehead, he turned and headed back downstairs.

Casey stared after him, uncertain whether to feel rejected, resentful, or touched by his thoughtfulness. Despite his admonition, she slept very little that night.

The next morning, long before sunrise, she tiptoed down the stairs carrying her overnight bag to find Alec waiting for her in the living room with a cup of hot coffee. She accepted the mug. "Thank you."

"You're welcome." His somber expression matched her mood.

Before she had finished half the cup, headlights flashed against the front widows. "That will be my ride." She handed the coffee back to him. "I'd better go."

He set the mug on the table and reached for her compact suitcase. "I'll carry your bag."

She slipped away before he could grab it and headed for the door. "That's okay. It doesn't weigh much. Give Grace a hug for me."

"Casey."

She hesitated then turned to meet his determined gaze. "Yes?"

"Wednesday."

That was all he said, but the single word was fraught with emotion. On the way to the airport, and later on the plane, she tried to picture what would happen when she returned. What Alec might say. How she should respond. But try as she might, she couldn't come up with a satisfactory scenario that allayed all her fears.

The same was still true Wednesday afternoon when she climbed into the cab at O'Hare. Her nerves tightened when the driver took the familiar exit off Lake Shore Drive and nearly snapped when they turned onto Alec's street. She had missed both Alec and Grace beyond measure but at the same time, was terrified to see them.

When the car pulled up in front of the big blue house, the porch light was on, and hanging over the porch was a hand-lettered paper sign, which read, *Welcome Home Casey*. A lump formed in her throat, and she blinked twice to banish incipient tears. Before she got halfway up the walk, Grace burst out of the house, ran down the steps, and threw herself into Casey's arms.

"I'm so glad you're home! Did you know Uncle Alec says Balthazar can visit us on weekends if Professor Huerta says it's okay because he saved us from Theo?"

Casey smiled, knowing what a concession that was for Alec. "That's wonderful. Balthazar was a real hero."

"And I've been back at school for three days, and our class got a new lizard in a big glass box, and I get to spend the night at Sophia's house tonight even though it's a school night!"

Casey hugged her then set her down and took her hand. Together they walked to the door where Alec waited with an enigmatic smile.

Casey suddenly felt shy. "Um...hi."

"Let me take that." He reached for her bag, and this time she let him have it. He set it in the foyer and helped her with her coat while Grace continued her non-stop monologue.

In the middle of a description of an upcoming field trip to the Museum of Science and Industry, the doorbell rang.

"I bet that's Sophia!" Grace yanked the door open to reveal Sophia and Carolyn Chiang standing on the porch.

"Are you ready to go?" Carolyn reached for her hand.

"Everything's in her backpack." Alec handed over the elephant-shaped pack, complete with flapping ears and dangling trunk.

Carolyn slung the pack over one slim shoulder and called to the girls, who were nearly to the gate, "Slow down, you two!" When she turned back, her dark eyes twinkled. "I'll take them to school in the morning, so you can relax and enjoy yourselves."

Alec leaned down and brushed a kiss against her cheek. "Thanks again."

Carolyn grinned and responded with a breezy, "Anytime."

When he closed the door, Casey eyed him with suspicion. "What did you tell her?"

"I didn't tell her anything. Carolyn's a very astute woman."

True, but his nonchalance raised her suspicions. "I need to go upstairs and freshen up."

"Take your time. Dinner will be on the table in fifteen minutes."

Alec was cooking? That ought to be interesting. She wondered if they were having frozen chicken nuggets.

Fifteen minutes later, he met her at the bottom of the stairs with a glass of red wine. A warm, spicy aroma that was definitely not chicken nuggets filled the air, and soft music played in the background.

Her curiosity—as well as her appetite—fully aroused, she followed him to the kitchen, where the lights were dimmed and the table set with candles. "This is a surprise."

"I considered taking you out, but I have things to say that I don't want to say in a public place." He pulled out her chair, as if they were in a fancy restaurant.

Casey sat and tried to tamp down her anxiety while he brought a pair of tossed salads from the refrigerator and removed a large foil container from the oven.

He pried off the cardboard lid and gave it a sniff. "Voila. Chicken Parmigiana from Luigi's. I know better than to try to impress you with my cooking."

So, he wanted to impress her. That had to be a sign of...something.

He dished up the plates and set one in front of her before taking his seat. "Dig in." He waved his fork. "Somebody slaved over this for hours, even if it wasn't me."

She gave a nervous little laugh and took a bite. The cheesy, tomato-y chicken melted in her mouth. "Mmm. It's perfect."

"Good. So, tell me about your trip."

She knew what he was asking but wasn't ready to dive into that yet. She set her fork on the edge of her plate and took a healthy swig of wine. "It was exhausting and annoying."

"Oh?" He looked so hopeful, she couldn't contain a smile.

"On the flight home, I was lucky enough to be seated next to a bona fide celebrity. At least, that's what she kept telling me. How much fun do you think you'd have spending four hours as the captive audience of a spoiled, entitled, seventeen-year-old, self-declared social media sensation with all the talent of a dead flea?"

He erupted in an outburst of laughter that brought tears to his eyes. After struggling a couple of minutes to regain control, he wiped his eyes with the corner of his napkin. "I have to admit, that doesn't sound like much fun."

"It wasn't."

"What did you think of the Institute?" The question might have been casual, but a tiny tremor shook his hand as he brought his water glass to his lips.

"It's an impressive place with a stately old building and perfectly manicured grounds."

His lips thinned. "Stop it. You know what I want to hear."

She took a deep breath and met the demand in his eyes. "I got the job."

The tension drained from his body, leaving his voice flat and lifeless. "I guess that's that."

Casey had spent almost three days mulling over her options for the future, as well as dissecting every aspect and nuance of their relationship. His assumption and ready acceptance infuriated her. "No, that is not that."

Alec straightened, and his expression grew wary. "What did you tell them?"

"That I needed a few days to think about it."

His gaze flared with renewed intensity. "In that case, let me throw out another option for your consideration. After I delivered Grace to her classroom yesterday, I stopped by the director's office."

"I'm sure she was glad to have Grace back at school."

He nodded. "She was. And in the course of our conversation, Mrs. Romero happened to mention the school is looking for a full-time psychologist. It might not have the cachet of the Wiseman Institute, but it's a highly-regarded pre-K-through-12 private school run by the university only a few blocks from here. I thought you might be interested."

A professional position. In her field. At Grace's school. The appeal was undeniable. "You didn't instigate this, did you?"

He tried to look injured, then reached across the table and took her hand. "It's a real job. They've been looking for a couple of months. I suggested I might know a good candidate. That's all. Will you at least think about it?"

She smiled. "I will definitely think about it." The job could be the answer to her prayers...depending. "Is that what you wanted to talk to me about?"

"That's part of it. The rest can wait. Right now, I want you to relax and enjoy your dinner. How about another glass of wine?" He picked up the bottle of Pinot Noir and poured.

"If you keep that up, I might fall asleep before you get a chance to tell me whatever it is you're putting off."

He added one last splash then tipped the bottle back up. "That's all for you, then."

The rest of the meal was comfortable and relaxed, with pleasant, low-key conversation, leaving Casey warm and only slightly light-headed by the time Alec cleared the table.

He piled the dishes in the sink then opened the refrigerator door and peered inside. "I bought a terrific-looking chocolate torte."

She groaned and closed her eyes. "That sounds fabulous, but I'm afraid I'm too full."

"Coffee?"

"That would be great."

"Coming up. You go sit in the living room, I'll bring it in."

She strolled into the living room where he'd lit the fireplace. The flames gave the darkened room an intimate, cozy atmosphere. A couple minutes later, Alec carried two cups into the room and settled next to her on the sofa.

She set her cup on the coffee table to cool and turned. "So, what else did you want to say to me?"

He reached for her hands. "Grace and I had a serious talk while you were gone. We want you to be part of our family."

*Whoa. No beating around the bush. No fancy prelude. Just come right out with it.*

"Why?"

"You're so good with Grace. I know you care about her, and she loves you."

"I do care about Grace," she admitted. "What exactly are you trying to say?"

"I'm obviously not doing it well, but I'm asking you to move in." His voice had a new edge, and his lips tightened.

"I can see how it would be convenient for you if I took the job at Grace's school. Everything else could stay the same, except you wouldn't have kidnappers to worry about."

"That's not how I meant it." He let out a breath. "I'm not great at expressing my feelings. I want you to live with us—with me—not because of Grace but because I love you. Is that clear enough?"

A fire kindled in her heart, but it still wasn't enough. She'd been wrong before. "Are you sure?"

"Of course, I'm sure. What about you? How do you feel?"

"I love you, too."

His tight expression eased with pleasure and relief. "Then there's no problem. We'll drive over and clean out your apartment tomorrow."

"But there is a problem. I don't know if I can trust my own emotions. What if you change your mind once you get to know me better?"

He took her hands again. "It's only been a couple of months, but I know you better than I've known any woman. We've shared responsibility for a child together. We've laughed, we've loved, we've been through hell together. You've seen me at my worst, and I've seen you at your...*you*-est. You are exactly what I want—what I need—for the rest of my life."

No woman could ask for more.

"Yes."

His lips curved in the start of smile. "I pour my heart out to you, and that's all you have to say?"

"Yes." She beamed at him.

"Lucky for you, it's enough." With that, he pulled her to him and sealed their bargain with a kiss brimming with a lifetime of promises.

# ABOUT THE AUTHOR

I haven't always been a writer, but I have always embraced creativity and relished new experiences. Seeking to expand my horizons beyond Kansas City, I chose a college in upstate New York. By the time I was twenty-one I had traveled the world from Tunisia to Japan. Little did I suspect I was collecting material for future characters and stories along the way.

I began writing when my daughter entered preschool (she's now a full-fledged adult) and became addicted to the challenge of translating the living, breathing images in my mind into words. I write romance because that's what I like to read. The world provides more than enough drama and tragedy. I want to give my readers the happily-ever-after we all crave.

I've been married to my personal hero for more than thirty years. After decades of living in the Midwest, we heeded the siren call of sun and sea and moved to the most breathtakingly beautiful place imaginable - the gorgeous central coast of California. I look forward to bringing you all the new stories this place inspires.

Alison

Made in the USA
Las Vegas, NV
08 January 2021

15372043R00184